ABOUT THE AUTHOR

ISAAC ASIMOV is regarded as one of the
greatest science-fiction writers of our time,
as well as a valued contributor to the world
of science. He holds a Ph.D. in Chemistry
from Columbia University (1948) and,
though he no longer lives in the Boston area,
is an Associate Professor of Biochemistry at
Boston University. He has received numerous awards for his inspiring scientific articles
covering a wide range of subjects.

In this novel, Dr. Asimov's probing imagination has created a fascinating adventure
set in the far-distant future—an adventure
that could change from fiction to fact any
day now.

THE NAKED SUN

isaac asimov

A FAWCETT CREST BOOK

Fawcett Books, Greenwich, Connecticut

THE NAKED SUN

THIS BOOK CONTAINS THE COMPLETE TEXT OF THE
ORIGINAL HARDCOVER EDITION.

Published by Fawcett Crest Books, CBS Publications, CBS Con-
sumer Publishing, a Division of CBS, Inc., by arrangement with
Doubleday and Company, Inc.

Selection of the Science Fiction Book Club, May 1971

Printed in the United States of America

19   18   17   16   15   14   13   12   11   10

To Noreen and Nick Falasca, for inviting me,
To Tony Boucher, for introducing me, and
To One Hundred Unusual Hours.

Contents

1   A Question Is Asked

STUBBORNLY Elijah Baley fought panic.

For two weeks it had been building up. Longer than that, even. It had been building up ever since they had called him to Washington and there calmly told him he was being reassigned.

The call to Washington had been disturbing enough in itself. It came without details, a mere summons; and that made it worse. It included travel slips directing round trip by plane and that made it still worse.

Partly it was the sense of urgency introduced by any order for plane travel. Partly it was the thought of the plane; simply that. Still, that was just the beginning of uneasiness and, as yet, easy to suppress.

After all, Lije Baley had been in a plane four times before. Once he had even crossed the continent. So, while plane travel is never pleasant, it would, at least, not be a complete step into the unknown.

And then, the trip from New York to Washington would take only an hour. The take-off would be from New York Runway Number 2, which, like all official Runways, was decently enclosed, with a lock opening to the unprotected atmosphere only after air speed had been achieved. The arrival would be at Washington Runway Number 5, which was similarly protected.

Furthermore, as Baley well knew, there would be no windows on the plane. There would be good lighting, decent food, all necessary conveniences. The radio-controlled flight would be smooth; there would scarcely be any sensation of motion once the plane was air-borne.

He explained all this to himself, and to Jessie, his wife, who had never been air-borne and who approached such matters with terror.

She said, "But I don't *like* you to take a plane, Lije. It isn't natural. Why can't you take the Expressways?"

"Because that would take ten hours"—Baley's long face was set in dour lines—"and because I'm a member of the City Police Force and have to follow the orders of my superiors. At least, I do if I want to keep my C-6 rating."

There was no arguing with that.

Baley took the plane and kept his eyes firmly on the news-strip that unreeled smoothly and continuously from the eye-level dispenser. The City was proud of that service: news, features, humorous articles, educational bits, occasional fiction. Someday the strips would be converted to film, it was said, since enclosing the eyes with a viewer would be an even more efficient way of distracting the passenger from his surroundings.

Baley kept his eyes on the unreeling strip, not only for the sake of distraction, but also because etiquette required it. There were five other passengers on the plane (he could not help noticing that much) and each one of them had his private right to whatever degree of fear and anxiety his nature and upbringing made him feel.

Baley would certainly resent the intrusion of anyone else on his own uneasiness. He wanted no strange eyes on the whiteness of his knuckles where his hands gripped the armrest, or the dampish stain they would leave when he took them away.

He told himself: I'm enclosed. This plane is just a little City.

But he didn't fool himself. There was an inch of steel at his left; he could feel it with his elbow. Past that, nothing——

Well, air! But that was nothing, really.

A thousand miles of it in one direction. A thousand in another. One mile of it, maybe two, straight down.

He almost wished he could see straight down, glimpse the top of the buried Cities he was passing over; New York, Philadelphia, Baltimore, Washington. He imagined the rolling, low-slung cluster-complexes of domes he had never seen but knew to be there. And under them, for a mile underground and dozens of miles in every direction, would be the Cities.

The endless, hiving corridors of the Cities, he thought, alive with people; apartments, community kitchens, factories, Expressways; all comfortable and warm with the evidence of man.

And he himself was isolated in the cold and featureless air in a small bullet of metal, moving through emptiness.

His hands trembled, and he forced his eyes to focus on the strip of paper and read a bit.

It was a short story dealing with Galactic exploration and it was quite obvious that the hero was an Earthman.

Baley muttered in exasperation, then held his breath momentarily in dismay at his boorishness in making a sound.

It was completely ridiculous, though. It was pandering to childishness, this pretense that Earthmen could invade space. Galactic exploration! The Galaxy was closed to Earthmen. It was pre-empted by the Spacers, whose ancestors had been Earthmen centuries before. Those ancestors had reached the Outer Worlds first, found themselves comfortable, and their descendants had lowered the bars to immigration. They had penned in Earth and their Earthman cousins. And Earth's City civilization completed the task, imprisoning Earthmen within the Cities by a wall of fear of open spaces that barred them from the robot-run farming and mining areas of their own planet; from even that.

Baley thought bitterly: Jehoshaphat! If we don't like it, let's do something about it. Let's not just waste time with fairy tales.

But there was nothing to do about it, and he knew it.

Then the plane landed. He and his fellow-passengers emerged and scattered away from one another, never looking.

Baley glanced at his watch and decided there was time for freshening before taking the Expressway to the Justice Department. He was glad there was. The sound and clamor of life, the huge vaulted chamber of the airport with City corridors leading off on numerous levels, everything else he saw and heard, gave him the feeling of being safely and warmly enclosed in the bowels and womb of the City. It washed away anxiety and only a shower was necessary to complete the job.

He needed a transient's permit to make use of one of the community bathrooms, but presentation of his travel orders eliminated any difficulties. There was only the routine stamping, with private-stall privileges (the date carefully marked to prevent abuse) and a slim strip of directions for getting to the assigned spot.

Baley was thankful for the feel of the strips beneath his feet. It was with something amounting to luxury that he felt himself accelerate as he moved from strip to moving strip inward toward the speeding Expressway. He swung himself aboard lightly, taking the seat to which his rating entitled him.

It wasn't a rush hour; seats were available. The bathroom, when he reached it, was not unduly crowded either. The stall assigned to him was in decent order with a launderette that worked well.

With his water ration consumed to good purpose and his clothing freshened he felt ready to tackle the Justice Department. Ironically enough, he even felt cheerful.

Undersecretary Albert Minnim was a small, compact man, ruddy of skin, and graying, with the angles of his body smoothed down and softened. He exuded an air of cleanliness and smelled faintly of tonic. It all spoke of the good things of life that came with the liberal rations obtained by those high in Administration.

Baley felt sallow and rawboned in comparison. He was conscious of his own large hands, deep-set eyes, a general sense of cragginess.

Minnim said cordially, "Sit down, Baley. Do you smoke?"

"Only a pipe, sir," said Baley.

He drew it out as he spoke, and Minnim thrust back a cigar he had half drawn.

Baley was instantly regretful. A cigar was better than

12

nothing and he would have appreciated the gift. Even with the increased tobacco ration that went along with his recent promotion from C-5 to C-6 he wasn't exactly swimming in pipe fixings.

"Please light up, if you care to," said Minnim, and waited with a kind of paternal patience while Baley measured out a careful quantity of tobacco and affixed the pipe baffle.

Baley said, his eyes on his pipe, "I have not been told the reason for my being called to Washington, sir."

"I know that," said Minnim. He smiled. "I can fix that right now. You are being reassigned temporarily."

"Outside New York City?"

"Quite a distance."

Baley raised his eyebrows and looked thoughtful. "How temporarily, sir?"

"I'm not sure."

Baley was aware of the advantages and disadvantages of reassignment. As a transient in a City of which he was not a resident, he would probably live on a scale better than his official rating entitled him to. On the other hand, it would be very unlikely that Jessie and their son, Bentley, would be allowed to travel with him. They would be taken care of, to be sure, there in New York, but Baley was a domesticated creature and he did not enjoy the thought of separation.

Then, too, a reassignment meant a specific job of work, which was good, and a responsibility greater than that ordinarily expected of the individual detective, which could be uncomfortable. Baley had, not too many months earlier, survived the responsibility of the investigation of the murder of a Spacer just outside New York. He was not overjoyed at the prospect of another such detail, or anything approaching it.

He said, "Would you tell me where I'm going? The nature of the reassignment? What it's all about?"

He was trying to weigh the Undersecretary's "Quite a distance" and make little bets with himself as to his new base of operations. The "Quite a distance" had sounded emphatic and Baley thought: Calcutta? Sydney?

Then he noticed that Minnim was taking out a cigar after all and was lighting it carefully.

Baley thought: Jehoshaphat! He's having trouble telling me. He doesn't want to say.

Minnim withdrew his cigar from between his lips. He watched the smoke and said, "The Department of Justice is assigning you to temporary duty on Solaria."

For a moment Baley's mind groped for an illusive identification: Solaria, Asia; Solaria, Australia . . . ?

Then he rose from his seat and said tightly, "You mean, one of the Outer Worlds?"

Minnim didn't meet Baley's eyes. "That is right!"

Baley said, "But that's impossible. They wouldn't allow an Earthman on an Outer World."

"Circumstances do alter cases, Plainclothesman Baley. There has been a murder on Solaria."

Baley's lips quirked into a sort of reflex smile. "That's a little out of our jurisdiction, isn't it?"

"They've requested help."

"From us? From Earth?" Baley was torn between confusion and disbelief. For an Outer World to take any attitude other than contempt toward the despised mother planet or, at best, a patronizing social benevolence was unthinkable. To come for help?

"From Earth?" he repeated.

"Unusual," admitted Minnim, "but there it is. They want a Terrestrial detective assigned to the case. It's been handled through diplomatic channels on the highest levels."

Baley sat down again. "Why me? I'm not a young man. I'm forty-three. I've got a wife and child. I couldn't leave Earth."

"That's not our choice, Plainclothesman. You were specifically asked for."

"*I?*"

"Plainclothesman Elijah Baley, C-6, of the New York City Police Force. They knew what they wanted. Surely you see why."

Baley said stubbornly, "I'm not qualified."

"They think you are. The way you handled the Spacer murder has apparently reached them."

"They must have got it all mixed up. It must have seemed better than it was."

Minnim shrugged. "In any case, they've asked for you and we have agreed to send you. You are reassigned. The papers have all been taken care of and you must go. During your absence, your wife and child will be taken care of at a C-7 level since that will be your temporary rating during your discharge of this assignment." He paused significantly. "Satisfactory completion of the assignment may make the rating permanent."

It was happening too quickly for Baley. None of this could be so. He *couldn't* leave Earth. Didn't they see that?

He heard himself ask in a level voice that sounded unnatural in his own ears, "What kind of a murder? What are the circumstances? Why can't they handle it themselves?"

Minnim rearranged small objects on his desk with carefully kept fingers. He shook his head. "I don't know anything about the murder. I don't know the circumstances."

"Then who does, sir? You don't expect me to go there cold, do you?" And again a despairing inner voice: But I *can't* leave Earth.

"Nobody knows anything about it. Nobody on Earth. The Solarians didn't tell us. That will be your job; to find out what is so important about the murder that they must have an Earthman to solve it. Or, rather, that will be *part* of your job."

Baley was desperate enough to say, "What if I refuse?" He knew the answer, of course. He knew exactly what declassification would mean to himself and, more than that, to his family.

Minnim said nothing about declassification. He said softly, "You can't refuse, Plainclothesman. You have a job to do."

"For Solaria? The hell with them."

"For *us,* Baley. For us." Minnim paused. Then he went on, "You know the position of Earth with respect to the Spacers. I don't have to go into that."

Baley knew the situation and so did every man on Earth. The fifty Outer Worlds, with a far smaller population, in combination, than that of Earth alone, nevertheless maintained a military potential perhaps a hundred times greater. With their underpopulated worlds resting on a positronic robot economy, their energy production per human was thousands of times that of Earth. And it was the amount of energy a single human could produce that dictated military potential, standard of living, happiness, and all besides.

Minnim said, "One of the factors that conspires to keep us in that position is ignorance. Just that. Ignorance. The Spacers know all about us. They send missions enough to Earth, heaven knows. We know nothing about them except what they tell us. No man on Earth has ever as much as set foot on an Outer World. *You* will, though."

Baley began, "I can't . . ."

But Minnim repeated, "You *will.* Your position will be unique. You will be on Solaria on their invitation, doing a job to which they will assign you. When you return, you will have information useful to Earth."

Baley watched the Undersecretary through somber eyes. "You mean I'm to spy for Earth."

"No question of spying. You need do nothing they don't ask you to do. Just keep your eyes and mind open. Observe! There will be specialists on Earth when you return to analyze and interpret your observations."

Baley said, "I take it there's a crisis, sir."

"Why do you say that?"

"Sending an Earthman to an Outer World is risky. The Spacers hate us. With the best will in the world and even though I'm there on invitation, I could cause an interstellar incident. The Terrestrial Government could easily avoid sending me if they chose. They could say I was ill. The Spacers are pathologically afraid of disease. They

16

wouldn't want me for any reason if they thought I were ill."

"Do you suggest," said Minnim, "we try that trick?"

"No. If the government had no other motive for sending me, they would think of that or something better without my help. So it follows that it is the question of spying that is the real essential. And if that is so, there must be more to it than just a see-what-you-can-see to justify the risk."

Baley half expected an explosion and would have half welcomed one as a relief of pressure, but Minnim only smiled frostily and said, "You can see past the non-essentials, it seems. But then, I expected no less."

The Undersecretary leaned across his desk toward Baley. "Here is certain information which you will discuss with no one, not even with other government officials. Our sociologists have been coming to certain conclusions concerning the present Galactic situation. Fifty Outer Worlds, underpopulated, roboticized, powerful, with people that are healthy and long-lived. We ourselves, crowded, technologically underdeveloped, short-lived, under their domination. It is unstable."

"Everything is in the long run."

"This is unstable in the short run. A hundred years is the most we're allowed. The situation will last our time, to be sure, but we have children. Eventually we will become too great a danger to the Outer Worlds to be allowed to survive. There are eight billions on Earth who hate the Spacers."

Baley said, "The Spacers exclude us from the Galaxy, handle our trade to their own profit, dictate to our government, and treat us with contempt. What do they expect? Gratitude?"

"True, and yet the pattern is fixed. Revolt, suppression, revolt, suppression—and within a century Earth will be virtually wiped out as a populated world. So the sociologists say."

Baley stirred uneasily. One didn't question sociologists

17

and their computers. "But what do you expect me to accomplish if all this is so?"

"Bring us information. The big flaw in sociological forecast is our lack of data concerning the Spacers. We've had to make assumptions on the basis of the few Spacers they sent out here. We've had to rely on what they choose to tell us of themselves, so it follows we know their strengths and only their strengths. Damn it, they have their robots and their low numbers and their long lives. But do they have weaknesses? Is there some factor or factors which, if we but knew, would alter the sociologic inevitability of destruction; something that could guide our actions and better the chance of Earth's survival."

"Hadn't you better send a sociologist, sir?"

Minnim shook his head. "If we could send whom we pleased, we would have sent someone out ten years ago, when these conclusions were first being arrived at. This is our first excuse to send someone and they ask for a detective and that suits us. A detective is a sociologist, too; a rule-of-thumb, practicing sociologist, or he wouldn't be a good detective. Your record proves you a good one."

"Thank you, sir," said Baley mechanically. "And if I get into trouble?"

Minnim shrugged. "That's the risk of a policeman's job." He dismissed the point with a wave of his hand and added, "In any case, you must go. Your time of departure is set. The ship that will take you is waiting."

Baley stiffened. "Waiting? When do I leave?"

"In two days."

"I've got to get back to New York then. My wife——"

"*We* will see your wife. She can't know the nature of your job, you know. She will be told not to expect to hear from you."

"But this is inhuman. I must see her. I may never see her again."

Minnim said, "What I say now may sound even more inhuman, but isn't it true that there is never a day you set about your duties on which you cannot tell yourself she may never see you again? Plainclothesman Baley, we must all do our duty."

Baley's pipe had been out for fifteen minutes. He had never noticed it.

No one had more to tell him. No one knew anything about the murder. Official after official simply hurried him on to the moment when he stood at the base of a spaceship, all unbelieving still.

It was like a gigantic cannon aimed at the heavens, and Baley shivered spasmodically in the raw, open air. The night closed in (for which Baley was thankful) like dark black walls melting into a black ceiling overhead. It was cloudy, and though he had been to Planetaria, a bright star, stabbing through a rift in the cloud, startled him when it caught his eyes.

A little spark, far, far away. He stared curiously, almost unafraid of it. It looked quite close, quite insignificant, and yet around things like that circled planets of which the inhabitants were lords of the Galaxy. The sun was a thing like that, he thought, except much closer, shining now on the other side of the Earth.

He thought of the Earth suddenly as a ball of stone with a film of moisture and gas, exposed to emptiness on every side, with its Cities barely dug into the outer rim, clinging precariously between rock and air. His skin crawled!

The ship was a Spacer vessel, of course. Interstellar trade was entirely in Spacer hands. He was alone now, just outside the rim of the City. He had been bathed and scraped and sterilized until he was considered safe, by Spacer standards, to board the ship. Even so, they sent only a robot out to meet him, bearing as he did a hundred varieties of disease germs from the sweltering City to which he himself was resistant but to which the eugenically hothoused Spacers were not.

The robot bulked dimly in the night, its eyes a dull red glow.

"Plainclothesman Elijah Baley?"

19

"That's right," said Baley crisply, the hair on the nape of his neck stirring a bit. He was enough of an Earthman to get angry goose flesh at the sight of a robot doing a man's job. There had been R. Daneel Olivaw, who had partnered with him in the Spacer murder affair, but that had been different. Daneel had been——

"You will follow me, please," said the robot, and a white light flooded a path toward the ship.

Baley followed. Up the ladder and into the ship he went, along corridors, and into a room.

The robot said, "This will be your room, Plainclothesman Baley. It is requested that you remain in it for the duration of the trip."

Baley thought: Sure, seal me off. Keep me safe. Insulated.

The corridors along which he had traveled had been empty. Robots were probably disinfecting them now. The robot facing him would probably step through a germicidal bath when it left.

The robot said, "There is a water supply and plumbing. Food will be supplied. You will have viewing matter. The ports are controlled from this panel. They are closed now but if you wish to view space——"

Baley said with some agitation, "That's all right, boy. Leave the ports closed."

He used the "boy" address that Earthmen always used for robots, but the robot showed no adverse response. It couldn't, of course. Its responses were limited and controlled by the Laws of Robotics.

The robot bent its large metal body in the travesty of a respectful bow and left.

Baley was alone in his room and could take stock. It was better than the plane, at least. He could see the plane from end to end. He could see its limits. The spaceship was large. It had corridors, levels, rooms. It was a small City in itself. Baley could almost breathe freely.

Then lights flashed and a robot's metallic voice sounded over the communo and gave him specific instructions for guarding himself against take-off acceleration.

There was the push backward against webbing and a yielding hydraulic system, a distant rumble of force-jets heated to fury by the proton micro-pile. There was the hiss of tearing atmosphere, growing thinner and high-pitched and fading into nothingness after an hour.

They were in space.

It was as though all sensation had numbed, as though nothing were real. He told himself that each second found him thousands of miles farther from the Cities, from Jessie, but it didn't register.

On the second day (the third?—there was no way of telling time except by the intervals of eating and sleeping) there was a queer momentary sensation of being turned inside out. It lasted an instant and Baley knew it was a Jump, that oddly incomprehensible, almost mystical, momentary transition through hyperspace that transferred a ship and all it contained from one point in space to another, light-years away. Another lapse of time and another Jump, still another lapse, still another Jump.

Baley told himself now that he was light-years away, tens of light-years, hundreds, thousands.

He didn't know how many. No one on Earth as much as knew Solaria's location in space. He would bet on that. They were ignorant, every one of them.

He felt terribly alone.

There was the feel of deceleration and the robot entered. Its somber, ruddy eyes took in the details of Baley's harness. Efficiently it tightened a wing nut; quickly it surveyed the details of the hydraulic system.

It said, "We will be landing in three hours. You will remain, if you please, in this room. A man will come to escort you out and to take you to your place of residence."

"Wait," said Baley tensely. Strapped in as he was, he felt helpless. "When we land, what time of day will it be?"

The robot said at once, "By Galactic Standard Time, it will be——"

"Local time, boy. Local time! Jehoshaphat!"

21

The robot continued smoothly, "The day on Solaria is twenty-eight point thirty-five Standard hours in length. The Solarian hour is divided into ten decads, each of which is divided into a hundred centads. We are scheduled to arrive at an airport at which the day will be at the twentieth centad of the fifth decad."

Baley hated that robot. He hated it for its obtuseness in not understanding; for the way it was making him ask the question directly and exposing his own weakness.

He had to. He said flatly, "Will it be daytime?"

And after all that the robot answered, "Yes, sir," and left.

It would be day! He would have to step out onto the unprotected surface of a planet in daytime.

He was not quite sure how it would be. He had seen glimpses of planetary surfaces from certain points within the City; he had even been out upon it for moments. Always, though, he had been surrounded by walls or within reach of one. There was always safety at hand.

Where would there be safety now? Not even the false walls of darkness.

And because he would not display weakness before the Spacers—he'd be damned if he would—he stiffened his body against the webbing that held him safe against the forces of deceleration, closed his eyes, and stubbornly fought panic.

2   A Friend Is Encountered

BALEY WAS losing his fight. Reason alone was not enough.

Baley told himself over and over: Men live in the open all their lives. The Spacers do so now. Our ancestors on Earth did it in the past. There is no real harm in wall-lessness. It is only my mind that tells me differently, and it is wrong.

But all that did not help. Something above and beyond reason cried out for walls and would have none of space.

As time passed, he thought he would not succeed. He would be cowering at the end, trembling and pitiful. The Spacer they would send for him (with filters in his nose to keep out germs, and gloves on his hands to prevent contact) would not even honestly despise him. The Spacer would feel only disgust.

Baley held on grimly.

When the ship stopped and the deceleration harness automatically uncoupled, while the hydraulic system retracted into the wall, Baley remained in his seat. He was afraid, and determined not to show it.

He looked away at the first quiet sound of the door of his room opening. There was the eye-corner flash of a tall, bronze-haired figure entering; a Spacer, one of those proud descendants of Earth who had disowned their heritage.

The Spacer spoke. "Partner Elijah!"

Baley's head turned toward the speaker with a jerk. His eyes rounded and he rose almost without volition.

He stared at the face; at the broad, high cheekbones, the absolute calm of the facial lines, the symmetry of the body, most of all at that level look out of nerveless blue eyes.

"D-daneel."

The Spacer said, "It is pleasant that you remember me, Partner Elijah."

"Remember you!" Baley felt relief wash over him. This being was a bit of Earth, a friend, a comfort, a savior. He had an almost unbearable desire to rush to the Spacer and embrace him, to hug him wildly, and laugh and pound his back and do all the foolish things old friends did when meeting once again after a separation.

But he didn't. He couldn't. He could only step forward, and hold out his hand and say, "I'm not likely to forget you, Daneel."

"That is pleasant," said Daneel, nodding gravely. "As you are well aware, it is quite impossible for me, while in working order, to forget you. It is well that I see you again."

Daneel took Baley's hand and pressed it with firm

23

coolness, his fingers closing to a comfortable but not painful pressure and then releasing it.

Baley hoped earnestly that the creature's unreadable eyes could not penetrate Baley's mind and see that wild moment, just past and not yet entirely subsided, when all of Baley had concentrated into a feeling of an intense friendship that was almost love.

After all, one could not love as a friend this Daneel Olivaw, who was not a man at all, but only a robot.

The robot that looked so like a man said, "I have asked that a robot-driven ground-transport vessel be connected to this ship by air-tube——"

Baley frowned. "An air-tube?"

"Yes. It is a common technique, frequently used in space, in order that personnel and matériel be transferred from one vessel to another without the necessity of special equipment against vacuum. It would seem then that you are not acquainted with the technique."

"No," said Baley, "but I get the picture."

"It is, of course, rather complicated to arrange such a device between spaceship and ground vehicle, but I have requested that it be done. Fortunately, the mission on which you and I are engaged is one of high priority. Difficulties are smoothed out quickly."

"Are you assigned to the murder case too?"

"Have you not been informed of that? I regret not having told you at once." There was, of course, no sign of regret on the robot's perfect face. "It was Dr. Han Fastolfe, whom you met on Earth during our previous partnership and whom I hope you remember, who first suggested you as an appropriate investigator in this case. He made it a condition that I be assigned to work with you once more."

Baley managed a smile. Dr. Fastolfe was a native of Aurora and Aurora was the strongest of the Outer Worlds. Apparently the advice of an Auroran bore weight.

Baley said, "A team that works shouldn't be broken up, eh?" (The first exhilaration of Daneel's appearance was fading and the compression about Baley's chest was returning.)

"I do not know if that precise thought was in his mind, Partner Elijah. From the nature of his orders to me, I should think that he was interested in having assigned to work with you one who would have experience with your world and would know of your consequent peculiarities."

"Peculiarities!" Baley frowned and felt offended. It was not a term he liked in connection with himself.

"So that I could arrange the air-tube, for example. I am well aware of your aversion to open spaces as a result of your upbringing in the Cities of Earth."

Perhaps it was the effect of being called "peculiar," the feeling that he had to counterattack or lose caste to a machine, that drove Baley to change the subject sharply. Perhaps it was just that life-long training prevented him from leaving any logical contradiction undisturbed.

He said, "There was a robot in charge of my welfare on board this ship; a robot" (a touch of malice intruded itself here) "that looks like a robot. Do you know it?"

"I spoke to it before coming on board."

"What's its designation? How do I make contact with it?"

"It is RX-2475. It is customary on Solaria to use only serial numbers for robots." Daneel's calm eyes swept the control panel near the door. "This contact will signal it."

Baley looked at the control panel himself and, since the contact to which Daneel pointed was labeled RX, its identification seemed quite unmysterious.

Baley put his finger over it and in less than a minute, the robot, the one that looked like a robot, entered.

Baley said, "You are RX-2475."

"Yes, sir."

"You told me earlier that someone would arrive to escort me off the ship. Did you mean him?" Baley pointed at Daneel.

The eyes of the two robots met. RX-2475 said, "His papers identify him as the one who was to meet you."

25

"Were you told in advance anything about him other than his papers? Was he described to you?"

"No, sir. I was given his name, however."

"Who gave you the information?"

"The captain of the ship, sir."

"Who is a Solarian?"

"Yes, sir."

Baley licked his lips. The next question would be decisive.

He said, "What were you told would be the name of the one you were expecting?"

RX-2475 said, "Daneel Olivaw, sir."

"Good boy! You may leave now."

There was the robotic bow and then the sharp about-face. RX-2475 left.

Baley turned to his partner and said thoughtfully, "You are not telling me all the truth, Daneel."

"In what way, Partner Elijah?" asked Daneel.

"While I was talking to you earlier, I recalled an odd point. RX-2475, when it told me I would have an escort said a *man* would come for me. I remember that quite well."

Daneel listened quietly and said nothing.

Baley went on. "I thought the robot might have made a mistake. I thought also that perhaps a man had indeed been assigned to meet me and had later been replaced by you, RX-2475 not being informed of the change. But you heard me check that. Your papers were described to it and it was given your name. But it was not quite given your name at that, was it, Daneel?"

"Indeed, it was not given my entire name," agreed Daneel.

"Your name is not Daneel Olivaw, but R. Daneel Olivaw, isn't it? Or, in full, Robot Daneel Olivaw."

"You are quite correct, Partner Elijah."

"From which it all follows that RX-2475 was never informed that you are a robot. It was allowed to think of you as a man. With your manlike appearance, such a masquerade is possible."

26

"I have no quarrel with your reasoning."

"Then let's proceed." Baley was feeling the germs of a kind of savage delight. He was on the track of something. It couldn't be anything much, but this was the kind of tracking he could do well. It was something he could do well enough to be called half across space to do. He said, "Now why should anyone want to deceive a miserable robot? It doesn't matter to it whether you are man or robot. It follows orders in either case. A reasonable conclusion then is that the Solarian captain who informed the robot and the Solarian officials who informed the Captain did not themselves know you were a robot. As I say, that is one reasonable conclusion, but perhaps not the only one. Is this one true?"

"I believe it is."

"All right, then. Good guess. Now why? Dr. Han Fastolfe, in recommending you as my partner allows the Solarians to think you are a human. Isn't that a dangerous thing? The Solarians, if they find out, may be quite angry. Why was it done?"

The humanoid robot said, "It was explained to me thus, Partner Elijah. Your association with a human of the Outer Worlds would raise your status in the eyes of the Solarians. Your association with a robot would lower it. Since I was familiar with your ways and could work with you easily, it was thought reasonable to allow the Solarians to accept me as a man without actually deceiving them by a positive statement to that effect."

Baley did not believe it. It seemed like the kind of careful consideration for an Earthman's feelings that did not come naturally to a Spacer, not even to as enlightened a one as Fastolfe.

He considered an alternative and said, "Are the Solarians well known among the Outer Worlds for the production of robots?"

"I am glad," said Daneel, "that you have been briefed concerning the inner economy of Solaria."

"Not a word," said Baley. "I can guess the spelling of the word Solaria and there my knowledge stops."

"Then I do not see, Partner Elijah, what it was that impelled you to ask that question, but it is a most pertinent one. You have hit the mark. My mind-store of information includes the fact that, of the fifty Outer Worlds, Solaria is by far the best known for the variety and excellence of robot models it turns out. It exports specialized models to all the other Outer Worlds."

Baley nodded in grim satisfaction. Naturally Daneel did not follow an intuitive mental leap that used human weakness as a starting point. Nor did Baley feel impelled to explain the reasoning. If Solaria turned out to be a world expert in robotics, Dr. Han Fastolfe and his associates might have purely personal and very human motives for demonstrating their own prize robot. It would have nothing at all to do with an Earthman's safety or feelings.

They would be asserting their own superiority by allowing the expert Solarians to be fooled into accepting a robot of Auroran handiwork as a fellow-man.

Baley felt much better. Strange that all the thought, all the intellectual powers he could muster, could not succeed in lifting him out of panic; and yet a sop to his own vainglory succeeded at once.

The recognition of the vainglory of the Spacers helped too.

He thought: Jehoshaphat, we're all human; even the Spacers.

Aloud he said, almost flippantly, "How long do we have to wait for the ground-car? I'm ready."

The air-tube gave signs of not being well adapted to its present use. Man and humanoid stepped out of the spaceship erect, moving along flexible mesh that bent and swayed under their weight. (In space, Baley imagined hazily, men transferring weightlessly from ship to ship might easily skim along the length of the tube, impelled by an initial Jump.)

Toward the other end the tube narrowed clumsily, its meshing bunching as though some giant hand had constricted it. Daneel, carrying the flashlight, got down on all fours and so did Baley. They traveled the last twenty feet in that fashion, moving at last into what was obviously a ground-car.

Daneel closed the door through which they had entered, sliding it shut carefully. There was a heavy, clicking noise that might have been the detachment of the air-tube.

Baley looked about curiously. There was nothing too exotic about the ground-car. There were two seats in tandem, each of which could hold three. There were doors at each end of each seat. The glossy sections that might ordinarily have been windows were black and opaque, as a result, undoubtedly, of appropriate polarization. Baley was acquainted with that.

The interior of the car was lit by two round spots of yellow illumination in the ceiling and, in short, the only thing Baley felt to be strange was the transmitter set into the partition immediately before the front seat and, of course, the added fact that there were no visible controls.

Baley said, "I suppose the driver is on the other side of this partition."

Daneel said, "Exactly so, Partner Elijah. And we can give our orders in this fashion." He leaned forward slightly and flicked a toggle switch that set a spot of red light to flickering. He said quietly, "You may start now. We are ready."

There was a muted whir that faded almost at once, a very slight, very transitory pressing against the back of the seat, and then nothing.

Baley said in surprise, "Are we moving?"

Daneel said, "We are. The car does not move on wheels but glides along a diamagnetic force-field. Except for acceleration and deceleration, you will feel nothing."

"What about curves?"

"The car will bank automatically to compensate. Its level is maintained when traveling up- or downhill."

"The controls must be complicated," said Baley dryly.

"Quite automatic. The driver of the vehicle is a robot."

"Umm." Baley had about all he wanted on the ground-car. He said, "How long will this take?"

"About an hour. Air travel would have been speedier, but I was concerned to keep you enclosed and the aircraft models available on Solaria do not lend themselves to complete enclosure as does a ground-car such as that in which we are now riding."

Baley felt annoyed at the other's "concern." He felt like a baby in the charge of its nurse. He felt almost as annoyed, oddly enough, at Daneel's sentences. It seemed to him that such needlessly formal sentence structure might easily betray the robotic nature of the creature.

For a moment Baley stared curiously at R. Daneel Olivaw. The robot, looking straight ahead, was motionless and unself-conscious under the other's gaze.

Daneel's skin texture was perfect, the individual hairs on head and body had been lovingly and intricately manufactured and placed. The muscle movement under the skin was most realistic. No pains, however extravagant, had been spared. Yet Baley knew, from personal knowledge, that limbs and chest could be split open along invisible seams so that repairs might be made. He knew there was metal and silicone under that realistic skin. He knew a positronic brain, most advanced but only positronic, nestled in the hollow of the skull. He knew that Daneel's "thoughts" were only short-lived positronic currents flowing along paths rigidly designed and foreordained by the manufacturer.

But what were the signs that would give that away to the expert eye that had no foreknowledge? The trifling unnaturalness of Daneel's manner of speech? The unemotional gravity that rested so steadily upon him? The very perfection of his humanity?

But he was wasting time. Baley said, "Let's get on with it, Daneel. I suppose that before arriving here, you were briefed on matters Solarian?"

"I was, Partner Elijah."

"Good. That's more than they did for me. How large is the world?"

"Its diameter is 9500 miles. It is the outermost of three planets and the only inhabited one. In climate and atmosphere it resembles Earth; its percentage of fertile land is higher; its useful mineral content lower, but of course less exploited. The world is self-supporting and can, with the aid of its robot exports, maintain a high standard of living."

Baley said, "What's the population?"

"Twenty thousand people, Partner Elijah."

Baley accepted that for a moment, then he said mildly, "You mean twenty million, don't you?" His scant knowledge of the Outer Worlds was enough to tell him that, although the worlds were underpopulated by Earthly standards, the individual populations *were* in the millions.

"Twenty thousand people, Partner Elijah," said the robot again.

"You mean the planet has just been settled?"

"Not at all. It has been independent for nearly two centuries, and it was settled for a century or more before that. The population is deliberately maintained at twenty thousand, that being considered optimum by the Solarians themselves."

"How much of the planet do they occupy?"

"All the fertile portions."

"Which is, in square miles?"

"Thirty million square miles, including marginal areas."

"For twenty thousand people?"

"There are also some two hundred million working positronic robots, Partner Elijah."

"Jehoshaphat! That's—that's ten thousand robots per human."

"It is by far the highest such ratio among the Outer Worlds, Partner Elijah. The next highest, on Aurora, is only fifty to one."

"What can they use so many robots for? What do they want with all that food?"

"Food is a relatively minor item. The mines are more important, and power production more important still."

Baley thought of all those robots and felt a trifle dizzy Two hundred million robots! So many among so few humans. The robots must litter the landscape. An observer from without might think Solaria a world of robots altogether and fail to notice the thin human leaven.

He felt a sudden need to see. He remembered the conversation with Minnim and the sociologic prediction of Earth's danger. It seemed far off, a bit unreal, but he remembered. His personal dangers and difficulties since leaving Earth dimmed the memory of Minnim's voice stating enormities with cool and precise enunciation, but never blotted it out altogether.

Baley had lived too long with duty to allow even the overwhelming fact of open space to stop him in its performance. Data collected from a Spacer's words, or from those of a Spacer robot for that matter, was the sort of thing that was already available to Earth's sociologists. What was needed was direct observation and it was his job, however unpleasant, to collect it.

He inspected the upper portion of the ground-car. "Is this thing a convertible, Daneel?"

"I beg your pardon, Partner Elijah, but I do not follow your meaning."

"Can the car's top be pushed back? Can it be made open to the—the sky?" (He had almost said "dome" out of habit.)

"Yes, it can."

"Then have that done, Daneel. I would like to take a look."

The robot responded gravely, "I am sorry, but I cannot allow that."

Baley felt astonished. He said, "Look, R. Daneel" (he stressed the R.). "Let's rephrase that. I order you to lower the top."

The creature was a robot, manlike or not. It *had* to follow orders.

But Daneel did not move. He said, "I must explain that it is my first concern to spare you harm. It has been clear to me on the basis both of my instructions and of my own personal experience that you would suffer harm at finding yourself in large, empty spaces. I cannot, therefore, allow you to expose yourself to that."

Baley could feel his face darkening with an influx of blood and at the same time could feel the complete uselessness of anger. The creature *was* a robot, and Baley knew the First Law of Robotics well.

It went: *A robot may not injure a human being, or, through inaction, allow a human being to come to harm.*

Everything else in a robot's positronic brain—that of any robot on any world in the Galaxy—had to bow to that prime consideration. Of course a robot had to follow orders, but with one major, all-important qualification. Following orders was only the Second Law of Robotics.

It went: *A robot must obey the orders given it by human beings except where such orders would conflict with the First Law.*

Baley forced himself to speak quietly and reasonably. "I think I can endure it for a short time, Daneel."

"That is not my feeling, Partner Elijah."

"Let me be the judge, Daneel."

"If that is an order, Partner Elijah, I cannot follow it."

Baley let himself lounge back against the softly upholstered seat. The robot would, of course, be quite beyond the reach of force. Daneel's strength, if exerted fully, would be a hundred times that of flesh and blood. He would be perfectly capable of restraining Baley without ever hurting him.

Baley was armed. He could point a blaster at Daneel, but, except for perhaps a momentary sensation of mastery, that action would only succeed in greater frustration. A threat of destruction was useless against a robot. Self-preservation was only the Third Law.

It went: *A robot must protect its own existence, as long as such protection does not conflict with the First or Second Laws.*

It would not trouble Daneel to be destroyed if the alternative were breaking the First Law. And Baley did not wish to destroy Daneel. Definitely not.

Yet he did want to see out the car. It was becoming an obsession with him. He couldn't allow this nurse-infant relationship to build up.

For a moment he thought of pointing the blaster at his own temple. Open the car top or I'll kill myself. Oppose one application of the First Law by a greater and more immediate one.

Baley knew he couldn't do it. Too undignified. He disliked the picture conjured up by the thought.

He said wearily, "Would you ask the driver how close in miles we are to destination?"

"Certainly, Partner Elijah."

Daneel bent forward and pushed the toggle switch. But as he did so, Baley leaned forward too, crying out, "Driver! Lower the top of the car!"

And it was the human hand that moved quickly to the toggle switch and closed it again. The human hand held its place firmly thereafter.

Panting a bit, Baley stared at Daneel.

For a second Daneel was motionless, as though his positronic paths were momentarily out of stability in their effort to adjust to the new situation. But that passed quickly and then the robot's hand was moving.

Baley had anticipated that. Daneel would remove the human hand from the switch (gently, not hurting it), reactivate the transmitter, and countermand the order.

Baley said, "You won't get my hand away without hurting me. I warn you. You will probably have to break my fingers."

That was not so. Baley knew that. But Daneel's movements stopped. Harm against harm. The positronic brain had to weigh probabilities and translate them into opposing potentials. It meant just a bit more hesitation.

Baley said, "It's too late."

His race was won. The top was sliding back and pouring into the car, now open, was the harsh white light of Solaria's sun.

Baley wanted to shut his eyes in initial terror, but fought the sensation. He faced the enormous wash of blue and green, incredible quantities of it. He could feel the undisciplined rush of air against his face, but could make out no details of anything. A moving something flashed past. It might have been a robot or an animal or an unliving something caught in a puff of air. He couldn't tell. The car went past it too quickly.

Blue, green, air, noise, motion——and over it all, beating down, furiously, relentlessly, frighteningly, was the white light that came from a ball in the sky.

For one fleeting split moment he bent his head back and stared directly at Solaria's sun. He stared at it, unprotected by the diffusing glass of the Cities' uppermost-Level sun-porches. He stared at the naked sun.

And at the very moment he felt Daneel's hands clamping down upon his shoulders. His mind crowded with thought during that unreal, whirling moment. He had to see! He had to see all he could. And Daneel must be there with him to keep him from seeing.

But surely a robot would not dare use violence on a man. That thought was dominant. Daneel could not prevent him forcibly, and yet Baley felt the robot's hands forcing him down.

Baley lifted his arms to force those fleshless hands away and lost all sensation.

3   A Victim Is Named

BALEY WAS back in the safety of enclosure. Daneel's face wavered before his eyes, and it was splotched with dark spots that turned to red when he blinked.

Baley said, "What happened?"

"I regret," said Daneel, "that you have suffered harm despite my presence. The direct rays of the sun are damaging to the human eye, but I believe that the damage from the short exposure you suffered will not be permanent. When you looked up, I was forced to pull you down and you lost consciousness."

Baley grimaced. That left the question open as to whether he had fainted out of overexcitement (or fright?) or had been knocked unconscious. He felt his jaw and

35

head and found no pain. He forbore asking the question direct. In a way he didn't want to know.

He said, "It wasn't so bad."

"From your reactions, Partner Elijah, I should judge you had found it unpleasant."

"Not at all," said Baley stubbornly. The splotches before his eyes were fading and they weren't tearing so. "I'm only sorry I saw so little. We were moving too fast. Did we pass a robot?"

"We passed a number of them. We are traveling across the Kinbald estate, which is given over to fruit orchards."

"I'll have to try again," said Baley.

"You must not, in my presence," said Daneel. "Meanwhile, I have done as you requested."

"As I requested?"

"You will remember, Partner Elijah, that before you ordered the driver to lower the top of the car, you had ordered me to ask the driver how close in miles we were to destination. We are ten miles away now and shall be there in some six minutes."

Baley felt the impulse to ask Daneel if he were angry at having been outwitted if only to see that perfect face become imperfect, but he repressed it. Of course Daneel would simply answer no, without rancor or annoyance. He would sit there as calm and as grave as ever, unperturbed and imperturbable.

Baley said quietly, "Just the same, Daneel, I'll have to get used to it, you know."

The robot regarded his human partner. "To what is it that you refer?"

"Jehoshaphat! To the—the outdoors. It's all this planet is made of."

"There will be no necessity for facing the outdoors," said Daneel. Then, as though that disposed of the subject, he said, "We are slowing down, Partner Elijah. I believe we have arrived It will be necessary to wait now for the connection of another air-tube leading to the dwelling that will serve as our base of operations."

"An air-tube is unnecessary, Daneel. If I am to be

working outdoors, there is no point in delaying the indoctrination."

"There will be no reason for you to work outdoors, Partner Elijah."

The robot started to say more, but Baley waved him quiet with a peremptory motion of the hand.

At the moment he was not in the mood for Daneel's careful consolations, for soothings, for assurances that all would be well and that he would be taken care of.

What he really wanted was an inner knowledge that he could take care of himself and fulfill his assignment. The sight and feel of the open had been hard to take. It might be that when the time came he would lack the hardihood to dare face it again, at the cost of his self-respect and, conceivably, of Earth's safety. All over a small matter of emptiness.

His face grew grim even at the glancing touch of that thought. He would face air, sun, and empty space yet!

Elijah Baley felt like an inhabitant of one of the smaller Cities, say Helsinki, visiting New York and counting the Levels in awe. He had thought of a "dwelling" as something like an apartment unit, but this was nothing like it at all. He passed from room to room endlessly. Panoramic windows were shrouded closely, allowing no hint of disturbing day to enter. Lights came to life noiselessly from hidden sources as they stepped into a room and died again as quietly when they left.

"So many rooms," said Baley with wonder. "So many. It's like a very tiny City, Daneel."

"It would seem so, Partner Elijah," said Daneel with equanimity.

It seemed strange to the Earthman. Why was it necessary to crowd so many Spacers together with him in close quarters? He said, "How many will be living here with me?"

Daneel said, "There will be myself, of course, and a number of robots."

37

Baley thought: He ought to have said, a number of *other* robots.

Again he found it obvious that Daneel had the intention of playing the man thoroughly even for no other audience than Baley, who knew the truth so well.

And then that thought popped into nothing under the force of a second, more urgent one. He cried, "*Robots?* How many *humans?*"

"None, Partner Elijah."

They had just stepped into a room, crowded from floor to ceiling with book films. Three fixed viewers with large twenty-four-inch viewing panels set vertically were in three corners of the room. The fourth contained an animation screen.

Baley looked about in annoyance. He said, "Did they kick everyone out just to leave me rattling around alone in this mausoleum?"

"It is meant only for you. A dwelling such as this for one person is customary on Solaria."

"Everyone lives like this?"

"Everyone."

"What do they need all the rooms for?"

"It is customary to devote a single room to a single purpose. This is the library. There is also a music room, a gymnasium, a kitchen, a bakery, a dining room, a machine shop, various robot-repair and testing rooms, two bedrooms——"

"Stop! How do you know all this?"

"It is part of the information pattern," said Daneel smoothly, "made available to me before I left Aurora."

"Jehoshaphat! Who takes care of all of this?" He swung his arm in a wide arc.

"There are a number of household robots. They have been assigned to you and will see to it that you are comfortable."

"But I don't need all this," said Baley. He had the urge to sit down and refuse to budge. He wanted to see no more rooms.

"We can remain in one room if you so desire, Partner

Elijah. That was visualized as a possibility from the start. Nevertheless, Solarian customs being what they are, it was considered wiser to allow this house to be built——"

"*Built!*" Baley stared. "You mean this was built for me? All this? Specially?"

"A thoroughly roboticized economy——"

"Yes, I see what you're going to say. What will they do with the house when all this is over?"

"I believe they will tear it down."

Baley's lips clamped together. Of course! Tear it down! Build a tremendous structure for the special use of one Earthman and then tear down everything he touched. Sterilize the soil the house stood on! Fumigate the air he breathed! The Spacers might seem strong, but they, too, had their foolish fears.

Daneel seemed to read his thoughts, or to interpret his expression at any rate. He said, "It may appear to you, Partner Elijah, that it is to escape contagion that they will destroy the house. If such are your thoughts, I suggest that you refrain from making yourself uncomfortable over the matter. The fear of disease on the part of Spacers is by no means so extreme. It is just that the effort involved in building the house is, to them, very little. Nor does the waste involved in tearing it down once more seem great to them.

"And by law, Partner Elijah, this place cannot be allowed to remain standing. It is on the estate of Hannis Gruer and there can only be one legal dwelling place on any estate, that of the owner. This house was built by special dispensation, for a specific purpose. It is meant to house us for a specific length of time, till our mission is completed."

"And who is Hannis Gruer?" asked Baley.

"The head of Solarian security. We are to see him on arrival."

"Are we? Jehoshaphat, Daneel, when do I begin to learn anything at all about anything? I'm working in a vacuum and I don't like it. I might as well go back to Earth. I might as well——"

He felt himself working up into resentment and cut himself short. Daneel never wavered. He merely waited his chance to speak. He said, "I regret the fact that you are annoyed. My general knowledge of Solaria does seem to be greater than yours. My knowledge of the murder case itself is as limited as is your own. It is Agent Gruer who will tell us what we must know. The Solarian Government has arranged this."

"Well, then, let's get to this Gruer. How long a trip will it be?" Baley winced at the thought of more travel and the familiar constriction in his chest was making itself felt again.

Daneel said, "No travel is necessary, Partner Elijah. Agent Gruer will be waiting for us in the conversation room."

"A room for conversation, too?" Baley murmured wryly. Then, in a louder voice, "Waiting for us now?"

"I believe so."

"Then let's get to him, Daneel!"

Hannis Gruer was bald, and that without qualification. There was not even a fringe of hair at the sides of his skull. It was completely naked.

Baley swallowed and tried, out of politeness, to keep his eyes off that skull, but couldn't. On Earth there was the continuous acceptance of Spacers at the Spacers' own evaluation. The Spacers were the unquestioned lords of the Galaxy; they were tall, bronze of skin and hair, handsome, large, cool, aristocratic.

In short, they were all R. Daneel Olivaw was, but with the fact of humanity in addition.

And the Spacers who were sent to Earth often did look like that; perhaps were deliberately chosen for that reason.

But here was a Spacer who might have been an Earthman for all his appearance. He was bald. And his nose was misshapen, too. Not much, to be sure, but on a Spacer even a slight asymmetry was noteworthy.

Baley said, "Good afternoon, sir. I am sorry if we kept you waiting."

40

No harm in politeness. He would have to work with these people.

He had the momentary urge to step across the expanse of room (how ridiculously large) and offer his hand in greeting. It was an urge easy to fight off. A Spacer certainly would not welcome such a greeting: a hand covered with Earthly germs?

Gruer sat gravely, as far away from Baley as he could get, his hands resting within long sleeves, and probably there were filters in his nostrils, although Baley couldn't see them.

It even seemed to him that Gruer cast a disapproving look at Daneel as though to say: You're a queer Spacer, standing that close to an Earthman.

That would mean Gruer simply did not know the truth. Then Baley noticed suddenly that Daneel was standing at some distance, at that; farther than he usually did.

Of course! Too close, and Gruer might find the proximity unbelievable. Daneel was intent on being accepted as human.

Gruer spoke in a pleasant, friendly voice, but his eyes tended to remain furtively on Daneel; looking away, then drifting back. He said, "I haven't been waiting long. Welcome to Solaria, gentlemen. Are you comfortable?"

"Yes, sir. Quite," said Baley. He wondered if etiquette would require that Daneel as the "Spacer" should speak for the two, but rejected that possibility resentfully. Jehoshaphat! It was he, himself, who had been requested for the investigation and Daneel had been added afterward. Under the circumstances Baley felt he would not play the secondary to a genuine Spacer; it was out of the question when a robot was involved, even such a robot as Daneel.

But Daneel made no attempt to take precedence over Baley, nor did Gruer seem surprised or displeased at that. Instead, he turned his attention at once to Baley to the exclusion of Daneel.

Gruer said, "You have been told nothing, Plainclothesman Baley, about the crime for which your services have been solicited. I imagine you are quite curious about that."

He shook his arms so that the sleeves fell backward and clasped his hands loosely in his lap. "Won't you gentlemen sit down?"

They did so and Baley said, "We *are* curious." He noted that Gruer's hands were not protected by gloves.

Gruer went on. "That was on purpose, Plainclothesman. We wanted you to arrive here prepared to tackle the problem with a fresh mind. We wanted no preconceived notions. You will have available to you shortly a full report of the details of the crime and of the investigations we have been able to conduct. I am afraid, Plainclothesman, that you will find our investigations ridiculously incomplete from the standpoint of your own experience. We have no police force on Solaria."

"None at all?" asked Baley.

Gruer smiled and shrugged. "No crime, you see. Our population is tiny and widely scattered. There is no occasion for crime; therefore no occasion for police."

"I see. But for all that, you *do* have crime now."

"True, but the first crime of violence in two centuries of history."

"Unfortunate, then, that you must begin with murder."

"Unfortunate, yes. More unfortunately still, the victim was a man we could scarcely afford to lose. A most inappropriate victim. And the circumstances of the murder were particularly brutal."

Baley said, "I suppose the murderer is completely unknown." (Why else would the crime be worth the importation of an Earthly detective?)

Gruer looked particularly uneasy. He glanced sideways at Daneel, who sat motionless, an absorptive, quiet mechanism. Baley knew than Daneel would, at any time in the future, be able to reproduce any conversation he heard, of whatever length. He was a recording machine that walked and talked like a man.

Did Gruer know that? His look at Daneel had certainly something of the furtive about it.

Gruer said, "No, I cannot say the murderer is completely unknown. In fact, there is only one person that can possibly have done the deed."

"Are you sure you don't mean only one person who is *likely* to have done the deed?" Baley distrusted overstatement and had no liking for the armchair deducer who discovered certainty rather than probability in the workings of logic.

But Gruer shook his bald head. "No. Only one possible person. Anyone else is impossible. Completely impossible."

"Completely?"

"I assure you."

"Then you have no problem."

"On the contrary. We do have a problem. That one person couldn't have done it either."

Baley said calmly, "Then no one did it."

"Yet the deed was done. Rikaine Delmarre is dead."

That's something, thought Baley. Jehoshaphat, I've got *something*. I've got the victim's name.

He brought out his notebook and solemnly made note of it, partly out of a wry desire to indicate that he had scraped up, at last, a nubbin of fact, and partly to avoid making it too obvious that he sat by the side of a recording machine who needed no notes.

He said, "How is the victim's name spelled?"

Gruer spelled it.

"His profession, sir?"

"Fetologist."

Baley spelled that as it sounded and let it go. He said, "Now who would be able to give me a personal account of the circumstances surrounding the murder? As firsthand as possible."

Gruer's smile was grim and his eyes shifted to Daneel again, and then away. "His wife, Plainclothesman."

"His wife . . . ?"

"Yes. Her name is Gladia." Gruer pronounced it in three syllables, accenting the second.

"Any children?" Baley's eyes were fixed on his notebook. When no answer came, he looked up. "Any children?"

But Gruer's mouth had pursed up as though he had tasted something sour. He looked sick. Finally he said, "I would scarcely know."

Baley said, "What?"

Gruer added hastily, "In any case, I think you had better postpone actual operations till tomorrow. I know you've had a hard trip, Mr. Baley, and that you are tired and probably hungry."

Baley, about to deny it, realized suddenly that the thought of food had an uncommon attraction for him at the moment. He said, "Will you join us at our meal?" He didn't think Gruer would, being a Spacer. (Yet he had been brought to the point of saying "Mr. Baley" rather than "Plainclothesman Baley," which was something.)

As expected, Gruer said, "A business engagement makes that impossible. I will have to leave. I am sorry."

Baley rose. The polite thing would be to accompany Gruer to the door. In the first place, however, he wasn't at all anxious to approach the door and the unprotected open. And in the second he wasn't sure where the door was.

He remained standing in uncertainty.

Gruer smiled and nodded. He said, "I will see you again. Your robots will know the combination if you wish to talk to me."

And he was gone.

Baley exclaimed sharply.

Gruer and the chair he was sitting on were simply not there. The wall behind Gruer, the floor under his feet changed with explosive suddenness.

Daneel said calmly, "He was not there in the flesh at any time. It was a trimensional image. It seemed to me you would know. You have such things on Earth."

"Not like this," muttered Baley.

A trimensional image on Earth was encased in a cubic force-field that glittered against the background. The image itself had a tiny flicker. On Earth there was no mistaking image for reality. Here . . .

No wonder Gruer had worn no gloves. He needed no nose filters, for that matter.

Daneel said, "Would you care to eat now, Partner Elijah?"

Dinner was an unexpected ordeal. Robots appeared. One set the table. One brought in the food.

"How many are there in the house, Daneel?" Baley asked.

"About fifty, Partner Elijah."

"Will they stay here while we eat?" (One had backed into a corner, his glossy, glowing-eyed face turned toward Baley.)

"It is the usual practice," said Daneel, "for one to do so in case its service is called upon. If you do not wish that, you have only to order it to leave."

Baley shrugged. "Let it stay!"

Under normal conditions Baley might have found the food delicious. Now he ate mechanically. He noted abstractedly that Daneel ate also, with a kind of unimpassioned efficiency. Later on, of course, he would empty the fluorocarbon sac within him into which the "eaten" food was now being stored. Meanwhile Daneel maintained his masquerade.

"Is it night outside?" asked Baley.

"It is," replied Daneel.

Baley stared somberly at the bed. It was too large. The whole bedroom was too large. There were no blankets to burrow under, only sheets. They would make a poor enclosure.

Everything was difficult! He had already gone through the unnerving experience of showering in a stall that actually adjoined the bedroom. It was the height of luxury in a way, yet, on the other hand, it seemed an unsanitary arrangement.

He said abruptly, "How is the light put out?" The

headboard of the bed gleamed with a soft light. Perhaps that was to facilitate book viewing before sleeping, but Baley was in no mood for that.

"It will be taken care of once you're in bed, if you compose yourself for sleep."

"The robots watch, do they?"

"It is their job."

"Jehoshaphat! What do these Solarians do for *themselves?*" Baley muttered. "I wonder now why a robot didn't scrub my back in the shower."

With no trace of humor Daneel said, "One would have, had you required it. As for the Solarians, they do what they choose. No robot performs his duty if ordered not to, except, of course, where the performance is necessary to the well-being of the human."

"Well, good night, Daneel."

"I will be in another bedroom, Partner Elijah. If, at any time during the night, you need anything———"

"I know. The robots will come."

"There is a contact patch on the side table. You have only to touch it. I will come too."

Sleep eluded Baley. He kept picturing the house he was in, balanced precariously at the outer skin of the world, with emptiness waiting just outside like a monster.

On Earth his apartment—his snug, comfortable, crowded apartment—sat nestled beneath many others. There were dozens of Levels and thousands of people between himself and the rim of Earth.

Even on Earth, he tried to tell himself, there were people on the topmost Level. They would be immediately adjacent to the outside. Sure! But that's what made those apartments low-rent.

Then he thought of Jessie, a thousand light-years away.

He wanted terribly to get out of bed right now, dress, and walk to her. His thoughts grew mistier. If there were only a tunnel, a nice, safe tunnel burrowing its way through safe, solid rock and metal from Solaria to Earth, he would walk and walk and walk. . . .

He would walk back to Earth, back to Jessie, back to comfort and security. . . .

Security.

Baley's eyes opened. His arms grew rigid and he rose up on his elbow, scarcely aware that he was doing so.

Security! This man, Hannis Gruer, was head of Solarian security. So Daneel had said. What did "security" mean? If it meant the same as it meant on Earth, and surely it must, this man Gruer was responsible for the protection of Solaria against invasion from without and subversion from within.

Why was he interested in a murder case? Was it because there were no police on Solaria and the Department of Security would come the closest to knowing what to do about a murder?

Gruer had seemed at ease with Baley, yet there had been those furtive glances, again and again, in the direction of Daneel.

Did Gruer suspect the motives of Daneel? Baley, himself, had been ordered to keep his eyes open and Daneel might very likely have received similar instructions.

It would be natural for Gruer to suspect that espionage was possible. His job made it necessary for him to suspect that in any case where it was conceivable. And he would not fear Baley overmuch, an Earthman, representative of the least formidable world in the Galaxy.

But Daneel was a native of Aurora, the oldest and largest and strongest of the Outer Worlds. That would be different.

Gruer, as Baley now remembered, had not addressed one word to Daneel.

For that matter, why should Daneel pretend so thoroughly to be a man? The earlier explanation that Baley had posed for himself, that it was a vainglorious game on the part of Daneel's Auroran designers, seemed trivial. It seemed obvious now that the masquerade was something more serious.

A man could be expected to receive diplomatic immunity; a certain courtesy and gentleness of treatment. A robot could not. But then why did not Aurora send a real man in the first place. Why gamble so desperately on a fake? The answer suggested itself instantly to Baley. A real man of Aurora, a real Spacer, would not care to associate too closely or for too long a time with an Earthman.

But if all this were true, why should Solaria find a single murder so important that it must allow an Earthman and an Auroran to come to their planet?

Baley felt trapped.

He was trapped on Solaria by the necessities of his assignment. He was trapped by Earth's danger, trapped in an environment he could scarcely endure, trapped by a responsibility he could not shirk. And, to add to all this, he was trapped somehow in the midst of a Spacer conflict the nature of which he did not understand.

4   A Woman Is Viewed

HE SLEPT at last. He did not remember when he actually made the transition to sleep. There was just a period when his thoughts grew more erratic and then the headboard of his bed was shining and the ceiling was alight with a cool, daytime glow. He looked at his watch.

Hours had passed. Tht robots who ran the house had decided it was time for him to wake up and had acted accordingly.

He wondered if Daneel were awake and at once realized the illogic of the thought. Daneel could not sleep. Baley wondered if he had counterfeited sleep as part of the role he was playing. Had he undressed and put on nightclothes?

As though on cue Daneel entered. "Good morning, Partner Elijah."

The robot was completely dressed and his face was in perfect repose. He said, "Did you sleep well?"

"Yes," said Baley dryly, "did you?"

He got out of bed and tramped into the bathroom for

a shave and for the remainder of the morning ritual. He shouted, "If a robot comes in to shave me, send him out again. They get on my nerves. Even if I don't see them, they get on my nerves."

He stared at his own face as he shaved, marveling a bit that it looked so like the mirrored face he saw on Earth. If only the image were another Earthman with whom he could consult instead of only the light-mimicry of himself. If he could go over what he had already learned, small as it was . . .

"Too small! Get more," he muttered to the mirror.

He came out, mopping his face, and pulled trousers over fresh shorts. (Robots supplied everything, damn them.)

He said, "Would you answer a few questions, Daneel?"

"As you know, Partner Elijah, I answer all questions to the best of my knowledge."

Or to the letter of your instructions, thought Baley. He said, "Why are there only twenty thousand people on Solaria?"

"That is a mere fact," said Daneel. "A datum. A figure that is the result of a counting process."

"Yes, but you're evading the matter. The planet can support millions; why, then, only twenty thousand? You said the Solarians consider twenty thousand optimum. Why?"

"It is their way of life."

"You mean they practice birth control?"

"Yes."

"And leave the planet empty?" Baley wasn't sure why he was pounding away at this one point, but the planet's population was one of the few hard facts he had learned about it and there was little else he could ask about.

Daneel said, "The planet is not empty. It is parceled out into estates, each of which is supervised by a Solarian."

"You mean each lives on his estate. Twenty thousand estates, each with a Solarian."

"Fewer estates than those, Partner Elijah. Wives share the estate."

"No Cities?" Baley felt cold.

"None at all, Partner Elijah. They live completely apart and never see one another except under the most extraordinary circumstances."

"Hermits?"

"In a way, yes. In a way, no."

"What does that mean?"

"Agent Gruer visited you yesterday by trimensional image. Solarians visit one another freely that way and in no other way."

Baley stared at Daneel. He said, "Does that include us? Are we expected to live that way?"

"It is the custom of the world."

"Then how do I investigate this case? If I want to see someone——"

"From this house, Partner Elijah, you can obtain a trimensional view of anyone on the planet. There will be no problem. In fact, it will save you the annoyance of leaving this house. It was why I said when we arrived that there would be no occasion for you to feel it necessary to grow accustomed to facing the outdoors. And that is well. Any other arrangement would be most distasteful to you."

"I'll judge what's distasteful to me," said Baley. "First thing today, Daneel, I get in touch with the Gladia woman, the wife of the murdered man. If the trimensional business is unsatisfactory, I will go out to her place, personally. It's a matter for my decision."

"We shall see what is best and most feasible, Partner Elijah," said Daneel noncommittally. "I shall arrange for breakfast." He turned to leave.

Baley stared at the broad robotic back and was almost amused. Daneel Olivaw acted the master. If his instructions had been to keep Baley from learning any more than was absolutely necessary, a trump card had been left in Baley's hand.

The other was only R. Daneel Olivaw, after all. All that was necessary was to tell Gruer, or any Solarian, that Daneel was a robot and not a man.

And yet, on the other hand, Daneel's pseudo humanity could be of great use, too. A trump card need not be played at once. Sometimes it was more useful in the hand.

Wait and see, he thought, and followed Daneel out to breakfast.

Baley said, "Now how does one go about establishing trimensional contact?"

"It is done for us, Partner Elijah," said Daneel, and his finger sought out one of the contact patches that summoned robots.

A robot entered at once.

Where do they come from, Baley wondered. As one wandered aimlessly about the uninhabited maze that constituted the mansion, not one robot was ever visible. Did they scramble out of the way as humans approached? Did they send messages to one another and clear the path?

Yet whenever a call went out, one appeared without delay.

Baley stared at the robotic newcomer. It was sleek, but not glossy. Its surface had a muted, grayish finish, with a checkerboard pattern on the right shoulder as the only bit of color. Squares in white and yellow (silver and gold, really, from the metallic luster) were placed in what seemed an aimless pattern.

Daneel said, "Take us to the conversation room."

The robot bowed and turned, but said nothing.

Baley said, "Wait, boy. What's your name?"

The robot faced Baley. It spoke in clear tones and without hesitation. "I have no name, master. My serial number"—and a metal finger lifted and rested on the shoulder patch—"is ACX-2745."

Daneel and Baley followed into a large room, which Baley recognized as having held Gruer and his chair the day before.

Another robot was waiting for them with the eternal, patient nonboredom of the machine. The first bowed and left.

Baley compared shoulder patches of the two as the

first bowed and started out. The pattern of silver and gold was different. The checkerboard was made up of a six-by-six square. The number of possible arrangements would be 2^{36} then, or seventy billion. More than enough.

Baley said, "Apparently, there is one robot for everything. One to show us here. One to run the viewer."

Daneel said, "There is much robotic specialization in Solaria, Partner Elijah."

"With so many of them, I can understand why." Baley looked at the second robot. Except for the shoulder patch, and, presumably, for the invisible positronic patterns within its spongy platinum-iridium brain it was the duplicate of the first. He said, "And your serial number?"

"ACC-1129, master."

"I'll just call you boy. Now I want to speak to a Mrs. Gladia Delmarre, wife of the late Rikaine Delmarre—— Daneel, is there an address, some way of pin-pointing her location?"

Daneel said gently, "I do not believe any further information is necessary. If I may question the robot——"

"Let me do that," Baley said. "All right, boy, do you know how the lady is to be reached?"

"Yes, master. I have knowledge of the connection pattern of all masters." This was said without pride. It was a mere fact, as though it were saying: I am made of metal, master.

Daneel interposed, "That is not surprising, Partner Elijah. There are less than ten thousand connections that need be fed into the memory circuits, and that is a small number."

Baley nodded. "Is there more than one Gladia Delmarre, by any chance? There might be that chance of confusion."

"Master?" After the question the robot remained blankly silent.

"I believe," said Daneel, "that this robot does not understand your question. It is my belief that duplicate names do not occur on Solaria. Names are registered at birth and no name may be adopted unless it is unoccupied at the time."

"All right," said Baley, "we learn something every minute. Now see here, boy, you tell me how to work whatever it is I am supposed to work; give me the connection pattern, or whatever you call it, and then step out."

There was a perceptible pause before the robot answered. It said, "Do you wish to make contact yourself, sir?"

"That's right."

Daneel touched Baley's sleeve gently. "One moment, Partner Elijah."

"Now what is it?"

"It is my belief that the robot could make the necessary contact with greater ease. It is his specialization."

Baley said grimly, "I'm sure he can do it better than I can. Doing it myself, I may make a mess of it." He stared levelly at the impassive Daneel. "Just the same, I prefer to make contact myself. Do I give the orders or don't I?"

Daneel said, "You give the orders, Partner Elijah, and your orders, where First Law permits, will be obeyed. However, with your permission, I would like to give you what pertinent information I have concerning the Solarian robots. Far more than on any other world, the robots on Solaria are specialized. Although Solarian robots are physically capable of many things, they are heavily equipped mentally for one particular type of job. To perform functions outside their specialty requires the high potentials produced by direct application of one of the Three Laws. Again, for them *not* to perform the duty for which they *are* equipped also requires the direct application of the Three Laws."

"Well, then, a direct order from me brings the Second Law into play, doesn't it?"

"True. Yet the potential set up by it is 'unpleasant' to the robot. Ordinarily, the matter would not come up, since almost never does a Solarian interfere with the day-to-day workings of a robot. For one thing, he would not care to do a robot's work; for another, he would feel no need to."

"Are you trying to tell me, Daneel, that it hurts the robot to have me do its work?"

"As you know, Partner Elijah, pain in the human sense is not applicable to robotic reactions."

Baley shrugged. "Then?"

"Nevertheless," went on Daneel, "the experience which the robot undergoes is as upsetting to it as pain is to a human, as nearly as I can judge."

"And yet," said Baley, "I'm not a Solarian. I'm an Earthman. I don't like robots doing what I want to do."

"Consider, too," said Daneel, "that to cause distress to a robot might be considered on the part of our hosts to be an act of impoliteness since in a society such as this there must be a number of more or less rigid beliefs concerning how it is proper to treat a robot and how it is not. To offend our hosts would scarcely make our task easier."

"All right," said Baley. "Let the robot do its job."

He settled back. The incident had not been without its uses. It was an educational example of how remorseless a robotic society could be. Once brought into existence, robots were not so easily removed, and a human who wished to dispense with them even temporarily found he could not.

His eyes half closed, he watched the robot approach the wall. Let the sociologists on Earth consider what had just occurred and draw their conclusions. He was beginning to have certain notions of his own.

Half a wall slid aside and the control panel that was revealed would have done justice to a City Section power station.

Baley longed for his pipe. He had been briefed that smoking on non-smoking Solaria would be a terrible breach of decorum, so he had not even been allowed to take his fixings. He sighed. There were moments when the feel of pipestem between teeth and a warm bowl in his hand would have been infinitely comforting.

The robot was working quickly, adjusting variable resistances a trifle here and there and intensifying field-forces in proper pattern by quick finger pressures.

Daneel said, "It is necessary first to signal the individual one desires to view. A robot will, of course, receive the message. If the individual being signaled is available and wishes to receive the view, full contact is established."

"Are all those controls necessary?" asked Baley. "The robot's hardly touching most of the panel."

"My information on the matter is not complete, Partner Elijah. There is, however, the necessity of arranging, upon occasion, for multiple viewings and for mobile viewings. The latter, particularly, call for complicated and continuing adjustments."

The robot said, "Masters, contact is made and approved. When you are ready, it will be completed."

"Ready," growled Baley, and as though the word were a signal, the far half of the room was alive with light.

Daneel said at once, "I neglected to have the robot specify that all visible openings to the outside be draped. I regret that and we must arrange———"

"Never mind," said Baley, wincing. "I'll manage. Don't interfere."

It was a bathroom he was staring at, or he judged it to be so from its fixtures. One end of it was, he guessed, a kind of beautician's establishment and his imagination pictured a robot (or robots?) working with unerring swiftness on the details of a woman's coiffure and on the externals that made up the picture she presented to the world.

Some gadgets and fittings he simply gave up on. There was no way of judging their purpose in the absence of experience. The walls were inlaid with an intricate pattern that all but fooled the eye into believing some natural object was being represented before fading away into an isaac asimov

abstraction. The result was soothing and almost hypnotic in the way it monopolized attention.

What might have been the shower stall, a large one, was shielded off by nothing that seemed material, but rather by a trick of lighting that set up a wall of flickering opacity. No human was in sight.

Baley's glance fell to the floor. Where did his room end and the other begin? It was easy to tell. There was a line where the quality of the light changed and that must be it.

He stepped toward the line and after a moment's hesitation pushed his hand beyond it.

He felt nothing, any more than he would have had he shoved the hand into one of Earth's crude trimensionals. There, at least, he would have seen his own hand still; faintly, perhaps, and overlaid by the image, but he would have seen it. Here it was lost completely. To his vision, his arm ended sharply at the wrist.

What if he stepped across the line altogether? Probably his own vision would become inoperative. He would be in a world of complete blackness. The thought of such efficient enclosure was almost pleasant.

A voice interrupted him. He looked up and stepped backward with an almost clumsy haste.

Gladia Delmarre was speaking. At least Baley assumed it was she. The upper portion of the flickering light across the shower stall had faded and a head was clearly visible.

It smiled at Baley. "I said hello, and I'm sorry to keep you waiting. I'll be dry soon."

Hers was a triangular face, rather broad at the cheekbones (which grew prominent when she smiled) and narrowing with a gentle curve past full lips to a small chin. Her head was not high above the ground. Baley judged her to be about five feet two in height. (This was not typical. At least not to Baley's way of thinking. Spacer women were supposed to lean toward the tall and stately.) Nor was her hair the Spacer bronze. It was light brown, tinging toward yellow, and worn moderately long. At the moment it was fluffed out in what Baley imagined must

56

be a stream of warm air. The whole picture was quite pleasing.

Baley said in confusion, "If you want us to break contact and wait till you're through——"

"Oh no. I'm almost done, and we can talk meanwhile. Hannis Gruer told me you would be viewing. You're from Earth, I understand." Her eyes rested full on him, seemed to drink him in.

Baley nodded and sat down. "My companion is from Aurora."

She smiled and kept her glance fixed on Baley as though *he* remained the curiosity nevertheless, and of course, Baley thought, so he was.

She lifted her arms above her head, running her fingers through the hair and spreading it out as though to hasten drying. Her arms were slim and graceful. Very attractive, Baley thought.

Then he thought uneasily: Jessie wouldn't like this.

Daneel's voice broke in. "Would it be possible, Mrs. Delmarre, to have the window we see polarized or draped. My partner is disturbed by the sight of daylight. On Earth, as you may have heard——"

The young woman (Baley judged her to be twenty-five but had the doleful thought that the apparent ages of Spacers could be most deceptive) put her hands to her cheeks and said, "Oh my, yes. I know all about that. How ridiculously silly of me. Forgive me, please, but it won't take a moment. I'll have a robot in here——"

She stepped out of the drying cabinet, her hand extended toward the contact-patch, still talking. "I'm always thinking I ought to have more than one contact-patch in this room. A house is just no good if it doesn't have a patch within reach no matter where you stand—say not more than five feet away. It just—— Why, what's the matter?"

She stared in shock at Baley, who, having jumped out of his chair and upset it behind him, had reddened to his hairline and hastily turned away.

Daneel said calmly, "It would be better, Mrs. Delmarre,

if, after you have made contact with the robot, you would return to the stall or, failing that, proceed to put on some articles of clothing."

Gladia looked down at her nudity in surprise and said, "Well, of course."

5   A Crime Is Discussed

"IT WAS only viewing, you see," said Gladia contritely. She was wrapped in something that left her arms and shoulders free. One leg showed to mid-thigh, but Baley, entirely recovered and feeling an utter fool, ignored it stoically.

He said, "It was the surprise, Mrs. Delmarre——"

"Oh, please. You can call me Gladia, unless—unless that's against your customs."

"Gladia, then. It's all right. I just want to assure you there was nothing repulsive about it, you understand. Just the surprise." Bad enough for him to have acted the fool, he thought, without having the poor girl think he found her unpleasant. As a matter of fact, it had been rather— rather . . .

Well, he didn't have the phrase, but he knew quite certainly that there was no way he would ever be able to talk of this to Jessie.

"I know I offended you," Gladia said, "but I didn't mean to. I just wasn't thinking. Of course I realize one must be careful about the customs of other planets, but the customs are so queer sometimes; at least, not queer," she hastened to add, "I don't mean queer. I mean strange, you know, and it's so easy to forget. As I forgot about keeping the windows darkened."

"Quite all right," muttered Baley. She was in another room now with all the windows draped and the light had the subtly different and more comfortable texture of artificiality.

"But about the other thing," she went on earnestly, "it's

58

just *viewing,* you see. After all, you didn't mind talking to me when I was in the drier and I wasn't wearing anything then, either."

"Well," said Baley, wishing she would run down as far as that subject was concerned, "hearing you is one thing, and seeing you is another."

"But that's exactly it. Seeing isn't involved." She reddened a trifle and looked down. "I hope you don't think I'd ever do anything like that, I mean, just step out of the drier, if anyone were *seeing* me. It was just *viewing.*"

"Same thing, isn't it?" said Baley.

"Not at all the same thing. You're viewing me right now. You can't touch me, can you, or smell me, or anything like that. You could if you were seeing me. Right now, I'm two hundred miles away from you at *least.* So how can it be the same thing?"

Baley grew interested. "But I see you with my eyes."

"No, you don't see me. You see my image. You're viewing me."

"And that makes a difference?"

"All the difference there is."

"I see." In a way he did. The distinction was not one he could make easily, but it had a kind of logic to it.

She said, bending her head a little to one side, "Do you *really* see?"

"Yes."

"Does that mean you wouldn't mind if I took off my wrapper?" She was smiling.

He thought: She's teasing and I ought to take her up on it.

But aloud he said, "No, it would take my mind off my job. We'll discuss it another time."

"Do you mind my being in the wrapper, rather than something more formal? Seriously."

"I don't mind."

"May I call you by your first name?"

"If you have the occasion."

"What is your first name?"

"Elijah."

"All right." She snuggled into a chair that looked hard and almost ceramic in texture, but it slowly gave as she sat until it embraced her gently.

Baley said, "To business, now."

She said, "To business."

Baley found it all extraordinarily difficult. There was no way even to make a beginning. On Earth he would ask name, rating, City and Sector of dwelling, a million different routine questions. He might even know the answers to begin with, yet it would be a device to ease into the serious phase. It would serve to introduce him to the person, make his judgment of the tactics to pursue something other than a mere guess.

But here? How could he be certain of anything? The very verb "to see" meant different things to himself and to the woman. How many other words would be different? How often would they be at cross-purposes without his being aware of it?

He said, "How long were you married, Gladia?"

"Ten years, Elijah."

"How old are you?"

"Thirty-three."

Baley felt obscurely pleased. She might easily have been a hundred thirty-three.

He said, "Were you happily married?"

Gladia looked uneasy. "How do you mean that?"

"Well——" For a moment Baley was at a loss. How do you define a happy marriage. For that matter, what would a Solarian consider a happy marriage? He said, "Well, you saw one another often?"

"What? I should hope not. We're not animals, you know."

Baley winced. "You did live in the same mansion? I thought——"

"Of course, we did. We were married. But I had my quarters and he had his. He had a very important career which took much of his time and I have my own work. We viewed each other whenever necessary."

"He *saw* you, didn't he?"

"It's not a thing one talks about but he *did* see me."

"Do you have any children?"

Gladia jumped to her feet in obvious agitation. "That's too much. Of all the indecent——"

"Now wait. *Wait!*" Baley brought his fist down on the arm of his chair. "Don't be difficult. This is a murder investigation. Do you understand? Murder. And it was your husband who was murdered. Do you want to see the murderer found and punished or don't you?"

"Then *ask* about the murder, not about—about——"

"I have to ask all sorts of things. For one thing I want to know whether you're sorry your husband is dead." He added with calculated brutality, "You don't seem to be."

She stared at him haughtily. "I'm sorry when anyone dies, especially when he's young and useful."

"Doesn't the fact that he was your husband make it just a little more than that?"

"He was assigned to me and, well, we *did* see each other when scheduled and——and"—she hurried the next words— "and, if you must know, we don't have children because none have been assigned us yet. I don't see what all that has to do with being sorry over someone being dead."

Maybe it had nothing to do with it, Baley thought. It depended on the social facts of life and with those he was not acquainted.

He changed the subject. "I'm told you have personal knowledge of the circumstances of the murder."

For a moment she seemed to grow taut. "I—discovered the body. Is that the way I should say it?"

"Then you didn't witness the actual murder?"

"Oh no," she said faintly.

"Well, suppose you tell me what happened. Take your time and use your own words." He sat back and composed himself to listen.

She began, "It was on three-two of the fifth——"

"When was that in Standard Time?" asked Baley quickly.

"I'm not sure. I really don't know. You can check, I suppose."

Her voice seemed shaky and her eyes had grown large. They were a little too gray to be called blue, he noted.

She said, "He came to my quarters. It was our assigned day for seeing and I knew he'd come."

"He always came on the assigned day?"

"Oh yes. He was a very conscientious man, a good Solarian. He never skipped an assigned day and always came at the same time. Of course, he didn't stay long. We have not been assigned ch——"

She couldn't finish the word, but Baley nodded.

"Anyway," she said, "he always came at the same time, you know, so that everything would be comfortable. We spoke a few minutes; seeing *is* an ordeal, but he spoke quite normally to me. It was his way. Then he left to attend to some project he was involved with; I'm not sure what. He had a special laboratory in my quarters to which he could retire on seeing days. He had a much bigger one in his quarters, of course."

Baley wondered what he did in those laboratories. Fetology, perhaps, whatever that was.

He said, "Did he seem unnatural in any way? Worried?"

"No. No. He was never worried." She came to the edge of a small laugh and buried it at the last moment. "He always had perfect control, like your friend there." For a brief moment her small hand reached out and indicated Daneel, who did not stir.

"I see. Well, go on."

Gladia didn't. Instead she whispered, "Do you mind if I have myself a drink?"

"Please do."

Gladia's hand slipped along the arm of her chair momentarily. In less than a minute, a robot moved in silently and a warm drink (Baley could see the steam) was in her hand. She sipped slowly, then set the drink down.

She said, "That's better. May I ask a personal question?"

Baley said, "You may always ask."

"Well, I've read a lot about Earth. I've always been

interested, you know. It's such a *queer* world." She gasped and added immediately, "I didn't mean that."

Baley frowned a little. "Any world is queer to people who don't live on it."

"I mean it's different. You know. Anyway, I want to ask a rude question. At least, I hope it doesn't seem rude to an Earthman. I wouldn't ask it of a Solarian, of course. Not for anything."

"Ask what, Gladia?"

"About you and your friend—Mr. Olivaw, is it?"

"Yes."

"You two aren't viewing, are you?"

"How do you mean?"

"I mean each other. You're seeing. You're there, both of you."

Baley said, "We're physically together. Yes."

"You could touch him, if you wanted to."

"That's right."

She looked from one to the other and said, "Oh."

It might have meant anything. Disgust? Revulsion?

Baley toyed with the idea of standing up, walking to Daneel and placing his hand flat on Daneel's face. It might be interesting to watch her reaction.

He said, "You were about to go on with the events of that day when your husband came to see you." He was morally certain that her digression, however interesting it might have been intrinsically to her, was primarily motivated by a desire to avoid just that.

She returned to her drink for a moment. Then: "There isn't much to tell. I saw he would be engaged, and I knew he would be, anyway, because he was always at some sort of constructive work, so I went back to my own work. Then, perhaps fifteen minutes later, I heard a shout."

There was a pause and Baley prodded her. "What kind of a shout?"

She said, "Rikaine's. My husband's. Just a shout. No words. A kind of fright. No! Surprise, shock. Something like that. I'd never heard him shout before."

She lifted her hands to her ears as though to shut out

even the memory of the sound and her wrapper slipped slowly down to her waist. She took no notice and Baley stared firmly at his notebook.

He said, "What did you do?"

"I ran. I ran. I didn't know where he was———"

"I thought you said he had gone to the laboratory he maintained in your quarters."

"He did, E-Elijah, but *I* didn't know where that was. Not for sure, anyway. I never went there. It was his. I had a general idea of its direction. I knew it was somewhere in the west, but I was so upset, I didn't even think to summon any robot. One of them would have guided me easily, but of course none came without being summoned. When I did get there—I found it somehow—he was dead."

She stopped suddenly and, to Baley's acute discomfort, she bent her head and wept. She made no attempt to obscure her face. Her eyes simply closed and tears slowly trickled down her cheeks. It was quite soundless. Her shoulders barely trembled.

Then her eyes opened and looked at him through swimming tears. "I never saw a dead man before. He was all bloody and his head was—just—all—— I managed to get a robot and he called others and I suppose they took care of me and of Rikaine. I don't remember. I don't———"

Baley said, "What do you mean, they took care of Rikaine?"

"They took him away and cleaned up." There was a small wedge of indignation in her voice, the lady of the house careful of its condition. "Things were a mess."

"And what happened to the body?"

She shook her head. "I don't know. Burned, I suppose. Like any dead body."

"You didn't call the police?"

She looked at him blankly and Baley thought: No police!

He said, "You told somebody, I suppose. People found out about the matter."

She said, "The robots called a doctor. And I had to

call Rikaine's place of work. The robots there had to know he wouldn't be back."

"The doctor was for you, I suppose."

She nodded. For the first time, she seemed to notice her wrapper draped about her hips. She pulled it up into position, murmuring forlornly, "I'm sorry, I'm sorry."

Baley felt uncomfortable, watching her as she sat there helpless, shivering, her face contorted with the absolute terror that had come over her with the memory.

She had never seen a dead body before. She had never seen blood and a crushed skull. And if the husband-wife relationship on Solaria was something thin and shallow, it was still a dead human being with whom she had been confronted.

Baley scarcely knew what to say or do next. He had the impulse to apologize, and yet, as a policeman, he was doing only his duty.

But there were no police on this world. Would she understand that this was his duty?

Slowly, and as gently as he could, he said, "Gladia, did you hear anything at all? Anything besides your husband's shout."

She looked up, her face as pretty as ever, despite its obvious distress—perhaps because of it. She said, "Nothing."

"No running footsteps? No other voice?"

She shook her head. "I didn't hear anything."

"When you found your husband, he was completely alone? You two were the only ones present?"

"Yes."

"No signs of anyone else having been there?"

"None that I could see. I don't see how anyone could have been there, anyway."

"Why do you say that?"

For a moment she looked shocked. Then she said dispiritedly, "You're from Earth. I keep forgetting. Well, it's just that nobody could have been there. My husband never saw anybody except me; not since he was a boy.

He certainly wasn't the sort to see anybody. Not Rikaine. He was very strict; very custom-abiding."

"It might not have been his choice. What if someone had just come to see him without an invitation, without your husband knowing anything about it? He couldn't have helped seeing the intruder regardless of how custom-abiding he was."

She said, "Maybe, but he would have called robots at once and had the man taken away. He would have! Besides, no one would try to see my husband without being invited to. I couldn't conceive of such a thing. And Rikaine certainly would never invite anyone to see him. It's ridiculous to think so."

Baley said softly, "Your husband was killed by being struck on the head, wasn't he? You'll admit that."

"I suppose so. He was—all——"

"I'm not asking for the details at the moment. Was there any sign of some mechanical contrivance in the room that would have enabled someone to crush his skull by remote control."

"Of course not. At least, I didn't see any."

"If anything like that had been there, I imagine you would have seen it. It follows then that a hand held something capable of crushing a man's skull and that hand swung it. Some person had to be within four feet of your husband to do that. So someone did see him."

"No one would," she said earnestly. "A Solarian just wouldn't see anyone."

"A Solarian who would commit murder wouldn't stick at a bit of seeing, would he?"

(To himself that statement sounded dubious. On Earth he had known the case of a perfectly conscienceless murderer who had been caught only because he could not bring himself to violate the custom of absolute silence in the community bathroom.)

Gladia shook her head. "You don't understand about seeing. Earthmen just see anybody they want to all the time, so you don't understand it. . . ."

Curiosity seemed to be struggling within her. Her eyes

lightened a bit. "Seeing does seem perfectly normal to you, doesn't it?"

"I've always taken it for granted," said Baley.

"It doesn't trouble you?"

"Why should it?"

"Well, the films don't say, and I've always wanted to know—— Is it all right if I ask a question?"

"Go ahead," said Baley stolidly.

"Do you have a wife assigned to you?"

"I'm married. I don't know about the assignment part."

"And I know you see your wife any time you want to and she sees you and neither of you thinks anything of it."

Baley nodded.

"Well, when you see her, suppose you just want to——" She lifted her hands elbow-high, pausing as though searching for the proper phrase. She tried again, "Can you just—any time . . ." She let it dangle.

Baley didn't try to help.

She said, "Well, never mind. I don't know why I should bother you with that sort of thing now anyway. Are you through with me?" She looked as though she might cry again.

Baley said, "One more try, Gladia. Forget that no one would see your husband. Suppose someone *did*. Who might it have been?"

"It's just useless to guess. It couldn't be anyone."

"It has to be someone. Agent Gruer says there is reason to suspect some one person. So you see there must be someone."

A small, joyless smile flickered over the girl's face. "I know who he thinks did it."

"All right. Who?"

She put a small hand on her breast. "I."

6   A Theory Is Refuted

"I should have said, Partner Elijah," said Daneel, speaking suddenly, "that that is an obvious conclusion."

Baley cast a surprised look at his robot partner. "Why obvious?" he asked.

"The lady herself," said Daneel, "states that she was the only person who did or who would see her husband. The social situation on Solaria is such that even she cannot plausibly present anything else as the truth. Certainly Agent Gruer would find it reasonable, even obligatory, to believe that a Solarian husband would be seen only by his wife. Since only one person could be in seeing range, only one person could be the murderer. Or murderess, rather. Agent Gruer, you will remember, said that only one person could have done it. Anyone else he considered impossible. Well?"

"He also said," said Baley, "that that one person couldn't have done it, either."

"By which he probably meant that there was no weapon found at the scene of the crime. Presumably Mrs. Delmarre could explain that anomaly."

He gestured with cool robotic politeness toward where Gladia sat, still in viewing focus, her eyes cast down, her small mouth compressed.

Jehoshaphat, thought Baley, we're forgetting the lady.

Perhaps it was annoyance that had caused him to forget. It was Daneel who annoyed him, he thought, with his unemotional approach to problems. Or perhaps it was himself, with his emotional approach. He did not stop to analyze the matter.

He said, "That will be all for now, Gladia. However one goes about it, break contact. Good-by."

She said softly, "Sometimes one says, 'Done viewing,' but I like 'Good-by' better. You seem disturbed, Elijah.

I'm sorry, because I'm used to having people think I did it, so you don't need to feel disturbed."

Daneel said, *"Did* you do it, Gladia?"

"No," she said angrily.

"Good-by, then."

With the anger not yet washed out of her face she was gone. For a moment, though, Baley could still feel the impact of those quite extraordinary gray eyes.

She might say she was used to having people think her a murderess, but that was very obviously a lie. Her anger spoke more truly than her words. Baley wondered of how many other lies she was capable.

And now Baley found himself alone with Daneel. He said, "All right, Daneel, I'm not altogether a fool."

"I have never thought you were, Partner Elijah."

"Then tell me what made you say there was no murder weapon found at the site of the crime? There was nothing in the evidence so far, nothing in anything I've heard that would lead us to that conclusion."

"You are correct. I have additional information not yet available to you."

"I was sure of that. What kind?"

"Agent Gruer said he would send a copy of the report of their own investigation. I have that copy. It arrived this morning."

"Why haven't you shown it to me?"

"I felt that it would perhaps be more fruitful for you to conduct your investigation, at least in the initial stages, according to your own ideas, without being prejudiced by the conclusions of other people who, self-admittedly, have reached no satisfactory conclusion. It was because I, myself, felt my logical processes might be influenced by those conclusions that I contributed nothing to the discussion."

Logical processes! Unbidden, there leaped into Baley's mind the fragment of a conversation he had once had with a roboticist. A robot, the man had said, is logical but not reasonable.

He said, "You entered the discussion at the end."

"So I did, Partner Elijah, but only because by that time I had independent evidence bearing out Agent Gruer's suspicions."

"What kind of independent evidence?"

"That which could be deduced from Mrs. Delmarre's own behavior."

"Let's be specific, Daneel."

"Consider that if the lady were guilty and were attempting to prove herself innocent, it would be useful to her to have the detective in the case believe her innocent."

"Well?"

"If she could warp his judgment by playing upon a weakness of his, she might do so, might she not?"

"Strictly hypothetical."

"Not at all," was the calm reply. "You will have noticed, I think, that she concentrated her attention entirely on you."

"I was doing the talking," said Baley.

"Her attention was on you from the start; even before she could guess that you would be doing the talking. In fact, one might have thought she would, logically, have expected that I, as an Auroran, would take the lead in the investigation. Yet she concentrated on you."

"And what do you deduce from this?"

"That it was upon you, Partner Elijah, that she pinned her hopes. You were the Earthman."

"What of that?"

"She had studied Earth. She implied that more than once. She knew what I was talking about when I asked her to blank out the outer daylight at the very start of the interview. She did not act surprised or uncomprehending, as she would most certainly have done had she not had actual knowledge of conditions on Earth."

"Well?"

"Since she has studied Earth, it is quite reasonable to suppose that she discovered one weakness Earthmen possess. She must know of the nudity tabu, and of how such a display must impress an Earthman."

"She—she explained about viewing——"

"So she did. Yet did it seem entirely convincing to you? Twice she allowed herself to be seen in what you would consider a state of improper clothing——"

"Your conclusion," said Baley, "is that she was trying to seduce me. Is that it?"

"Seduce you away from your professional impersonality. So it would seem to me. And though I cannot share human reactions to stimuli, I would judge, from what has been imprinted on my instruction circuits, that the lady meets any reasonable standard of physical attractiveness. From your behavior, moreover, it seems to me that you were aware of that and that you approved her appearance. I would even judge that Mrs. Delmarre acted rightly in thinking her mode of behavior would predispose you in her favor."

"Look," said Baley uncomfortably, "regardless of what effect she might have had on me, I am still an officer of the law in full possession of my sense of professional ethics. Get that straight. Now let's see the report."

Baley read through the report in silence. He finished, turned back, and read it through a second time.

"That brings in a new item," he said. "The robot."

Daneel Olivaw nodded.

Baley said thoughtfully, "She didn't mention it."

Daneel said, "You asked the wrong question. You asked if he was alone when she found the body. You asked if anyone else had been present at the death scene. A robot isn't 'anybody else.' "

Baley nodded. If he himself were a suspect and were asked who else had been at the scene of a crime, he would scarcely have replied: "No one but this table."

He said, "I suppose I should have asked if any robots were present?" (Damn it, what questions does one ask anyway on a strange world?) He said, "How legal is robotic evidence, Daneel?"

"What do you mean?"

71

"Can a robot bear witness on Solaria? Can it give evidence?"

"Why should you doubt it?"

"A robot isn't human, Daneel. On Earth, it cannot be a legal witness."

"And yet a footprint can, Partner Elijah, although that is much less a human than a robot is. The position of your planet in this respect is illogical. On Solaria, robotic evidence, when competent, is admissible."

Baley did not argue the point. He rested his chin on the knuckles of one hand and went over this matter of the robot in his mind.

In the extremity of terror Gladia Delmarre, standing over her husband's body, had summoned robots. By the time they came she was unconscious.

The robots reported having found her there together with the dead body. And something else was present as well; a robot. That robot had not been summoned; it was already there. It was not one of the regular staff. No other robot had seen it before or knew its function or assignment.

Nor could anything be discovered from the robot in question. It was not in working order. When found, its motions were disorganized and so, apparently, was the functioning of its positronic brain. It could give none of the proper responses, either verbal or mechanical, and after exhaustive investigation by a robotics expert it was declared a total loss.

Its only activity that had any trace of organization was its constant repetition of "You're going to kill me—you're going to kill me—you're going to kill me . . ."

No weapon that could possibly have been used to crush the dead man's skull was located.

Baley said suddenly, "I'm going to eat, Daneel, and then we see Agent Gruer again—or view him, anyway."

Hannis Gruer was still eating when contact was established. He ate slowly, choosing each mouthful carefully from a variety of dishes, peering at each anxiously as though searching for some hidden combination he would find most satisfactory.

Baley thought: He may be a couple of centuries old. Eating may be getting dull for him.

Gruer said, "I greet you, gentlemen. You received our report, I believe." His bald head glistened, as he leaned across the table to reach a titbit.

"Yes. We have spent an interesting session with Mrs. Delmarre also," said Baley.

"Good, good," said Gruer. "And to what conclusion, if any, did you come?"

Baley said, "That she is innocent, sir."

Gruer looked up sharply. "Really?"

Baley nodded.

Gruer said, "And yet she was the only one who could see him, the only one who could possibly be within reach. . . ."

Baley said, "That's been made clear to me, and no matter how firm social customs are on Solaria, the point is not conclusive. May I explain?"

Gruer had returned to his dinner. "Of course."

"Murder rests on three legs," said Baley, "each equally important. They are motive, means, and opportunity. For a good case against any suspect, each of the three must be satisfied. Now I grant you that Mrs. Delmarre had the opportunity. As for the motive, I've heard of none."

Gruer shrugged. "We know of none." For a moment his eyes drifted to the silent Daneel.

"All right. The suspect has no known motive, but perhaps she's a pathological killer. We can let the matter ride for a while, and continue. She is in his laboratory with him and there's some reason why she wants to kill him. She waves some club or other heavy object threateningly. It takes him a while to realize that his wife really intends to hurt him. He shouts in dismay, 'You're going to kill me,' and so she does. He turns to run as the blow descends and it crushes the back of his head. Did a doctor examine the body, by the way?"

"Yes and no. The robots called a doctor to attend Mrs.

73

Delmarre and, as a matter of course, he looked at the dead body, too."

"That wasn't mentioned in the report."

"It was scarcely pertinent. The man was dead. In fact, by the time the doctor could view the body, it had been stripped, washed, and prepared for cremation in the usual manner."

"In other words, the robots had destroyed evidence," said Baley, annoyed. Then: "Did you say he *viewed* the body? He didn't *see* it?"

"Great Space," said Gruer, "what a morbid notion. He viewed it, of course, from all necessary angles and at close focus, I'm sure. Doctors can't avoid seeing patients under some conditions, but I can't conceive of any reason why they should have to see corpses. Medicine is a dirty job, but even doctors draw the line somewhere."

"Well, the point is this. Did the doctor report anything about the nature of the wound that killed Dr. Delmarre?"

"I see what you're driving at. You think that perhaps the wound was too severe to have been caused by a woman."

"A woman is weaker than a man, sir. And Mrs. Delmarre is a small woman."

"But quite athletic, Plainclothesman. Given a weapon of the proper type, gravity and leverage would do most of the work. Even not allowing for that, a woman in frenzy can do surprising things."

Baley shrugged. "You speak of a weapon. Where is it?"

Gruer shifted position. He held out his hand toward an empty glass and a robot entered the viewing field and filled it with a colorless fluid that might have been water.

Gruer held the filled glass momentarily, then put it down as though he had changed his mind about drinking. He said, "As is stated in the report, we have not been able to locate it."

"I know the report says that. I want to make absolutely certain of a few things. The weapon was searched for?"

"Thoroughly."

"By yourself?"

"By robots, but under my own viewing supervision at all times. We could locate nothing that might have been the weapon."

"That weakens the case against Mrs. Delmarre, doesn't it?"

"It does," said Gruer calmly. "It is one of several things about the case we don't understand. It is one reason why we have not acted against Mrs. Delmarre. It is one reason why I told you that the guilty party could not have committed the crime, either. Perhaps I should say that she apparently could not have committed the crime."

"Apparently?"

"She must have disposed of the weapon someway. So far, we have lacked the ingenuity to find it."

Baley said dourly, "Have you considered all possibilities?"

"I think so."

"I wonder. Let's see. A weapon has been used to crush a man's skull and it is not found at the scene of the crime. The only alternative is that it has been carried away. It could not have been carried away by Rikaine Delmarre. He was dead. Could it have been carried away by Gladia Delmarre?"

"It must have been," said Gruer.

"How? When the robots arrived, she was on the floor unconscious. Or she may have been feigning unconsciousness, but anyway she was there. How long a time between the murder and the arrival of the first robot?"

"That depends upon the exact time of the murder, which we don't know," said Gruer uneasily.

"I read the report, sir. One robot reported hearing a disturbance and a cry it identified as Dr. Delmarre's. It was apparently the closest to the scene. The summoning signal flashed five minutes afterward. It would take the robot less than a minute to appear on the scene." (Baley remembered his own experiences with the rapid-fire appearance of robots when summoned.) "In five minutes, even ten, how far could Mrs. Delmarre have carried a weapon and returned in time to assume unconsciousness?"

"She might have destroyed it in a disposer unit."

"The disposer unit was investigated, according to the report, and the residual gamma-ray activity was quite low. Nothing sizable had been destroyed in it for twenty-four hours."

"I know that," said Gruer. "I simply present it as an example of what might have been done."

"True," said Baley, "but there may be a very simple explanation. I suppose the robots belonging to the Delmarre household have been checked and all were accounted for."

"Oh yes."

"And all in reasonable working order?"

"Yes."

"Could any of those have carried away the weapon, perhaps without being aware of what it was?"

"Not one of them had removed anything from the scene of the crime. Or touched anything, for that matter."

"That's not so. They certainly removed the body and prepared it for cremation."

"Well, yes, of course, but that scarcely counts. You would expect them to do that."

"Jehoshaphat!" muttered Baley. He had to struggle to keep calm.

He said, "Now suppose someone else had been on the scene."

"Impossible," said Gruer. "How could someone invade Dr. Delmarre's personal presence?"

"Suppose!" cried Baley. "Now there was never any thought in the robots' minds that an intruder might have been present. I don't suppose any of them made an immediate search of the grounds about the house. It wasn't mentioned in the report."

"There was no search till we looked for the weapon, but that was a considerable time afterward."

"Nor any search for signs of a ground-car or an air vehicle on the grounds?"

"No."

"Then if someone had nerved himself to invade Dr.

Delmarre's personal presence, as you put it, he could have killed him and then walked away leisurely. No one would have stopped him or even seen him. Afterward, he could rely on everyone being sure no one could have been there."

"And no one could," said Gruer positively.

Baley said, "One more thing. Just one more. There was a robot involved. A robot was at the scene."

Daneel interposed for the first time. "The robot was not at the scene. Had it been there, the crime would not have been committed."

Baley turned his head sharply. And Gruer, who had lifted his glass a second time as though about to drink, put it down again to stare at Daneel.

"Is that not so?" asked Daneel.

"Quite so," said Gruer. "A robot would have stopped one person from harming another. First Law."

"All right," said Baley. "Granted. But it must have been close. It was on the scene when the other robots arrived. Say it was in the next room. The murderer is advancing on Delmarre and Delmarre cries out, 'You're going to kill me.' The robots of the household did not hear those words; at most they heard a cry, so, unsummoned, they did not come. But this particular robot heard the words and First Law made it come unsummoned. It was too late. Probably, it actually saw the murder committed."

"It must have seen the last stages of the murder," agreed Gruer. "That is what disordered it. Witnessing harm to a human without having prevented it is a violation of the First Law and, depending upon circumstances, more or less damage to the positronic brain is induced. In this case, it was a great deal of damage."

Gruer stared at his fingertips as he turned the glass of liquid to and fro, to and fro.

Baley said, "Then the robot was a witness. Was it questioned?"

"What use? He was disordered. It could only say 'You're going to kill me.' I agree with your reconstruction that far. They were probably Delmarre's last words burned into

77

the robot's consciousness when everything else was destroyed."

"But I'm told Solaria specializes in robots. Was there no way in which the robot could be repaired? No way in which its circuits could be patched?"

"None," said Gruer sharply.

"And where is the robot, now?"

"Scrapped," said Gruer.

Baley raised his eyebrows. "This is a rather peculiar case. No motive, no means, no witnesses, no evidence. Where there was some evidence to begin with, it was destroyed. You have only one suspect and everyone seems convinced of her guilt; at least, everyone is certain no one else can be guilty. That's your opinion, too, obviously. The question then is: Why was I sent for?"

Gruer frowned. "You seem upset, Mr. Baley." He turned abruptly to Daneel. "Mr. Olivaw."

"Yes, Agent Gruer."

"Won't you please go through the dwelling and make sure all windows are closed and blanked out? Plainclothesman Baley may be feeling the effects of open space."

The statement astonished Baley. It was his impulse to deny Gruer's assumption and order Daneel to keep his place when, on the brink, he caught something of panic in Gruer's voice, something of glittering appeal in his eyes.

He sat back and let Daneel leave the room.

It was as though a mask had dropped from Gruer's face, leaving it naked and afraid. Gruer said, "That was easier than I had thought. I'd planned so many ways of getting you alone. I never thought the Auroran would leave at a simple request, and yet I could think of nothing else to do."

Baley said, "Well, I'm alone now."

Gruer said, "I couldn't speak freely in his presence. He's an Auroran and he is here because he was forced on us as the price of having you." The Solarian leaned forward. "There's something more to this than murder. I am not concerned only with the matter of who did it. There are parties on Solaria, secret organizations. . . ."

Baley stared. "Surely, I can't help you there."

"Of course you can. Now understand this: Dr. Delmarre was a Traditionalist. He believed in the old ways, the good ways. But there are new forces among us, forces for change, and Delmarre has been silenced."

"By Mrs. Delmarre?"

"Hers must have been the hand. That doesn't matter. There is an organization behind her and that is the important matter."

"Are you sure? Do you have evidence?"

"Vague evidence, only. I can't help that. Rikaine Delmarre was on the track of something. He assured me *his* evidence was good, and I believe him. I knew him well enough to know him as neither fool nor child. Unfortunately, he told me very little. Naturally, he wanted to complete his investigation before laying the matter completely open to the authorities. He must have gotten close to completion, too, or they wouldn't have dared the risk of having him openly slaughtered by violence. One thing Delmarre told me, though. The whole human race is in danger."

Baley felt himself shaken. For a moment it was as though he were listening to Minnim again, but on an even larger scale. Was *everyone* going to turn to him with cosmic dangers?

"Why do you think I can help?" he asked.

"Because you're an Earthman," said Gruer. "Do you understand? We on Solaria have no experience with these things. In a way, we don't understand people. There are too few of us here."

He looked uneasy. "I don't like to say this, Mr. Baley. My colleagues laugh at me and some grow angry, but it is a definite feeling I have. It seems to me that you Earthmen *must* understand people far better than we do, just by living among such crowds of them. And a detective more than anyone. Isn't that so?"

Baley half nodded and held his tongue.

Gruer said, "In a way, this murder was fortunate. I have not dared speak to the others about Delmarre's investigation, since I wasn't sure who might be involved in the conspiracy, and Delmarre himself was not ready to give any details till his investigation was complete. And even if Delmarre had completed his work, how would we deal with the matter afterward? How does one deal with hostile human beings? I don't know. From the beginning, I felt we needed an Earthman. When I heard of your work in connection with the murder in Spacetown on Earth, I knew we needed you. I got in touch with Aurora, with whose men you have worked most closely, and through them approached the Earth government. Yet my own colleagues could not be persuaded into agreeing to this. Then came the murder and that was enough of a shock to give me the agreement I needed. At the moment, they would have agreed to anything."

Gruer hesitated, then added, "It's not easy to ask an Earthman to help, but I must do so. Remember, whatever it is, the human race is in danger. Earth, too."

Earth was doubly in danger, then. There was no mistaking the desperate sincerity in Gruer's voice.

But then, if the murder were so fortunate a pretext for allowing Gruer to do what he so desperately wanted to do all the time, was it entirely fortune? It opened new avenues of thought that were not reflected in Baley's face, eyes, or voice.

Baley said, "I have been sent here, sir, to help. I will do so to the best of my ability."

Gruer finally lifted his long-delayed drink and looked over the rim of the glass at Baley. "Good," he said. "Not a word to the Auroran, please. Whatever this is about, Aurora may be involved. Certainly they took an unusually intense interest in the case. For instance, they insisted on including Mr. Olivaw as your partner. Aurora is powerful; we had to agree. They say they include Mr. Olivaw only because he worked with you before, but it may well be that they wish a reliable man of their own on the scene, eh?"

He sipped slowly, his eyes on Baley.

Baley passed the knuckles of one hand against his long cheek, rubbing it thoughtfully. "Now if that——"

He didn't finish, but leaped from his chair and almost hurled himself toward the other, before remembering it was only an image he was facing.

For Gruer, staring wildly at his drink, clutched his throat, whispering hoarsely, "Burning . . . burning . . ."

The glass fell from his hand, its contents spilling. And Gruer dropped with it, his face distorted with pain.

7 A Doctor Is Prodded

DANEEL STOOD in the doorway. "What happened, Partner Eli——"

But no explanation was needed. Daneel's voice changed to a loud ringing shout. "Robots of Hannis Gruer! Your master is hurt! Robots!"

At once a metal figure strode into the dining room and after it, in a minute or two, a dozen more entered. Three carried Gruer gently away. The others busily engaged in straightening the disarray and picking up the tableware strewn on the floor.

Daneel called out suddenly, "You there, robots, never mind the crockery. Organize a search. Search the house for any human being. Alert any robots on the grounds outside. Have them go over every acre of the estate. If you find a master, hold him. Do not hurt him" (unnecessary advice) "but do not let him leave, either. If you find no master present, let me know. I will remain at this viewer combination."

Then, as robots scattered, Elijah muttered to Daneel, "That's a beginning. It was poison, of course."

"Yes. That much is obvious, Partner Elijah." Daneel sat down queerly, as though there were a weakness in his knees. Baley had never seen him give way so, not for an instant, to any action that resembled anything so human as a weakness in the knees.

Daneel said, "It is not well with my mechanism to see a human being come to harm."

"There was nothing you could do."

"That I understand and yet it is as though there were certain cloggings in my thought paths. In human terms what I feel might be the equivalent to shock."

"If that's so, get over it." Baley felt neither patience nor sympathy for a queasy robot. "We've got to consider the little matter of responsibility. There is no poison without a poisoner."

"It might have been food-poisoning."

"Accidental food-poisoning? On a world this neatly run? Never. Besides, the poison was in a liquid and the symptoms were sudden and complete. It was a poisoned dose and a large one. Look, Daneel, I'll go into the next room to think this out a bit. You get Mrs. Delmarre. Make sure she's at home and check the distance between her estate and Gruer's."

"Is it that you think she——"

Baley held up a hand. "Just find out, will you?"

He strode out of the room, seeking solitude. Surely there could not be two independent attempts at murder so close together in time on a world like Solaria. And if a connection existed, the easiest assumption to make was that Gruer's story of a conspiracy was true.

Baley felt a familiar excitement growing within him. He had come to this world with Earth's predicament in his mind, and his own. The murder itself had been a faraway thing, but now the chase was really on. The muscles in his jaw knotted.

After all, the murderer or murderers (or murderess) had struck in his presence and he was stung by that. Was he held in so little account? It was professional pride that was hurt and Baley knew it and welcomed the fact. At least it gave him a firm reason to see this thing through as a murder case, simply, without reference to Earth's dangers.

Daneel had located him now and was striding toward him. "I have done as you asked me to, Partner Elijah. I have viewed Mrs. Delmarre. She is at home, which is somewhat over a thousand miles from the estate of Agent Gruer."

Baley said, "I'll see her myself later. View her, I mean." He stared thoughtfully at Daneel. "Do you think she has any connection with this crime?"

"Apparently not a direct connection, Partner Elijah."

"Does that imply there might be an indirect connection?"

"She might have persuaded someone else to do it."

"Someone else?" Baley asked quickly. "Who?"

"That, Partner Elijah, I cannot say."

"If someone were acting for her, that someone would have to be at the scene of the crime."

"Yes," said Daneel, "someone must have been there to place the poison in the liquid."

"Isn't it possible that the poisoned liquid might have been prepared earlier in the day? Perhaps much earlier?"

Daneel said quietly, "I had thought of that, Partner Elijah, which is why I used the word 'apparently' when I stated that Mrs. Delmarre had no direct connection with the crime. It is within the realm of possibility for her to have been on the scene earlier in the day. It would be well to check her movements."

"We will do that. We will check whether she was physically present at any time."

Baley's lips twitched. He had guessed that in some ways robotic logic must fall short and he was convinced of it now. As the roboticist had said: Logical but not reasonable.

He said, "Let's get back into the viewing room and get Gruer's estate back in view."

The room sparkled with freshness and order. There was no sign at all that less than an hour before a man had collapsed in agony.

Three robots stood, backs against the wall, in the usual robotic attitude of respectful submission.

Baley said, "What news concerning your master?"

The middle robot said, "The doctor is attending him, master."

"Viewing or seeing?"

"Viewing, master."

"What does the doctor say? Will your master live?"

"It is not yet certain, master."

Baley said, "Has the house been searched?"

"Thoroughly, master."

"Was there any sign of another master beside your own?"

"No, master."

"Were there any signs of such presence in the near past?"

"Not at all, master."

"Are the grounds being searched?"

"Yes, master."

"Any results so far?"

"No, master."

Baley nodded and said, "I wish to speak to the robot that served at the table this night."

"It is being held for inspection, master. Its reactions are erratic."

"Can it speak?"

"Yes, master."

"Then get it here without delay."

There *was* delay and Baley began again. "I said——"

Daneel interrupted smoothly. "There is interradio communication among these Solarian types. The robot you desire is being summoned. If it is slow in coming, it is part of the disturbance that has overtaken it as the result of what has occurred."

Baley nodded. He might have guessed at interradio. In a world so thoroughly given over to robots some sort of intimate communication among them would be necessary if the system were not to break down. It explained how a dozen robots could follow when one robot had been summoned, but only when needed and not otherwise.

A robot entered. It limped, one leg dragging. Baley wondered why and then shrugged. Even among the primitive robots on Earth reactions to injury of the positronic paths were never obvious to the layman. A disrupted circuit might strike a leg's functioning, as here, and the fact would be most significant to a roboticist and completely meaningless to anyone else.

Baley said cautiously, "Do you remember a colorless liquid on your master's table, some of which you poured into a goblet for him?"

The robot said, "Yeth, mathter."

A defect in oral articulation, too!

Baley said, "What was the nature of the liquid?"

"It wath water, mathter."

"Just water? Nothing else?"

"Jutht water, mathter."

"Where did you get it?"

"From the rethervoir tap, mathter."

"Had it been standing in the kitchen before you brought it in?"

"The mathter preferred it not too cold, mathter. It wath a thtanding order that it be poured an hour before mealth."

How convenient, thought Baley, for anyone who knew that fact.

He said, "Have one of the robots connect me with the doctor viewing your master as soon as he is available. And while that is being done, I want another one to explain how the reservoir tap works. I want to know about the water supply here."

The doctor was available with little delay. He was the oldest Spacer Baley had ever seen, which meant, Baley thought, that he might be over three hundred years old. The veins stood out on his hands and his close-cropped hair was pure white. He had a habit of tapping his ridged front teeth with a fingernail, making a little clicking noise that Baley found annoying. His name was Altim Thool.

The doctor said, "Fortunately, he threw up a good deal of the dose. Still, he may not survive. It is a tragic event." He sighed heavily.

"What was the poison, Doctor?" asked Baley.

"I'm afraid I don't know." (Click-click-click.)

Baley said, "What? Then how are you treating him?"

"Direct stimulation of the neuromuscular system to prevent paralysis, but except for that I am letting nature take its course." His face, with its faintly yellow skin, like well-worn leather of superior quality, wore a pleading expression. "We have very little experience with this sort of thing. I don't recall another case in over two centuries of practice."

Baley stared at the other with contempt. "You know there are such things as poisons, don't you?"

"Oh yes." (Click-click.) "Common knowledge."

"You have book-film references where you can gain some knowledge."

"It would take days. There are numerous mineral poisons. We make use of insecticides in our society, and it is not impossible to obtain bacterial toxins. Even with descriptions in the films it would take a long time to gather the equipment and develop the techniques to test for them."

"If no one on Solaria knows," said Baley grimly, "I'd suggest you get in touch with one of the other worlds and find out. Meanwhile, you had better test the reservoir tap in Gruer's mansion for poison. Get there in person, if you have to, and do it."

Baley was prodding a venerable Spacer roughly, ordering him about like a robot and was quite unconscious of the incongruity of it. Nor did the Spacer make any protest.

Dr. Thool said doubtfully, "How could the reservoir tap be poisoned? I'm sure it couldn't be."

"Probably not," agreed Baley, "but test it anyway to make sure."

The reservoir tap was a dim possibility indeed. The robot's explanation had shown it to be a typical piece of

Solarian self-care. Water might enter it from whatever source and be tailored to suit. Microorganisms were removed and non-living organic matter eliminated. The proper amount of aeration was introduced, as were various ions in just those trace amounts best suited to the body's needs. It was very unlikely that any poison could survive one or another of the control devices.

Still, if the safety of the reservoir were directly established, then the time element would be clear. There would be the matter of the hour before the meal, when the pitcher of water (exposed to *air*, thought Baley sourly) was allowed to warm slowly, thanks to Gruer's idiosyncrasy.

But Dr. Thool, frowning, was saying, "But how would I test the reservoir tap?"

"Jehoshaphat! Take an animal with you. Inject some of the water you take out of the tap into its veins, or have it drink some. Use your head, man. And do the same for what's left in the pitcher, and if that's poisoned, as it must be, run some of the tests the reference films describe. Find some simple one. Do *some*thing."

"Wait, wait. What pitcher?"

"The pitcher in which the water was standing. The pitcher from which the robot poured the poisoned drink."

"Well, dear me—I presume it has been cleaned up. The household retinue would surely not leave it standing about."

Baley groaned. Of course not. It was *impossible* to retain evidence with eager robots forever destroying it in the name of household duty. He should have *ordered* it preserved, but of course, this society was not his own and he never reacted properly to it.

Jehoshaphat!

Word eventually came through that the Gruer estate was clear; no sign of any unauthorized human present anywhere.

Daneel said, "That rather intensifies the puzzle, Partner

Elijah, since it seems to leave no one in the role of poisoner."

Baley, absorbed in thought, scarcely heard. He said, "What? . . . Not at all. Not at all. It clarifies the matter." He did not explain, knowing quite well that Daneel would be incapable of understanding or believing what Baley was certain was the truth.

Nor did Daneel ask for an explanation. Such an invasion of a human's thoughts would have been most unrobotic.

Baley prowled back and forth restlessly, dreading the approach of the sleep period, when his fears of the open would rise and his longing for Earth increase. He felt an almost feverish desire to keep things happening.

He said to Daneel, "I might as well see Mrs. Delmarre again. Have the robot make contact."

They walked to the viewing room and Baley watched a robot work with deft metal fingers. He watched through a haze of obscuring thought that vanished in startled astonishment when a table, elaborately spread for dinner, suddenly filled half the room.

Gladia's voice said, "Hello." A moment later she stepped into view and sat down. "Don't look surprised, Elijah. It's just dinnertime. And I'm very carefully dressed. See?"

She was. The dominant color of her dress was a light blue and it shimmered down the length of her limbs to wrists and ankles. A yellow ruff clung about her neck and shoulders, a little lighter than her hair, which was now held in disciplined waves.

Baley said, "I did not mean to interrupt your meal."

"I haven't begun yet. Why don't you join me?"

He eyed her suspiciously. "Join you?"

She laughed. "You Earthmen are so funny. I don't mean join me in personal presence. How could you do that? I mean, go to your own dining room and then you and the other one can dine with me."

"But if I leave——"

"Your viewing technician can maintain contact."

Daneel nodded gravely at that, and with some uncertainty Baley turned and walked toward the door. Gladia, together with her table, its setting, and its ornaments moved with him.

Gladia smiled encouragingly. "See? Your viewing technician is keeping us in contact."

Baley and Daneel traveled up a moving ramp that Baley did not recall having traversed before. Apparently there were numerous possible routes between any two rooms in this impossible mansion and he knew only few of them. Daneel, of course, knew them all.

And, moving through walls, sometimes a bit below floor level, sometimes a bit above, there was always Gladia and her dinner table.

Baley stopped and muttered, "This takes getting used to."

Gladia said at once, "Does it make you dizzy?"

"A little."

"Then I tell you what. Why don't you have your technicians freeze me right here. Then when you're in your dining room and all set, he can join us up."

Daneel said, "I will order that done, Partner Elijah."

Their own dinner table was set when they arrived, the plates steaming with a dark brown soup in which diced meat was bobbing, and in the center a large roast fowl was ready for the carving. Daneel spoke briefly to the serving robot and, with smooth efficiency, the two places that had been set were drawn to the same end of the table.

As though that were a signal, the opposite wall seemed to move outward, the table seemed to lengthen and Gladia was seated at the opposite end. Room joined to room and table to table so neatly that but for the varying pattern in wall and floor covering and the differing designs in tableware it would have been easy to believe they were all dining together in actual fact.

"There," said Gladia with satisfaction. "Isn't this comfortable?"

"Quite," said Baley. He tasted his soup gingerly, found

it delicious, and helped himself more generously. "You know about Agent Gruer?"

Trouble shadowed her face at once and she put her spoon down. "Isn't it terrible? Poor Hannis."

"You use his first name. Do you know him?"

"I know almost all the important people on Solaria. Most Solarians do know one another. Naturally."

Naturally, indeed, thought Baley. How many of them were there, after all?

Baley said, "Then perhaps you know Dr. Altim Thool. He's taking care of Gruer."

Gladia laughed gently. Her serving robot sliced meat for her and added small, browned potatoes and slivers of carrots. "Of course I know him. He treated me."

"Treated you when?"

"Right after the—the trouble. About my husband, I mean."

Baley said in astonishment, "Is he the only doctor on the planet?"

"Oh no." For a moment her lips moved as though she were counting to herself. "There are at least ten. And there's one youngster I know of who's studying medicine. But Dr. Thool is one of the best. He has the most experience. Poor Dr. Thool."

"Why poor?"

"Well, you know what I mean. It's such a nasty job, being a doctor. Sometimes you just have to see people when you're a doctor and even touch them. But Dr. Thool seems so resigned to it and he'll always do some seeing when he feels he must. He's always treated me since I was a child and was always so friendly and kind and I honestly feel I almost wouldn't mind if he did have to see me. For instance, he saw me this last time."

"After your husband's death, you mean?"

"Yes. You can imagine how he felt when he saw my husband's dead body and me lying there."

"I was told he viewed the body," said Baley.

"The body, yes. But after he made sure I was alive and in no real danger, he ordered the robots to put a pillow under my head and give me an injection of something or other, and then get out. He came over by jet. Really! By jet. It took less than half an hour and he took care of me and made sure all was well. I was so woozy when I came to that I was sure I was only viewing him, you know, and it wasn't till he touched me that I knew we were seeing, and I screamed. Poor Dr. Thool. He was awfully embarrassed, but I knew he meant well."

Baley nodded. "I suppose there's not much use for doctors on Solaria?"

"I should hope *not*."

"I know there are no germ diseases to speak of. What about metabolic disorders? Atherosclerosis? Diabetes? Things like that?"

"It happens and it's pretty awful when it does. Doctors can make life more livable for such people in a physical way, but that's the least of it."

"Oh?"

"Of course. It means the gene analysis was imperfect. You don't-suppose we allow defects like diabetes to develop on purpose. Anyone who develops such things has to undergo very detailed re-analysis. The mate assignment has to be retracted, which is terribly embarrassing for the mate. And it means no—no"—her voice sank to a whisper—"children."

Baley said in a normal voice, "No children?"

Gladia flushed. "It's a terrible thing to say. Such a word! Ch-children!"

"It comes easy after a while," said Baley dryly.

"Yes, but if I get into the habit, I'll say it in front of another Solarian someday and I'll just sink into the ground. . . . Anyway, if the two of them have had children (see, I've said it again) already, the children have to be found and examined—that was one of Rikaine's jobs, by the way—and well, it's just a mess."

So much for Thool, thought Baley. The doctor's incompetence was a natural consequence of the society, and held nothing sinister. Nothing *necessarily* sinister. Cross him off, he thought, but lightly.

He watched Gladia as she ate. She was neat and precisely delicate in her movements and her appetite seemed normal. (His own fowl was delightful. In one respect, anyway—food—he could easily be spoiled by these Outer Worlds.)

He said, "What is your opinion of the poisoning, Gladia?"

She looked up. "I'm trying not to think of it. There are so many horrors lately. Maybe it wasn't poisoning."

"It was."

"But there wasn't anyone around?"

"How do you know?"

"There couldn't have been. He has no wife, these days, since he's all through with his quota of ch—you know what. So there was no one to put the poison in anything, so how could he be poisoned?"

"But he was poisoned. That's a fact and must be accepted."

Her eyes clouded over. "Do you suppose," she said, "he did it himself?"

"I doubt it. Why should he? And so publicly?"

"Then it couldn't be done, Elijah. It just couldn't."

Baley said, "On the contrary, Gladia. It could be done very easily. And I'm sure I know exactly how."

8   A Spacer Is Defied

GLADIA SEEMED to be holding her breath for a moment. It came out through puckered lips in what was almost a whistle. She said, "I'm sure *I* don't see how. Do you know *who* did it?"

Baley nodded. "The same one who killed your husband."

"Are you sure?"

"Aren't you? Your husband's murder was the first in the history of Solaria. A month later there is another murder. Could that be a coincidence? Two separate murderers striking within a month of each other on a crime-free world? Consider, too, that the second victim was investigating the first crime and therefore represented a violent danger to the original murderer."

"Well!" Gladia applied herself to her dessert and said between mouthfuls, "If you put it that way, I'm innocent."

"How so, Gladia?"

"Why, Elijah. I've never been near the Gruer estate, never in my whole life. So I certainly couldn't have poisoned Agent Gruer. And if I haven't—why, neither did I kill my husband."

Then, as Baley maintained a stern silence, her spirit seemed to fade and the corners of her small mouth drooped. "Don't you think so, Elijah?"

"I can't be sure," said Baley. "I've told you I know the method used to poison Gruer. It's an ingenious one and anyone on Solaria could have used it, whether they were on the Gruer estate or not; whether they were ever on the Gruer estate or not."

Gladia clenched her hands into fists. "Are you saying I did it?"

"I'm not saying that."

"You're implying it." Her lips were thin with fury and her high cheekbones were splotchy. "Is that all your interest in viewing me? To ask me sly questions? To trap me?"

"Now wait——"

"You seemed so sympathetic. So understanding. You—you Earthman!"

Her contralto had become a tortured rasp with the last word.

Daneel's perfect face leaned toward Gladia and he said, "If you will pardon me, Mrs. Delmarre, you are holding a knife rather tightly and may cut yourself. Please be careful."

Gladia stared wildly at the short, blunt, and undoubtedly quite harmless knife she held in her hand. With a spasmodic movement she raised it high.

Baley said, "You couldn't reach me, Gladia."

She gasped. "Who'd want to reach you? Ugh!" She shuddered in exaggerated disgust and called out, "Break contact at once!"

The last must have been to a robot out of the line of sight, and Gladia and her end of the room were gone and the original wall sprang back.

Daneel said, "Am I correct in believing you now consider this woman guilty?"

"No," said Baley flatly. "Whoever did this needed a great deal more of certain characteristics than this poor girl has."

"She has a temper."

"What of that? Most people do. Remember, too, that she has been under a considerable strain for a considerable time. If I had been under a similar strain and someone had turned on me as she imagined I had turned on her, I might have done a great deal more than wave a foolish little knife."

Daneel said, "I have not been able to deduce the technique of poisoning at a distance, as you say you have."

Baley found it pleasant to be able to say, "I know you haven't. You lack the capacity to decipher this particular puzzle."

He said it with finality and Daneel accepted the statement as calmly and as gravely as ever.

Baley said, "I have two jobs for you, Daneel."

"And what are they, Partner Elijah?"

"First, get in touch with this Dr. Thool and find out Mrs. Delmarre's condition at the time of the murder of her husband. How long she required treatment and so on."

"Do you want to determine something in particular?"

"No. I'm just trying to accumulate data. It isn't easy on this world. Secondly, find out who will be taking Gruer's place as head of security and arrange a viewing session for me first thing in the morning. As for me," he said without pleasure in his mind, and with none in his voice,

"I'm going to bed and eventually, I hope, I'll sleep." Then, almost petulantly, "Do you suppose I could get a decent book-film in this place?"

Daneel said, "I would suggest that you summon the robot in charge of the library."

Baley felt only irritation at having to deal with the robot. He would much rather have browsed at will.

"No," he said, "not a classic; just an ordinary piece of fiction dealing with everyday life on contemporary Solaria. About half a dozen of them."

The robot submitted (it would have to) but even as it manipulated the proper controls that plucked the requisite book-films out of their niches and transferred them first to an exit slot and then to Baley's hand, it rattled on in respectful tones about all the other categories in the library.

The master might like an adventure romance of the days of exploration, it suggested, or an excellent view of chemistry, perhaps, with animated atom models, or a fantasy, or a Galactography. The list was endless.

Baley waited grimly for his half dozen, said, "These will do," reached with his own hands (his *own* hands) for a scanner and walked away.

When the robot followed and said, "Will you require help with the adjustment, master?" Baley turned and snapped, "No. Stay where you are."

The robot bowed and stayed.

Lying in bed, with the headboard aglow, Baley almost regretted his decision. The scanner was like no model he had ever used and he began with no idea at all as to the method for threading the film. But he worked at it obstinately, and, eventually, by taking it apart and working it out bit by bit, he managed something.

At least he could view the film and, if the focus left a bit to be desired, it was small payment for a moment's independence from the robots.

In the next hour and a half he had skipped and switched through four of the six films and was disappointed.

He had had a theory. There was no better way, he had thought, to get an insight into Solarian ways of life and thought than to read their novels. He needed that insight if he were to conduct the investigation sensibly.

But now he had to abandon his theories. He had viewed novels and had succeeded only in learning of people with ridiculous problems who behaved foolishly and reacted mysteriously. Why should a woman abandon her job on discovering her child had entered the same profession and refuse to explain her reasons until unbearable and ridiculous complications had resulted? Why should a doctor and an artist be humiliated at being assigned to one another and what was so noble about the doctor's insistence on entering robotic research?

He threaded the fifth novel into the scanner and adjusted it to his eyes. He was bone-weary.

So weary, in fact, that he never afterward recalled anything of the fifth novel (which he believed to be a suspense story) except for the opening in which a new estate owner entered his mansion and looked through the past account films presented him by a respectful robot.

Presumably he fell asleep then with the scanner on his head and all lights blazing. Presumably a robot, entering respectfully, had gently removed the scanner and put out the lights.

In any case, he slept and dreamed of Jessie. All was as it had been. He had never left Earth. They were ready to travel to the community kitchen and then to see a subetheric show with friends. They would travel over the Expressways and see people and neither of them had a care in the world. He was happy.

And Jessie was beautiful. She had lost weight somehow. Why should she be so slim? And so beautiful?

And one other thing was wrong. Somehow the sun shone down on them. He looked up and there was only the vaulted base of the upper Levels visible, yet the sun shone down, blazing brightly on everything, and no one was afraid.

Baley woke up, disturbed. He let the robots serve breakfast and did not speak to Daneel. He said nothing, asked nothing, downed excellent coffee without tasting it.

Why had he dreamed of the visible-invisible sun? He could understand dreaming of Earth and of Jessie, but what had the sun to do with it? And why should the thought of it bother him, anyway?

"Partner Elijah," said Daneel gently.

"What?"

"Corwin Attlebish will be in viewing contact with you in half an hour. I have arranged that."

"Who the hell is Corwin Whatchamacullum?" asked Baley sharply, and refilled his coffee cup.

"He was Agent Gruer's chief aide, Partner Elijah, and is now Acting Head of Security."

"Then get him now."

"The appointment, as I explained, is for half an hour from now."

"I don't care when it's for. Get him now. That's an order."

"I will make the attempt, Partner Elijah. He may not, however, agree to receive the call."

"Let's take the chance, and get on with it, Daneel."

The Acting Head of Security accepted the call and, for the first time on Solaria, Baley saw a Spacer who looked like the usual Earthly conception of one. Attlebish was tall, lean, and bronze. His eyes were a light brown, his chin large and hard.

He looked faintly like Daneel. But whereas Daneel was idealized, almost godlike, Corwin Attlebish had lines of humanity in his face.

Attlebish was shaving. The small abrasive pencil gave out its spray of fine particles that swept over cheek and chin, biting off the hair neatly and then disintegrating into impalpable dust.

Baley recognized the instrument through hearsay but had never seen one used before.

"You the Earthman?" asked Attlebish slurringly through

barely cracked lips, as the abrasive dust passed under his nose.

Baley said, "I'm Elijah Baley, Plainclothesman C-7. I'm from Earth."

"You're early." Attlebish snapped his shaver shut and tossed it somewhere outside Baley's range of vision. "What's on your mind, Earthman?"

Baley would not have enjoyed the other's tone of voice at the best of times. He burned now. He said, "How is Agent Gruer?"

Attlebish said, "He's still alive. He may stay alive."

Baley nodded. "Your poisoners here on Solaria don't know dosages. Lack of experience. They gave Gruer too much and he threw it up. Half the dose would have killed him."

"Poisoners? There is no evidence for poison."

Baley stared. "Jehoshaphat! What else do you think it is?"

"A number of things. Much can go wrong with a person." He rubbed his face, looking for roughness with his fingertips. "You would scarcely know the metabolic problems that arise past the age of two fifty."

"If that's the case, have you obtained competent medical advice?"

"Dr. Thool's report——"

That did it. The anger that had been boiling inside Baley since waking burst through. He cried at the top of his voice, "I don't care about Dr. Thool. I said competent medical advice. Your doctors don't know anything, any more than your detectives would, if you had any. You had to get a detective from Earth. Get a doctor as well."

The Solarian looked at him coolly. "Are you telling me what to do?"

"Yes, and without charge. Be my guest. Gruer *was* poisoned. I witnessed the process. He drank, retched, and yelled that his throat was burning. What do you call it when you consider that he was investigating——" Baley came to a sudden halt.

"Investigating what?" Attlebish was unmoved.

Baley was uncomfortably aware of Daneel at his usual position some ten feet away. Gruer had not wanted Daneel, as an Auroran, to know of the investigation. He said lamely, "There were political implications."

Attlebish crossed his arms and looked distant, bored, and faintly hostile. "We have no politics on Solaria in the sense we hear of it on other worlds. Hannis Gruer has been a good citizen, but he is imaginative. It was he who, having heard some story about you, urged that we import you. He even agreed to accept an Auroran companion for you as a condition. I did not think it necessary. There is no mystery. Rikaine Delmarre was killed by his wife and we shall find out how and why. Even if we do not, she will be genetically analyzed and the proper measures taken. As for Gruer, your fantasy concerning poisoning is of no importance."

Baley said incredulously, "You seem to imply that I'm not needed here."

"I believe not. If you wish to return to Earth, you may do so. I may even say we urge you to."

Baley was amazed at his own reaction. He cried, "No, sir. I don't budge."

"We hired you, Plainclothesman. We can discharge you. You will return to your home planet."

"*No!* You listen to me. I'd advise you to. You're a big-time Spacer and I'm an Earthman, but with all respect, with deepest and most humble apologies, you're scared."

"Withdraw that statement!" Attlebish drew himself to his six-foot-plus, and stared down at the Earthman haughtily.

"You're scared as hell. You think you'll be next if you pursue this thing. You're giving in so they'll let you alone; so they'll leave you your miserable life." Baley had no notion who the "they" might be or if there were any "they" at all. He was striking out blindly at an arrogant Spacer and enjoying the thud his phrases made as they hit against the other's self-control.

"You will leave," said Attlebish, pointing his finger in

cold anger, "within the hour. There'll be no diplomatic considerations about this, I assure you."

"Save your threats, Spacer. Earth is nothing to you, I admit, but I'm not the only one here. May I introduce my partner, Daneel Olivaw. He's from Aurora. He doesn't talk much. He's not here to talk. I handle that department. But he listens awfully well. He doesn't miss a word.

"Let me put it straight, Attlebish"—Baley used the unadorned name with relish—"whatever monkeyshines are going on here on Solaria, Aurora and forty-odd other Outer Worlds are interested. If you kick us off, the next deputation to visit Solaria will consist of warships. I'm from Earth and I know how the system works. Hurt feelings mean warships by return trip."

Attlebish transferred his regard to Daneel and seemed to be considering. His voice was gentler. "There is nothing going on here that need concern anyone outside the planet."

"Gruer thought otherwise and my partner heard him." This was no time to cavil at a lie.

Daneel turned to look at Baley, at the Earthman's last statement, but Baley paid no attention. He drove on: "I intend to pursue this investigation. Ordinarily, there's nothing I wouldn't do to get back to Earth. Even just dreaming about it gets me so restless I can't sit. If I owned this robot-infested palace I'm living in now, I'd give it with the robots thrown in and you and all your lousy world to boot for a ticket home.

"But I won't be ordered off by you. Not while there's a case to which I've been assigned that's still open. Try getting rid of me against my will and you'll be looking down the throats of space-based artillery.

"What's more, from now on, this murder investigation is going to be run *my* way. I'm in charge. I see the people I want to see. I *see* them. I don't view them. I'm used to seeing and that's the way it's going to be. I'll want the official approval of your office for all of that."

"This is impossible, unbearable——"

"Daneel, you tell him."

The humanoid's voice said dispassionately, "As my partner has informed you, Agent Attlebish, we have been sent here to conduct a murder investigation. It is essential that we do so. We, of course, do not wish to disturb any of your customs and perhaps actual seeing will be unnecessary, although it would be helpful if you were to give approval for such seeing as becomes necessary as Plainclothesman Baley has requested. As to leaving the planet against our will, we feel that would be inadvisable, although we regret any feeling on your part or on the part of any Solarian that our remaining would be unpleasant."

Baley listened to the stilted sentence structure with a dour stretching of his lips that was not a smile. To one who knew Daneel as a robot, it was all an attempt to do a job without giving offense to any human, not to Baley and not to Attlebish. To one who thought Daneel was an Auroran, a native of the oldest and most powerful militarily of the Outer Worlds, it sounded like a series of subtly courteous threats.

Attlebish put the tips of his fingers to his forehead. "I'll think about it."

"Not too long," said Baley, "because I have some visiting to do within the hour, and not by viewer. Done viewing!"

He signaled the robot to break contact, then he stared with surprise and pleasure at the place where Attlebish had been. None of this had been planned. It had all been impulse born of his dream and of Attlebish's unnecessary arrogance. But now that it had happened, he was glad. It was what he had wanted, really—to take control.

He thought: Anyway, that was telling the dirty Spacer!

He wished the entire population of Earth could have been here to watch. The man *looked* such a Spacer, and that made it all the better, of course. All the better.

Only, why this feeling of vehemence in the matter of seeing? Baley scarcely understood that. He knew what he planned to do, and seeing (not viewing) was part of

101

it. All right. Yet there had been the tight lift to his spirit when he spoke of seeing, as though he were ready to break down the walls of this mansion even though it served no purpose.

Why?

There was something impelling him besides, the case, something that had nothing to do even with the question of Earth's safety: But what?

Oddly, he remembered his dream again; the sun shining down through all the opaque layers of the gigantic underground Cities of Earth.

Daneel said with thoughtfulness (as far as his voice could carry a recognizable emotion), "I wonder, Partner Elijah, if this is entirely safe."

"Bluffing this character? It worked. And it wasn't really a bluff. I think it *is* important to Aurora to find out what's going on on Solaria, and that Aurora knows it. Thank you, by the way, for not catching me out in a misstatement."

"It was the natural decision. To have borne you out did Agent Attlebish a certain rather subtle harm. To have given you the lie would have done you a greater and more direct harm."

"Potentials countered and the higher one won out, eh, Daneel?"

"So it was, Partner Elijah. I understand that this process, in a less definable way, goes on within the human mind. I repeat, however, that this new proposal of yours is not safe."

"Which new proposal is this?"

"I do not approve your notion of seeing people. By that I mean seeing as opposed to viewing."

"I understand you. I'm not asking for your approval."

"I have my instructions, Partner Elijah. What it was that Agent Hannis Gruer told you during my absence last night I cannot know. That he did say something is obvious from the change in your attitude toward this problem. However, in the light of my instructions, I can guess. He must have warned you of the possibility of danger to other planets arising from the situation on Solaria."

Slowly Baley reached for his pipe. He did that occasionally and always there was the feeling of irritation when he found nothing and remembered he could not smoke. He said, "There are only twenty thousand Solarians. What danger can they represent?"

"My masters on Aurora have for some time been uneasy about Solaria. I have not been told all the information at their disposal——"

"And what little you have been told you have been told not to repeat to me. Is that it?" demanded Baley.

Daneel said, "There is a great deal to find out before this matter can be discussed freely."

"Well, what are the Solarians doing? New weapons? Paid subversion? A campaign of individual assassination? What can twenty thousand people do against hundreds of millions of Spacers?"

Daneel remained silent.

Baley said, "I intend to find out, you know."

"But not the way you have now proposed, Partner Elijah. I have been instructed most carefully to guard your safety."

"You would have to anyway. First Law!"

"Over and above that, as well. In conflict between your safety and that of another I must guard yours."

"Of course. I understand that. If anything happens to me, there is no further way in which you can remain on Solaria without complications that Aurora is not yet ready to face. As long as I'm alive, I'm here at Solaria's original request and so we can throw our weight around, if necessary, and make them keep us. If I'm dead, the whole situation is changed. Your orders are, then, to keep Baley alive. Am I right, Daneel?"

Daneel said, "I cannot presume to interpret the reasoning behind my orders."

Baley said, "All right, don't worry. The open space won't kill me, if I do find it necessary to see anyone. I'll survive. I may even get used to it."

"It is not the matter of open space alone, Partner Elijah," said Daneel. "It is this matter of seeing Solarians. I do not approve of it."

"You mean the Spacers won't like it. Too bad if they don't. Let them wear nose filters and gloves. Let them spray the air. And if it offends their nice morals to see me in the flesh, let them wince and blush. But I intend to see them. I consider it necessary to do so and I *will* do so."

"But I cannot allow you to."

"*You* can't allow *me*?"

"Surely you see why, Partner Elijah."

"I do not."

"Consider, then, that Agent Gruer, the key Solarian figure in the investigation of this murder, has been poisoned. Does it not follow that if I permit you to proceed in your plan for exposing yourself indiscriminately in actual person, the next victim will necessarily be you yourself. How then can I possibly permit you to leave the safety of this mansion?"

"How will you stop me, Daneel?"

"By force, if necessary, Partner Elijah," said Daneel calmly. "Even if I must hurt you. If I do not do so, you will surely die."

9   A Robot Is Stymied

BALEY SAID, "So the higher potential wins out again, Daneel. You will hurt me to keep me alive."

"I do not believe hurting you will be necessary, Partner Elijah. You know that I am superior to you in strength and you will not attempt a useless resistance. If it should become necessary, however, I will be compelled to hurt you."

"I could blast you down where you stand," said Baley. "Right now! There is nothing in *my* potentials to prevent me."

"I had thought you might take this attitude at some time in our present relationship, Partner Elijah. Most particularly, the thought occurred to me during our trip to this mansion, when you grew momentarily violent in the ground-car. The destruction of myself is unimportant in comparison with your safety, but such destruction would cause you distress eventually and disturb the plans of my masters. It was one of my first cares, therefore, during your first sleeping period, to deprive your blaster of its charge."

Baley's lips tightened. He was left without a charged blaster! His hand dropped instantly to his holster. He drew his weapon and stared at the charge reading. It hugged zero.

For a moment he balanced the lump of useless metal as though to hurl it directly into Daneel's face. What good? The robot would dodge efficiently.

Baley put the blaster back. It could be recharged in good time.

Slowly, thoughtfully, he said, "I'm not fooled by you, Daneel."

"In what way, Partner Elijah?"

"You are too much the master. I am too completely stopped by you. Are you a robot?"

"You have doubted me before," said Daneel.

"On Earth last year, I doubted whether R. Daneel Olivaw was truly a robot. It turned out he was. I believe he still is. My question, however is this: Are you R. Daneel Olivaw?"

"I am."

"Yes? Daneel was designed to imitate a Spacer closely. Why could not a Spacer be made up to imitate Daneel closely?"

"For what reason?"

"To carry on an investigation here with greater initiative and capacity than ever a robot could. And yet by assuming Daneel's role, you could keep me safely under control by giving me a false consciousness of mastery. After all, you are working through me and I must be kept pliable."

"All this is not so, Partner Elijah."

"Then why do all the Solarians we meet assume you to be human? They are robotic experts. Are they so easily fooled? It occurs to me that I cannot be one right against many wrong. It is far more likely that I am one wrong against many right."

"Not at all, Partner Elijah."

"Prove it," said Baley, moving slowly toward an end table and lifting a scrap-disposal unit. "You can do that easily enough, if you *are* a robot. Show the metal beneath your skin."

Daneel said, "I assure you——"

"Show the metal," said Baley crisply. "That is an order! Or don't you feel compelled to obey orders?"

Daneel unbuttoned his shirt. The smooth, bronze skin of his chest was sparsely covered with light hair. Daneel's fingers exerted a firm pressure just under the right nipple, and flesh and skin split bloodlessly the length of the chest, with the gleam of metal showing beneath.

And as that happened, Baley's fingers, resting on the end table, moved half an inch to the right and stabbed at a contact patch. Almost at once a robot entered.

"Don't move, Daneel," cried Baley. "That's an order! Freeze!"

Daneel stood motionless, as though life, or the robotic imitation thereof, had departed from him.

Baley shouted to the robot, "Can you get two more of the staff in here without yourself leaving? If so, do it."

The robot said, "Yes, master."

Two more robots entered, answering a radioed call. The three lined up abreast.

"Boys!" said Baley. "Do you see this creature whom you thought a master?"

Six ruddy eyes had turned solemnly on Daneel. They said in unison, "We see him, master."

Baley said, "Do you also see that this so-called master is actually a robot like yourself since it is metal within. It is only designed to look like a man."

"Yes, master."

106

"You are not required to obey any order it gives you. Do you understand that?"

"Yes, master."

"I, on the other hand," said Baley, "am a true man."

For a moment the robots hesitated. Baley wondered if, having had it shown to them that a thing might seem a man yet be a robot, they would accept *anything* in human appearance as a man, anything at all.

But then one robot said, "You are a man, master," and Baley drew breath again.

He said, "Very well, Daneel. You may relax."

Daneel moved into a more natural position and said calmly, "Your expressed doubt as to my identity, then, was merely a feint designed to exhibit my nature to these others, I take it."

"So it was," said Baley, and looked away. He thought: The thing is a machine, not a man. You can't double-cross a machine.

And yet he couldn't entirely repress a feeling of shame. Even as Daneel stood there, chest open, there seemed something so human about him, something capable of being betrayed.

Baley said, "Close your chest, Daneel, and listen to me. Physically, you are no match for three robots. You see that, don't you?"

"That is clear, Partner Elijah."

"Good! . . . Now you boys," and he turned to the other robots again. "You are to tell no one, human or master, that this creature is a robot. Never at any time, without further instructions from myself and myself alone."

"I thank you," interposed Daneel softly.

"However," Baley went on, "this manlike robot is not to be allowed to interfere with my actions in any way. If it attempts any such interference, you will restrain it by force, taking care not to damage it unless absolutely necessary. Do not allow it to establish contact with humans other than myself, or with robots other than yourselves, either by seeing or by viewing. And do not leave it at any time. Keep it in this room and remain here yourselves. Your other duties are suspended until further notice. Is all this clear?"

"Yes, master," they chorused.

Baley turned to Daneel again. "There is nothing you can do now, so don't try to stop me."

Daneel's arms hung loosely at his side. He said, "I may not, through inaction, allow you to come to harm, Partner Elijah. Yet under the circumstances, nothing but inaction is possible. The logic is unassailable. I shall do nothing. I trust you will remain safe and in good health."

There it was, thought Baley. Logic was logic and robots had nothing else. Logic told Daneel he was completely stymied. Reason might have told him that all factors are rarely predictable, that the opposition might make a mistake.

None of that. A robot is logical only, not reasonable.

Again Baley felt a twinge of shame and could not forbear an attempt at consolation. He said, "Look, Daneel, even if I were walking into danger, *which I'm not*" (he added that hurriedly, with a quick glance at the other robots) "it would only be my job. It is what I'm paid to do. It is as much my job to prevent harm to mankind as a whole as yours is to prevent harm to man as an individual. Do you see?"

"I do not, Partner Elijah."

"Then that is because you're not made to see. Take my word for it that if you were a man, you would see."

Daneel bowed his head in acquiescence and remained standing, motionless, while Baley walked slowly toward the door of the room. The three robots parted to make room for him and kept their photo-electric eyes fixed firmly on Daneel.

Baley was walking to a kind of freedom and his heart beat rapidly in anticipation of the fact, then skipped a beat. Another robot was approaching the door from the other side.

Had something gone wrong?

"What is it, boy?" he snapped.

"A message has been forwarded to you, master, from the office of Acting Head of Security Attlebish."

Baley took the personal capsule handed to him and it opened at once. A finely inscribed strip of paper unrolled. (He wasn't startled. Solaria would have his fingerprints on file and the capsule would be adjusted to open at the touch of his particular convolutions.)

He read the message and his long face mirrored satisfaction. It was his official permission to arrange "seeing" interviews, subject to the wishes of the interviewees, who were nevertheless urged to give "Agents Baley and Olivaw" every possible co-operation.

Attlebish had capitulated, even to the extent of putting the Earthman's name first. It was an excellent omen with which to begin, finally, an investigation conducted as it should be conducted.

Baley was in an air-borne vessel again, as he had been on that trip from New York to Washington. This time, however, there was a difference. The vessel was not closed in. The windows were left transparent.

It was a clear, bright day and from where Baley sat the windows were so many patches of blue. Unrelieved, featureless. He tried not to huddle. He buried his head in his knees only when he could absolutely no longer help it.

The ordeal was of his own choosing. His state of triumph, his unusual sense of freedom at having beaten down first Attlebish and then Daneel, his feeling of having asserted the dignity of Earth against the Spacers, almost demanded it.

He had begun by stepping across open ground to the waiting plane with a kind of lightheaded dizziness that was almost enjoyable, and he had ordered the windows left unblanked in a kind of manic self-confidence.

I have to get used to it, he thought, and stared at the blue until his heart beat rapidly and the lump in his throat swelled beyond endurance.

He had to close his eyes and bury his head under the protective cover of his arms at shortening intervals.

Slowly his confidence trickled away and even the touch of the holster of his freshly recharged blaster could not reverse the flow.

He tried to keep his mind on his plan of attack. First, learn the ways of the planet. Sketch in the background against which everything must be placed or fail to make sense.

See a sociologist!

He had asked a robot for the name of the Solarian most eminent as a sociologist. And there was that comfort about robots; they asked no questions.

The robot gave the name and vital statistics, and paused to remark that the sociologist would most probably be at lunch and would, therefore, possibly ask to delay contact.

"Lunch!" said Baley sharply. "Don't be ridiculous. It's not noon by two hours."

The robot said, "I am using local time, master."

Baley stared, then understood. On Earth, with its buried Cities, day and night, waking and sleeping, were man-made periods, adjusted to suit the needs of the community and the planet. On a planet such as this one, exposed nakedly to the sun, day and night were not a matter of choice at all, but were imposed on man willy-nilly.

Baley tried to picture a world as a sphere being lit and unlit as it turned. He found it hard to do and felt scornful of the so-superior Spacers who let such an essential thing as time be dictated to them by the vagaries of planetary movements.

He said, "Contact him anyway."

Robots were there to meet the plane when it landed and Baley, stepping out into the open again, found himself trembling badly.

He muttered to the nearest of the robots, "Let me hold your arm, boy."

The sociologist waited for him down the length of a hall, smiling tightly. "Good afternoon, Mr. Baley."

Baley nodded breathlessly. "Good evening, sir. Would you blank out the windows?"

The sociologist said, "They are blanked out already. I know something of the ways of Earth. Will you follow me?"

Baley managed it without robotic help, following at a considerable distance, across and through a maze of hall-ways. When he finally sat down in a large and elaborate room, he was glad of the opportunity to rest.

The walls of the room were set with curved, shallow alcoves. Statuary in pink and gold occupied each niche; abstract figures that pleased the eye without yielding instant meaning. A large, boxlike affair with white and dangling cylindrical objects and numerous pedals suggested a musical instrument.

Baley looked at the sociologist standing before him. The Spacer looked precisely as he had when Baley had viewed him earlier that day. He was tall and thin and his hair was pure white. His face was strikingly wedge-shaped, his nose prominent, his eyes deep-set and alive.

His name was Anselmo Quemot.

They stared at one another until Baley felt he could trust his voice to be reasonably normal. And then his first remark had nothing to do with the investigation. In fact it was nothing he had planned.

He said, "May I have a drink?"

"A drink?" The sociologist's voice was a trifle too high-pitched to be entirely pleasant. He said, "You wish water?"

"I'd prefer something alcoholic."

The sociologist's look grew sharply uneasy, as though the obligations of hospitality were something with which he was unacquainted.

And that, thought Baley, was literally so. In a world where viewing was the thing, there would be no sharing of food and drink.

A robot brought him a small cup of smooth enamel. The drink was a light pink in color. Baley sniffed at it cautiously and tasted it even more cautiously. The small

111

sip of liquid evaporated warmly in his mouth and sent a pleasant message along the length of his esophagus. His next sip was more substantial.

Quemot said, "If you wish more——"

"No, thank you, not now. It is good of you, sir, to agree to see me."

Quemot tried a smile and failed rather markedly, "It has been a long time since I've done anything like this. Yes."

He almost squirmed as he spoke.

Baley said, "I imagine you find this rather hard."

"Quite." Quemot turned away sharply and retreated to a chair at the opposite end of the room. He angled the chair so that it faced more away from Baley than toward him and sat down. He clasped his gloved hands and his nostrils seemed to quiver.

Baley finished his drink and felt warmth in his limbs and even the return of something of his confidence.

He said, "Exactly how *does* it feel to have me here, Dr. Quemot?"

The sociologist muttered, "That is an uncommonly personal question."

"I know it is. But I think I explained when I viewed you earlier that I was engaged in a murder investigation and that I would have to ask a great many questions, some of which were bound to be personal."

"I'll help if I can," said Quemot. "I hope the questions will be decent ones." He kept looking away as he spoke. His eyes, when they struck Baley's face, did not linger, but slipped away.

Baley said, "I don't ask about your feelings out of curiosity only. This is essential to the investigation."

"I don't see how."

"I've got to know as much as I can about this world. I must understand how Solarians feel about ordinary matters. Do you see that?"

Quemot did not look at Baley at all now. He said slowly, "Ten years ago, my wife died. Seeing her was never very easy, but, of course, it is something one learns

112

to bear in time and she was not the intrusive sort. I have been assigned no new wife since I am past the age of—of"—he looked at Baley as though requesting him to supply the phrase, and when Baley did not do so, he continued in a lower voice—"siring. Without even a wife, I have grown quite unused to this phenomenon of seeing."

"But how does it feel?" insisted Baley. "Are you in panic?" He thought of himself on the plane.

"No. Not in panic." Quemot angled his head to catch a glimpse of Baley and almost instantly withdrew. "But I will be frank, Mr. Baley. I imagine I can smell you."

Baley automatically leaned back in his chair, painfully self-conscious. "Smell me?"

"Quite imaginary, of course," said Quemot. "I cannot say whether you do have an odor or how strong it is, but even if you had a strong one, my nose filters would keep it from me. Yet, imagination . . ." He shrugged.

"I understand."

"It's worse. You'll forgive me, Mr. Baley, but in the actual presence of a human, I feel strongly as though something slimy were about to touch me. I keep shrinking away. It is most unpleasant."

Baley rubbed his ear thoughtfully and fought to keep down annoyance. After all, it was the other's neurotic reaction to a simple state of affairs.

He said, "If all this is so, I'm surprised you agreed to see me so readily. Surely you anticipated this unpleasantness."

"I did. But you know, I was curious. You're an Earthman."

Baley thought sardonically that that should have been another argument against seeing, but he said only, "What does that matter?"

A kind of jerky enthusiasm entered Quemot's voice. "It's not something I can explain easily. Not even to myself, really. But I've worked on sociology for ten years now. Really worked. I've developed propositions that are quite new and startling, and yet basically true. It is one of these propositions that makes me most extraordinarily interested in Earth and Earthmen. You see, if you were to consider Solaria's society and way of life carefully, it will become obvious to you that the said society and way of life is modeled directly and closely on that of Earth itself."

10   A Culture Is Traced

BALEY COULD not prevent himself from crying out, "What!"

Quemot looked over his shoulder as the moments of silence passed and said finally, "Not Earth's present culture. No."

Baley said, "Oh."

"But in the past, yes. Earth's ancient history. As an Earthman, you know it, of course."

"I've viewed books," said Baley cautiously.

"Ah. Then you understand."

Baley, who did not, said, "Let me explain exactly what I want, Dr. Quemot. I want you to tell me what you can about why Solaria is so different from the other Outer Worlds, why there are so many robots, why you behave as you do. I'm sorry if I seem to be changing the subject."

Baley most definitely wanted to change the subject. Any discussion of a likeness or unlikeness between Solaria's culture and Earth's would prove too absorbing by half. He might spend the day there and come away none the wiser as far as useful information was concerned.

Quemot smiled. "You want to compare Solaria and the other Outer Worlds and not Solaria and Earth."

"I know Earth, sir."

"As you wish." The Solarian coughed slightly. "Do you mind if I turn my chair completely away from you? It would be more—more comfortable."

"As you wish, Dr. Quemot," said Baley stiffly.

"Good." A robot turned the chair at Quemot's low-voiced order, and as the sociologist sat there, hidden from

Baley's eyes by the substantial chair back, his voice took on added life and even deepened and strengthened in tone.

Quemot said, "Solaria was first settled about three hundred years ago. The original settlers were Nexonians. Are you acquainted with Nexon?"

"I'm afraid not."

"It is close to Solaria, only about two parsecs away. In fact, Solaria and Nexon represent the closest pair of inhabited worlds in the Galaxy. Solaria, even when uninhabited by man, was life-bearing and eminently suited for human occupation. It represented an obvious attraction to the well-to-do of Nexon, who found it difficult to maintain a proper standard of living as their own planet filled up."

Baley interrupted. "Filled up? I thought Spacers practiced population control."

"Solaria does, but the Outer Worlds in general control it rather laxly. Nexon was completing its second million of population at the time I speak of. There was sufficient crowding to make it necessary to regulate the number of robots that might be owned by a particular family. So those Nexonians who could established summer homes on Solaria, which was fertile, temperate, and without dangerous fauna.

"The settlers on Solaria could still reach Nexon without too much trouble and while on Solaria they could live as they pleased. They could use as many robots as they could afford or felt a need for. Estates could be as large as desired since, with an empty planet, room was no problem, and with unlimited robots, exploitation was no problem.

"Robots grew to be so many that they were outfitted with radio contact and that was the beginning of our famous industries. We began to develop new varieties, new attachments, new capabilities. Culture dictates invention; a phrase I believe I have invented." Quemot chuckled.

A robot, responding to some stimulus Baley could not see beyond the barrier of the chair, brought Quemot a drink similar to that Baley had had earlier. None was brought to Baley, and he decided not to ask for one.

Quemot went on, "The advantages of life on Solaria were obvious to all who watched. Solaria became fashionable. More Nexonians established homes, and Solaria became what I like to call a 'villa planet.' And of the settlers, more and more took to remaining on the planet all year round and carrying on their business on Nexon through proxies. Robot factories were established on Solaria. Farms and mines began to be exploited to the point where exports were possible.

"In short, Mr. Baley, it became obvious that Solaria, in the space of a century or less, would be as crowded as Nexon had been. It seemed ridiculous and wasteful to find such a new world and then lose it through lack of foresight.

"To spare you a great deal of complicated politics, I need say only that Solaria managed to establish its independence and make it stick without war. Our usefulness to other Outer Worlds as a source of specialty robots gained us friends and helped us, of course.

"Once independent, our first care was to make sure that population did not grow beyond reasonable limits. We regulate immigration and births and take care of all needs by increasing and diversifying the robots we use."

Baley said, "Why is it the Solarians object to seeing one another?" He felt annoyed at the manner in which Quemot chose to expound sociology.

Quemot peeped round the corner of his chair and retreated almost at once. "It follows inevitably. We have huge estates. An estate ten thousand square miles in area is not uncommon, although the largest ones contain considerable unproductive areas. My own estate is nine hundred fifty square miles in area but every bit of it is good land.

"In any case, it is the size of an estate, more than anything else, that determines a man's position in society. And one property of a large estate is this: You can wander about in it almost aimlessly with little or no danger of entering a neighbor's territory and thus encountering your neighbor. You see?"

Baley shrugged. "I suppose I do."

"In short, a Solarian takes pride in not meeting his neighbor. At the same time, his estate is so well run by robots and so self-sufficient that there is no reason for him to have to meet his neighbor. The desire not to do so led to the development of ever more perfect viewing equipment, and as the viewing equipment grew better there was less and less need ever to see one's neighbor. It was a reinforcing cycle, a kind of feed-back. Do you see?"

Baley said, "Look here, Dr. Quemot. You don't have to make all this so simple for me. I'm not a sociologist but I've had the usual elementary courses in college. It's only an Earth college, of course," Baley added with a reluctant modesty designed to ward off the same comment, in more insulting terms, from the other, "but I can follow mathematics."

"Mathematics?" said Quemot, his voice squeaking the last syllable.

"Well, not the stuff they use in robotics, which I *wouldn't* follow, but sociological relationships I can handle. For instance, I'm familiar with the Teramin Relationship."

"The what, sir?"

"Maybe you have a different name for it. The differential of inconveniences suffered with privileges granted: dee eye sub jay taken to the nth——"

"What are you talking about?" It was the sharp and peremptory tone of a Spacer that Baley heard and he was silenced in bewilderment.

Surely the relationship between inconveniences suffered and privileges granted was part of the very essentials of learning how to handle people without an explosion. A private stall in the community bathroom for one person, given for cause, would keep x persons waiting patiently for the same lightning to strike them, the value of x varying in known ways with known variations in environment and human temperament, as quantitatively described in the Teramin Relationship.

But then again, in a world where all was privilege and nothing inconvenience, the Teramin Relationship might reduce to triviality. Perhaps he had chosen the wrong example.

He tried again. "Look, sir, it's one thing to get a qualitative fill-in on the growth of this prejudice against seeing, but it isn't helpful for my purposes. I want to know the exact analysis of the prejudice so I can counteract it effectively. I want to persuade people to see me, as you are doing now."

"Mr. Baley," said Quemot, "you can't treat human emotions as though they were built about a positronic brain."

"I'm not saying you can. Robotics is a deductive science and sociology an inductive one. But mathematics can be made to apply in either case."

There was silence for a moment. Then Quemot spoke in a voice that trembled. "You have admitted you are not a sociologist."

"I know. But I was told you *were* one. The best on the planet."

"I am the only one. You might almost say I have invented the science."

"Oh?" Baley hesitated over the next question. It sounded impertinent even to himself. "Have you viewed books on the subject?"

"I've looked at some Auroran books."

"Have you looked at books from Earth?"

"Earth?" Quemot laughed uneasily. "It wouldn't have occurred to me to read any of Earth's scientific productions. No offense intended."

"Well, I'm sorry. I had thought I would be able to get specific data that would make it possible for me to interview others face to face without having to——"

Quemot made a queer, grating, inarticulate sound and the large chair in which he sat scraped backward, then went over with a crash.

A muffled "My apologies" was caught by Baley.

Baley had a momentary glimpse of Quemot running with an ungainly stride, then he was out the room and gone.

Baley's eyebrows lifted. What the devil had he said this time? Jehoshaphat! What wrong button had he pushed?

Tentatively he rose from his seat, and stopped halfway as a robot entered.

"Master," said the robot, "I have been directed to inform you that the master will view you in a few moments."

"*View* me, boy?"

"Yes, master. In the meanwhile, you may desire further refreshment."

Another beaker of the pink liquid was at Baley's elbow and this time a dish of some confectionary, warm and fragrant, was added.

Baley took his seat again, sampled the liquor cautiously and put it down. The confectionary was hard to the touch and warm, but the crust broke easily in the mouth and the inner portion was at once considerably warmer and softer. He could not identify the components of the taste and wondered if it might not be a product of the native spices or condiments of Solaria.

Then he thought of the restricted, yeast-derived dietary of Earth and wondered if there might be a market for yeast strains designed to imitate the tastes of Outer World products.

But his thoughts broke off sharply as sociologist Quemot appeared out of nowhere and faced him. *Faced* him this time! He sat in a smaller chair in a room in which the walls and floor clashed sharply with those surrounding Baley. And he was smiling now, so that fine wrinkles in his face deepened and, paradoxically, gave him a more youthful appearance by accentuating the life in his eyes.

He said, "A thousand pardons, Mr. Baley. I thought I was enduring personal presence so well, but that was a delusion. I was quite on edge and your phrase pushed me over it, in a manner of speaking."

"What phrase was that, sir?"

"You said something about interviewing people face to——" He shook his head, his tongue dabbing quickly

119

isaac asimov

at his lips. "I would rather not say it. I think you know what I mean. The phrase conjured up the most striking picture of the two of us breathing—breathing one another's breath." The Solarian shuddered. "Don't you find that repulsive?"

"I don't know that I've ever thought of it so."

"It seems so filthy a habit. And as you said it and the picture arose in my mind, I realized that after all we *were* in the same room and even though I was not facing you, puffs of air that had been in your lungs must be reaching me and entering mine. With my sensitive frame of mind——"

Baley said, "Molecules all over Solaria's atmosphere have been in thousands of lungs. Jehoshaphat! They've been in the lungs of animals and the gills of fish."

"That *is* true," said Quemot with a rueful rub of his cheek, "and I'd just as soon not think of that, either. However there was a sense of immediacy to the situation with yourself actually there and with both of us inhaling and exhaling. It's amazing the relief I feel in viewing."

"I'm still in the same house, Dr. Quemot."

"That's precisely what is so amazing about the relief. You are in the same house and yet just the use of the trimensionals makes all the difference. At least I know what seeing a stranger feels like now. I won't try it again."

"That sounds as though you were experimenting with seeing."

"In a way," said the Spacer, "I suppose I was. It was a minor motivation. And the results were interesting, even if they were disturbing as well. It was a good test and I may record it."

"Record what?" asked Baley, puzzled.

"My feelings!" Quemot returned puzzled stare for puzzled stare.

Baley sighed. Cross-purposes. Always cross-purposes. "I only asked because somehow I assumed you would have instruments of some sort to measure emotional responses. An electroencephalograph, perhaps." He looked about fruitlessly, "Though I suppose you could have a pocket

120

version of the same that works without direct electrical connection. We don't have anything like that on Earth."

"I trust," said the Solarian stiffly, "that I am able to estimate the nature of my own feelings without an instrument. They were pronounced enough."

"Yes, of course, but for quantitative analysis . . ." began Baley.

Quemot said querulously, "I don't know what you're driving at. Besides, I'm trying to tell you something else, my own theory, in fact, something I have viewed in no books, something I am quite proud of——"

Baley said, "Exactly what is that, sir?"

"Why, the manner in which Solaria's culture is based on one existing in Earth's past."

Baley sighed. If he didn't allow the other to get it off his chest, there might be very little co-operation thereafter. He said, "And that is?"

"Sparta!" said Quemot, lifting his head so that for a moment his white hair glistened in the light and seemed almost a halo. "I'm sure you've heard of Sparta!"

Baley felt relieved. He had been mightily interested in Earth's ancient past in his younger days (it was an attractive study to many Earthmen—an Earth supreme because it was an Earth alone; Earthmen the masters because there were no Spacers), but Earth's past was a large one. Quemot might well have referred to some phase with which Baley was unacquainted and that would have been embarrassing.

As it was, he could say cautiously, "Yes. I've viewed films on the subject."

"Good. Good. Now Sparta in its heyday consisted of a relatively small number of Spartiates, the only full citizens, plus a somewhat larger number of second-class individuals, the Perioeci, and a really large number of outright slaves, the Helots. The Helots outnumbered the Spartiates a matter of twenty to one, and the Helots were men with human feelings and human failings.

"In order to make certain that a Helot rebellion could never be successful despite their overwhelming numbers,

121

the Spartans became military specialists. Each lived the life of a military machine, and the society achieved its purpose. There was never a successful Helot revolt.

"Now we human beings on Solaria are equivalent, in a way, to the Spartiates. We have our Helots, but our Helots aren't men but machines. They cannot revolt and need not be feared even though they outnumber us a thousand times as badly as the Spartans' human Helots outnumbered them. So we have the advantage of Spartiate exclusiveness without any need to sacrifice ourselves to rigid mastery. We can, instead, model ourselves on the artistic and cultural way of life of the Athenians, who were contemporaries of the Spartans and who——"

Baley said, "I've viewed films on the Athenians, too."

Quemot grew warmer as he spoke. "Civilizations have always been pyramidal in structure. As one climbs toward the apex of the social edifice, there is increased leisure and increasing opportunity to pursue happiness. As one climbs, one finds also fewer and fewer people to enjoy this more and more. Invariably, there is a preponderance of the dispossessed. And remember this, no matter how well off the bottom layers of the pyramid might be on an absolute scale, they are always dispossessed in comparison with the apex. For instance, even the most poorly off humans on Aurora are better off than Earth's aristocrats, but they are dispossessed with respect to Aurora's aristocrats, and it is with the masters of their own world that they compare themselves.

"So there is always social friction in ordinary human societies. The action of social revolution and the reaction of guarding against such revolution or combating it once it has begun are the causes of a great deal of the human misery with which history is permeated.

"Now here on Solaria, for the first time, the apex of the pyramid stands alone. In the place of the dispossessed are the robots. We have the first new society, the first really new one, the first great social invention since the farmers of Sumeria and Egypt invented cities."

He sat back now, smiling.

Baley nodded. "Have you published this?"

"I may," said Quemot with an affectation of careless-ness, "someday. I haven't yet. This is my third contribu-tion."

"Were the other two as broad as this?"

"They weren't in sociology. I have been a sculptor in my time. The work you see about you"—he indicated the statuary—"is my own. And I have been a composer, too. But I am getting older and Rikaine Delmarre always argued strongly in favor of the applied arts rather than the fine arts and I decided to go into sociology."

Baley said, "That sounds as though Delmarre was a good friend of yours."

"We knew one another. At my time in life, one knows all adult Solarians. But there is no reason not to agree that Rikaine Delmarre and I were well acquainted."

"What sort of a man was Delmarre?" (Strangely enough, the name of the man brought up the picture of Gladia in Baley's mind and he was plagued with a sudden, sharp recall of her as he had last seen her, furious, her face distorted with anger at him.)

Quemot looked a bit thoughtful. "He was a worthy man; devoted to Solaria and to its way of life."

"An idealist, in other words."

"Yes. Definitely. You could see that in the fact that he volunteered for his job as—as fetal engineer. It was an applied art, you see, and I told you his feelings about that."

"Was volunteering unusual?"

"Wouldn't *you* say—— But I forget you're an Earth-man. Yes, it is unusual. It's one of those jobs that must be done, yet finds no voluntary takers. Ordinarily, some-one must be assigned to it for a period of so many years and it isn't pleasant to be the one chosen. Delmarre volunteered, and for life. He felt the position was too important to be left to reluctant draftees, and he per-suaded me into that opinion, too. Yet I certainly would never have volunteered. I couldn't possibly make the personal sacrifice. And it was more of a sacrifice for

123

him, since he was almost a fanatic in personal hygiene."

"I'm still not certain I understand the nature of his job."

Quemot's old cheeks flushed gently. "Hadn't you better discuss that with his assistant?"

Baley said, "I would certainly have done so by now, sir, if anyone had seen fit to tell me before this moment that he had an assistant."

"I'm sorry about that," said Quemot, "but the existence of the assistant is another measure of his social responsibility. No previous occupant of the post provided for one. Delmarre, however, felt it necessary to find a suitable youngster and conduct the necessary training himself so as to leave a professional heir behind when the time came for him to retire or, well, to die." The old Solarian sighed heavily. "Yet I outlived him and he was so much younger. I used to play chess with him. Many times."

"How did you manage that?"

Quemot's eyebrows lifted. "The usual way."

"You saw one another?"

Quemot looked horrified. "What an idea! Even if I could stomach it, Delmarre would never allow it for an instant. Being fetal engineer didn't blunt his sensibilities. He was a finicky man."

"Then how——"

"With two boards as any two people would play chess." The Solarian shrugged in a sudden gesture of tolerance. "Well, you're an Earthman. My moves registered on his board, and his on mine. It's a simple matter."

Baley said, "Do you know Mrs. Delmarre?"

"We've viewed one another. She's a field colorist, you know, and I've viewed some of her showings. Fine work in a way but more interesting as curiosities than as creations. Still, they're amusing and show a perceptive mind."

"Is she capable of killing her husband, would you say?"

"I haven't given it thought. Women are surprising creatures. But then, there's scarcely room for argument, is there? Only Mrs. Delmarre could have been close enough to Rikaine to kill him. Rikaine would never, under any

124

circumstances, have allowed anyone else seeing privileges for any reason. Extremely finicky. Perhaps finicky is the wrong word. It was just that he lacked any trace of abnormality; anything of the perverse. He was a good Solarian."

"Would you call your granting me seeing privileges perverse?" asked Baley.

Quemot said, "Yes, I think I would. I should say there was a bit of scatophilia involved."

"Could Delmarre have been killed for political reasons?"

"What?"

"I've heard him called a Traditionalist."

"Oh, we all are."

"You mean there is no group of Solarians who are *not* Traditionalists?"

"I dare say there are some," said Quemot slowly, "who think it is dangerous to be too Traditionalist. They are overconscious of our small population, of the way the other worlds outnumber us. They think we are defenseless against possible aggression from the other Outer Worlds. They're quite foolish to think so and there aren't many of them. I don't think they're a force."

"Why do you say they are foolish? Is there anything about Solaria that would affect the balance of power in spite of the great disadvantage of numbers? Some new type of weapon?"

"A weapon, certainly. But not a new one. The people I speak of are more blind than foolish not to realize that such a weapon is in operation continuously and cannot be resisted."

Baley's eyes narrowed. "Are you serious?"

"Certainly."

"Do you know the nature of the weapon?"

"All of us must. *You* do, if you stop to think of it. I see it a trifle easier than most, perhaps, since I am a sociologist. To be sure, it isn't used as a weapon ordinarily is used. It doesn't kill or hurt, but it is irresistible even so. All the more irresistible because no one notices it."

125

Baley said with annoyance, "And just what is this non-lethal weapon?"

Quemot said, "The positronic robot."

11   A Farm Is Inspected

FOR A MOMENT Baley went cold. The positronic robot was the symbol of Spacer superiority over Earthmen. That was weapon enough.

He kept his voice steady. "It's an economic weapon. Solaria is important to the other Outer Worlds as a source of advanced models and so it will not be harmed by them."

"That's an obvious point," said Quemot indifferently. "That helped us establish our independence. What I have in mind is something else, something more subtle and more cosmic." Quemot's eyes were fixed on his fingers' ends and his mind was obviously fixed on abstractions.

Baley said, "Is this another of your sociological theories?"

Quemot's poorly suppressed look of pride all but forced a short smile out of the Earthman.

The sociologist said, "It is indeed mine. Original, as far as I know, and yet obvious if population data on the Outer Worlds is carefully studied. To begin with, ever since the positronic robot was invented, it has been used more and more intensively everywhere."

"Not on Earth," said Baley.

"Now, now, Plainclothesman. I don't know much of your Earth, but I know enough to know that robots are entering your economy. You people live in large Cities and leave most of your planetary surface unoccupied. Who runs your farms and mines, then?"

"Robots," admitted Baley. "But if it comes to that, Doctor, Earthmen invented the positronic robot in the first place."

"They did? Are you sure?"

"You can check. It's true."

"Interesting. Yet robots made the least headway there." The sociologist said thoughtfully, "Perhaps that is because of Earth's large population. It would take that much longer. Yes . . . Still, you have robots even in your Cities."

"Yes," said Baley.

"More now than, say, fifty years ago."

Baley nodded impatiently. "Yes."

"Then it fits. The difference is only one of time. Robots tend to displace human labor. The robot economy moves in only one direction. More robots and fewer humans. I've studied population data *very* carefully and I've plotted it and made a few extrapolations." He paused in sudden surprise. "Why, that's rather an application of mathematics to sociology, isn't it?"

"It is," said Baley.

"There may be something to it, at that. I will have to give the matter thought. In any case, these are the conclusions I have come to, and I am convinced there is no doubt as to their correctness. The robot-human ratio in any economy that has accepted robot labor tends continuously to increase despite any laws that are passed to prevent it. The increase is slowed, but never stopped. At first the human population increases, but the robot population increases much more quickly. Then, after a certain critical point is reached . . ."

Quemot stopped again, then said, "Now let's see. I wonder if the critical point could be determined exactly; if you could really put a figure to it. There's your mathematics again."

Baley stirred restlessly. "What happens after the critical point is reached, Dr. Quemot?"

"Eh? Oh, the human population begins actually to decline. A planet approaches a true social stability. Aurora will have to. Even your Earth will have to. Earth may take a few more centuries, but it is inevitable."

"What do you mean by social stability?"

"The situation here. In Solaria. A world in which the humans are the leisure class only. So there is no reason
127

to fear the other Outer Worlds. We need only wait a century perhaps and they shall all be Solarias. I suppose that will be the end of human history, in a way; at least, its fulfillment. Finally, finally, all men will have all they can need and want. You know, there is a phrase I once picked up; I don't know where it comes from; something about the pursuit of happiness."

Baley said thoughtfully, "All men are 'endowed by their Creator with certain unalienable rights . . . among these are life, liberty, and the pursuit of happiness.' "

"You've hit it. Where's that from?"

"Some old document," said Baley.

"Do you see how that is changed here on Solaria and eventually in all the Galaxy? The pursuit will be over. The rights mankind will be heir to will be life, liberty, and happiness. Just that. Happiness."

Baley said dryly, "Maybe so, but a man has been killed on your Solaria and another may yet die."

He felt regret almost the moment he spoke, for the expression on Quemot's face was as though he had been struck with an open palm. The old man's head bowed. He said without looking up, "I have answered your questions as well as I could. Is there anything else you wish?"

"I have enough. Thank you, sir. I am sorry to have intruded on your grief at your friend's death."

Quemot looked up slowly. "It will be hard to find another chess partner. He kept our appointments most punctually and he played an extraordinarily even game. He was a good Solarian."

"I understand," said Baley softly. "May I have your permission to use your viewer to make contact with the next person I must see?"

"Of course," said Quemot. "My robots are yours. And now I will leave you. Done viewing."

A robot was at Baley's side within thirty seconds of Quemot's disappearance and Baley wondered once again how these creatures were managed. He had seen Quemot's fingers move toward a contact as he had left and that was all.

Perhaps the signal was quite a generalized one, saying only, "Do your duty!" Perhaps robots listened to all that went on and were always aware of what a human might desire at any given moment, and if the particular robot was not designed for a particular job in either mind or body, the radio web that united all robots went into action and the correct robot was spurred into action.

For a moment Baley had the vision of Solaria as a robotic net with holes that were small and continually growing smaller, with every human being caught neatly in place. He thought of Quemot's picture of worlds turning into Solarias; of nets forming and tightening even on Earth, until——

His thoughts were disrupted as the robot who had entered spoke with the quiet and even respect of the machine.

"I am ready to help you, master."

Baley said, "Do you know how to reach the place where Rikaine Delmarre once worked?"

"Yes, master."

Baley shrugged. He would never teach himself to avoid asking useless questions. The robots knew. Period. It occurred to him that, to handle robots with true efficiency, one must needs be expert, a sort of roboticist. How well did the average Solarian do, he wondered? Probably only so-so.

He said, "Get Delmarre's place and contact his assistant. If the assistant is not there, locate him wherever he is."

"Yes, master."

As the robot turned to go, Baley called after it, "Wait! What time is it at the Delmarre workplace?"

"About 0630, master."

"In the morning?"

"Yes, master."

Again Baley felt annoyance at a world that made itself victim of the coming and going of a sun. It was what came of living on bare planetary surface.

He thought fugitively of Earth, then tore his mind away. While he kept firmly to the matter in hand, he managed well. Slipping into homesickness would ruin him.

He said, "Call the assistant, anyway, boy, and tell him it's government business—and have one of the other boys bring something to eat. A sandwich and a glass of milk will do."

He chewed thoughtfully at the sandwich, which contained a kind of smoked meat, and with half his mind thought that Daneel Olivaw would certainly consider every article of food suspect after what had happened to Gruer. And Daneel might be right, too.

He finished the sandwich without ill effects, however (immediate ill effects, at any rate), and sipped at the milk. He had not learned from Quemot what he had come to learn, but he had learned something. As he sorted it out in his mind, it seemed he had learned a good deal.

Little about the murder, to be sure, but more about the larger matter.

The robot returned. "The assistant will accept contact, master."

"Good. Was there any trouble about it?"

"The assistant was asleep, master."

"Awake now, though?"

"Yes, master."

The assistant was facing him suddenly, sitting up in bed and wearing an expression of sullen resentment.

Baley reared back as though a force-barrier had been raised before him without warning. Once again a piece of vital information had been withheld from him. Once again he had not asked the right questions.

No one had thought to tell him that Rikaine Delmarre's assistant was a woman.

Her hair was a trifle darker than ordinary Spacer bronze and there was a quantity of it, at the moment in disorder. Her face was oval, her nose a trifle bulbous, and her chin large. She scratched slowly at her side just above the waist and Baley hoped the sheet would remain in position. He remembered Gladia's free attitude toward what was permitted while viewing.

Baley felt a sardonic amusement at his own disillusion at that moment. Earthmen assumed, somehow, that all Spacer women were beautiful, and certainly Gladia had reinforced that assumption. This one, though, was plain even by Earthly standards.

It therefore surprised Baley that he found her contralto attractive when she said, "See here, do you know what time it is?"

"I do," said Baley, "but since I will be seeing you, I felt I should warn you."

"Seeing me? Skies above——" Her eyes grew wide and she put a hand to her chin. (She wore a ring on one finger, the first item of personal adornment Baley had yet seen on Solaria.) "Wait, you're not my new assistant, are you?"

"No. Nothing like that. I'm here to investigate the death of Rikaine Delmarre."

"Oh? Well, investigate, then."

"What is your name?"

"Klorissa Cantoro."

"And how long have you been working with Dr. Delmarre?"

"Three years."

"I assume you're now at the place of business." (Baley felt uncomfortable at that noncommittal phrase, but he did not know what to call a place where a fetal engineer worked.)

"If you mean, am I at the farm?" said Klorissa discontentedly, "I certainly am. I haven't left it since the old man was done in, and I won't leave it, looks like, till an assistant is assigned me. Can *you* arrange that, by the way?"

"I'm sorry, ma'am. I have no influence with anyone here."

"Thought I'd ask."

Klorissa pulled off the sheet and climbed out of bed without any self-consciousness. She was wearing a one-piece sleeping suit and her hand went to the notch of the seam, where it ended at the neck.

Baley said hurriedly, "Just one moment. If you'll agree to see me, that will end my business with you for now and you may dress in privacy."

"In privacy?" She put out her lower lip and stared at Baley curiously. "You're finicky, aren't you? Like the boss."

"Will you see me? I would like to look over the farm."

"I don't get this business about seeing, but if you want to view the farm I'll tour you. If you'll give me a chance to wash and take care of a few things and wake up a little, I'll enjoy the break in routine."

"I don't want to view anything. I want to *see*."

The woman cocked her head to one side and her keen look had something of professional interest in it. "Are you a pervert or something? When was the last time you underwent a gene analysis?"

"Jehoshaphat!" muttered Baley. "Look, I'm Elijah Baley. I'm from Earth."

"From Earth?" She cried vehemently. "Skies above! Whatever are you doing here? Or is this some kind of complicated joke?"

"I'm not joking. I was called in to investigate Delmarre's death. I'm a plainclothesman, a detective."

"You mean that kind of investigation. But I thought everyone knew his wife did it."

"No, ma'am, there's some question about it in my mind. May I have your permission to see the farm and you. As an Earthman, you understand, I'm not accustomed to viewing. It makes me uncomfortable. I have permission from the Head of Security to see people who might help me. I will show you the document, if you wish."

"Let's see it."

Baley held the official strip up before her imaged eyes. She shook her head. "Seeing! It's filthy. Still, skies above, what's a little more filth in this filthy job? Look here, though, don't you come close to me. You stay a good distance away. We can shout or send messages by robot, if we have to. You understand?"

"I understand."

Her sleeping suit split open at the seam just as contact broke off and the last word he heard from her was a muttered: "Earthman!"

"That's close enough," said Klorissa.

Baley, who was some twenty-five feet from the woman, said, "It's all right this distance, but I'd like to get indoors quickly."

It had not been so bad this time, somehow. He had scarcely minded the plane trip, but there was no point in overdoing it. He kept himself from yanking at his collar to allow himself to breathe more freely.

Klorissa said sharply, "What's wrong with you? You look kind of beat."

Baley said, "I'm not used to the outdoors."

"That's right! Earthman! You've got to be cooped up or something. Skies above!" Her tongue passed over her lips as though it tasted something unappetizing. "Well, come in, then, but let me move out of the way first. All right. Get in."

Her hair was in two thick braids that wound about her head in a complicated geometrical pattern. Baley wondered how long it took to arrange like that and then remembered that, in all probability, the unerring mechanical fingers of a robot did the job.

The hair set off her oval face and gave it a kind of symmetry that made it pleasant if not pretty. She did not wear any facial make-up, nor, for that matter, were her clothes meant to do more than cover her serviceably. For the most part they were a subdued dark blue except for her gloves, which covered her to mid-arm and were a badly clashing lilac in color. Apparently they were not part of her ordinary costume. Baley noted the thickening of one finger of the gloves owing to the presence of the ring underneath.

133

They remained at opposite ends of the room, facing one another.

Baley said, "You don't like this, do you, ma'am?"

Klorissa shrugged. "Why should I like it? I'm not an animal. But I can stand it. You get pretty hardened, when you deal with—with"—she paused, and then her chin went up as though she had made up her mind to say what she had to say without mincing—"with children." She pronounced the word with careful precision.

"You sound as though you don't like the job you have."

"It's an important job. It must be done. Still, I don't like it."

"Did Rikaine Delmarre like it?"

"I suppose he didn't, but he never showed it. He was a good Solarian."

"And he was finicky."

Klorissa looked surprised.

Baley said, "You yourself said so. When we were viewing and I said you might dress in private, you said I was finicky like the boss."

"Oh. Well, he *was* finicky. Even viewing he never took any liberties. Always proper."

"Was that unusual?"

"It shouldn't be. Ideally, you're supposed to be proper, but no one ever is. Not when viewing. There's no personal presence involved so why take any pains? You know? I don't take pains when viewing, except with the boss. You had to be formal with him."

"Did you admire Dr. Delmarre?"

"He was a good Solarian."

Baley said, "You've called this place a farm and you've mentioned children. Do you bring up children here?"

"From the age of a month. Every fetus on Solaria comes here."

"Fetus?"

"Yes." She frowned. "We get them a month after conception. Does this embarrass you?"

"No," Baley said shortly. "Can you show me around?"

"I can. But keep your distance."

Baley's long face took on a stony grimness as he looked down the length of the long room from above. There was glass between the room and themselves. On the other side, he was sure, was perfectly controlled heat, perfectly controlled humidity, perfectly controlled asepsis. Those tanks, row on row, each contained its little creature floating in a watery fluid of precise composition, infused with a nutrient mixture of ideal proportions. Life and growth went on.

Little things, some smaller than half his fist, curled on themselves, with bulging skulls and tiny budding limbs and vanishing tails.

Klorissa, from her position twenty feet away, said, "How do you like it, Plainclothesman?"

Baley said, "How many do you have?"

"As of this morning, one hundred and fifty-two. We receive fifteen to twenty each month and we graduate as many to independence."

"Is this the only such institution on the planet?"

"That's right. It's enough to keep the population steady, counting on a life expectancy of three hundred years and a population of twenty thousand. This building is quite new. Dr. Delmarre supervised its construction and made many changes in our procedures. Our fetal death rate now is virtually zero."

Robots threaded their way among the tanks. At each tank they stopped and checked controls in a tireless, meticulous way, looking in at the tiny embryos within.

"Who operates on the mother?" asked Baley. "I mean, to get the little things."

"Doctors," answered Klorissa.

"Dr. Delmarre?"

"Of course not. *Medical* doctors. You don't think Dr. Delmarre would ever stoop to—— Well, never mind."

"Why can't robots be used?"

"Robots in surgery? First Law makes that very difficult, Plainclothesman. A robot might perform an appendectomy to save a human life, if he knew how, but I doubt that he'd be usable after that without major repairs. Cutting human flesh would be quite a traumatic experience for a

135

positronic brain. Human doctors can manage to get hardened to it. Even to the personal presence required."

Baley said, "I notice that robots tend the fetuses, though. Do you and Dr. Delmarre ever interfere?"

"We have to, sometimes, when things go wrong. If a fetus has developmental trouble, for instance. Robots can't be trusted to judge the situation accurately when human life is involved."

Baley nodded. "Too much risk of a misjudgment and a life lost, I suppose."

"Not at all. Too much risk of overvaluing a life and saving one improperly." The woman looked stern. "As fetal engineers, Baley, we see to it that healthy children are born; *healthy* ones. Even the best gene analysis of parents can't assure that all gene permutations and combinations will be favorable, to say nothing of the possibility of mutations. That's our big concern, the unexpected mutation. We've got the rate of those down to less than one in a thousand, but that means that, on the average, once a decade, we have trouble."

She motioned him along the balcony and he followed her.

She said, "I'll show you the infants' nurseries and the youngsters' dormitories. They're much more a problem than the fetuses are. With them, we can rely on robot labor only to a limited extent."

"Why is that?"

"You would know, Baley, if you ever tried to teach a robot the importance of discipline. First Law makes them almost impervious to that fact. And don't think youngsters don't learn that about as soon as they can talk. I've seen a three-year-old holding a dozen robots motionless by yelling, 'You'll hurt me. I'm hurt.' It takes an extremely advanced robot to understand that a child might be deliberately lying."

"Could Delmarre handle the children?"

"Usually."

"How did he do that? Did he get out among them and shake sense into them?"

"Dr. Delmarre? Touch them? Skies above! Of course not! But he could *talk* to them. And he could give a robot specific orders. I've seen him viewing a child for fifteen minutes, and keeping a robot in spanking position all that time, getting it to spank—spank—spank. A few like that and the child would risk fooling with the boss no more. And the boss was skillful enough about it so that usually the robot didn't need more than a routine readjustment afterward."

"How about you? Do you get out among the children?"

"I'm afraid I have to sometimes. I'm not like the boss. Maybe someday I'll be able to handle the long-distance stuff, but right now if I tried, I'd just ruin robots. There's an art to handling robots really well, you know. When I think of it, though. Getting out among the children. Little animals!"

She looked back at him suddenly. "I suppose you wouldn't mind seeing them."

"It wouldn't bother me."

She shrugged and stared at him with amusement. "Earthman!" She walked on again. "What's all this about, anyway? You'll have to end up with Gladia Delmarre as murderess. You'll *have* to."

"I'm not quite sure of that," said Baley.

"How could you be anything else but sure? Who else could it possibly be?"

"There are possibilities, ma'am."

"Who, for instance?"

"Well, you, for instance!"

And Klorissa's reaction to that quite surprised Baley.

12   A Target Is Missed

SHE LAUGHED.

The laughter grew and fed on itself till she was gasping for breath and her plump face had reddened almost to purple. She leaned against the wall and gasped for breath.

"No, don't come—closer," she begged. "I'm all right."

Baley said gravely, "Is the possibility that humorous?"

She tried to answer and laughed again. Then, in a whisper, she said, "Oh, you *are* an Earthman? How could it ever be me?"

"You knew him well," said Baley. "You knew his habits. You could have planned it."

"And you think I would *see* him? That I would get close enough to bash him over the head with something? You just don't know anything at all about it, Baley."

Baley felt himself redden. "Why couldn't you get close enough to him, ma'am. You've had practice—uh—mingling."

"With the *children*."

"One thing leads to another. You seem to be able to stand my presence."

"At twenty feet," she said contemptuously.

"I've just visited a man who nearly collapsed because he had to endure my presence for a while."

Klorissa sobered and said, "A difference in degree."

"I suggest that a difference in degree is all that is necessary. The habit of seeing children makes it possible to endure seeing Delmarre just long enough."

"I would like to point out, Mr. Baley," said Klorissa, no longer appearing the least amused, "that it doesn't matter a speck what I can endure. Dr. Delmarre was the finicky one. He was almost as bad as Leebig himself. Almost. Even if I could endure seeing him, he would never endure seeing me. Mrs. Delmarre is the only one he could possibly have allowed within seeing distance."

Baley said, "Who's this Leebig you mentioned?"

Klorissa shrugged. "One of these odd-genius types, if you know what I mean. He'd done work with the boss on robots."

Baley checked that off mentally and returned to the matter at hand. He said, "It could also be said you had a motive."

"What motive?"

"His death put you in charge of this establishment, gave you position."

"You call that a motive? Skies above, who could *want* this position? Who on Solaria? This is a motive for keeping him alive. It's a motive for hovering over him and protecting him. You'll have to do better than that, Earthman."

Baley scratched his neck uncertainly with one finger. He saw the justice of that.

Klorissa said, "Did you notice my ring, Mr. Baley?"

For a moment it seemed she was about to strip the glove from her right hand, but she refrained.

"I noticed it," said Baley.

"You don't know its significance, I suppose?"

"I don't." (He would never have done with ignorance, he thought bitterly.)

"Do you mind a small lecture, then?"

"If it will help me make sense of this damned world," blurted out Baley, "by all means."

"Skies above!" Klorissa smiled. "I suppose we seem to you as Earth would seem to us. Imagine. Say, here's an empty chamber. Come in here and we'll sit down—no, the room's not big enough. Tell you what, though. You take a seat in there and I'll stand out here."

She stepped farther down the corridor, giving him space to enter the room, then returned, taking up her stand against the opposite wall at a point from which she could see him.

Baley took his seat with only the slightest quiver of chivalry countering it. He thought rebelliously: Why not? Let the Spacer woman stand.

Klorissa folded her muscular arms across her chest and said, "Gene analysis is the key to our society. We don't analyze for genes directly, of course. Each gene, however, governs one enzyme, and we can analyze for enzymes. Know the enzymes, know the body chemistry. Know the body chemistry, know the human being. You see all that?"

"I understand the theory," said Baley. "I don't know how it's applied."

"That part's done here. Blood samples are taken while the infant is still in the late fetal stage. That gives us our rough first approximation. Ideally, we should catch all mutations at that point and judge whether birth can be risked. In actual fact, we still don't quite know enough to eliminate all possibility of mistake. Someday, maybe. Anyway, we continue testing after birth; biopsies as well as body fluids. In any case, long before adulthood, we know exactly what our little boys and girls are made of."

(Sugar and spice . . . A nonsense phrase went unbidden through Baley's mind.)

"We wear coded rings to indicate our gene constitution," said Klorissa. "It's an old custom, a bit of the primitive left behind from the days when Solarians had not yet been weeded eugenically. Nowadays, we're all healthy."

Baley said, "But you still wear yours. Why?"

"Because I'm exceptional," she said with an unembarrassed, unblunted pride. "Dr. Delmarre spent a long time searching for an assistant. He *needed* someone exceptional. Brains, ingenuity, industry, stability. Most of all, stability. Someone who could learn to mingle with children and not break down."

"He couldn't, could he? Was that a measure of his instability?"

Klorissa said, "In a way, it was, but at least it was a desirable type of instability under most circumstances. You wash your hands, don't you?"

Baley's eyes dropped to his hands. They were as clean as need be. "Yes," he said.

"All right. I suppose it's a measure of instability to feel such revulsion at dirty hands as to be unable to clean an oily mechanism by hand even in an emergency. Still, in the *ordinary* course of living, the revulsion keeps you clean, which is good."

"I see. Go ahead."

"There's nothing more. My genic health is the third-highest ever recorded on Solaria, so I wear my ring. It's a record I enjoy carrying with me."

"I congratulate you."

140

"You needn't sneer. It may not be my doing. It may be the blind permutation of parental genes, but it's a proud thing to own, anyway. And no one would believe me capable of so seriously psychotic an act as murder. Not with my gene make-up. So don't waste accusations on me."

Baley shrugged and said nothing. The woman seemed to confuse gene make-up and evidence and presumably the rest of Solaria would do the same.

Klorissa said, "Do you want to see the youngsters now?"

"Thank you. Yes."

The corridors seemed to go on forever. The building was obviously a tremendous one. Nothing like the huge banks of apartments in the Cities of Earth, of course, but for a single building clinging to the outside skin of a planet it must be a mountainous structure.

There were hundreds of cribs, with pink babies squalling, or sleeping, or feeding. Then there were playrooms for the crawlers.

"They're not too bad even at this age," said Klorissa grudgingly, "though they take up a tremendous sum of robots. It's practically a robot per baby till walking age."

"Why is that?"

"They sicken if they don't get individual attention."

Baley nodded. "Yes, I suppose the requirement for affection is something that can't be done away with."

Klorissa frowned and said brusquely, "Babies require attention."

Baley said, "I am a little surprised that robots can fulfill the need for affection."

She whirled toward him, the distance between them not sufficing to hide her displeasure. "See here, Baley, if you're trying to shock me by using unpleasant terms, you won't succeed. Skies above, don't be childish."

"Shock you?"

"I can use the word too. Affection! Do you want a short word, a good four-letter word. I can say that, too. Love! Love! Now if it's out of your system, behave yourself."

Baley did not trouble to dispute the matter of obscenity. He said, "Can robots really give the necessary attention, then?"

"Obviously, or this farm would not be the success it is. They fool with the child. They nuzzle it and snuggle it. The child doesn't care that it's only a robot. But then, things grow more difficult between three and ten."

"Oh?"

"During that interval, the children insist on playing with one another. Quite indiscriminately."

"I take it you let them."

"We have to, but we never forget our obligation to teach them the requirements of adulthood. Each has a separate room that can be closed off. Even from the first, they must sleep alone. We insist on that. And then we have an isolation time every day and that increases with the years. By the time a child reaches ten, he is able to restrict himself to viewing for a week at a time. Of course, the viewing arrangements are elaborate. They can view outdoors, under mobile conditions, and can keep it up all day."

Baley said, "I'm surprised you can counter an instinct so thoroughly. You do counter it; I see that. Still, it surprises me."

"What instinct?" demanded Klorissa.

"The instinct of gregariousness. There is one. You say yourself that as children they insist on playing with each other."

Klorissa shrugged. "Do you call that instinct? But then, what if it is? Skies above, a child has an instinctive fear of falling, but adults can be trained to work in high places even where there is constant danger of falling. Haven't you ever seen gymnastic exhibitions on high wires? There are some worlds where people live in tall buildings. And children have instinctive fear of loud noises, too, but are you afraid of them?"

"Not within reason," said Baley.

"I'm willing to bet that Earth people couldn't sleep if things were really quiet. Skies above, there isn't an instinct around that can't give way to a good, persistent education. Not in human beings, where instincts are weak anyway. In fact, if you go about it right, education gets easier with each generation. It's a matter of evolution."

Baley said, "How is that?"

"Don't you see? Each individual repeats his own evolutionary history as he develops. Those fetuses back there have gills and a tail for a time. Can't skip those steps. The youngster has to go through the social-animal stage in the same way. But just as a fetus can get through in one month a stage that evolution took a hundred million years to get through, so our children can hurry through the social-animal stage. Dr. Delmarre was of the opinion that with the generations, we'd get through that stage faster and faster."

"Is that so?"

"In three thousand years, he estimated, at the present rate of progress, we'd have children who'd take to viewing at once. The boss had other notions, too. He was interested in improving robots to the point of making them capable of disciplining children without becoming mentally unstable. Why not? Discipline today for a better life tomorrow is a true expression of First Law if robots could only be made to see it."

"Have such robots been developed yet?"

Klorissa shook her head. "I'm afraid not. Dr. Delmarre and Leebig had been working hard on some experimental models."

"Did Dr. Delmarre have some of the models sent out to his estate? Was he a good enough roboticist to conduct tests himself?"

"Oh yes. He tested robots frequently."

"Do you know that he had a robot with him when he was murdered?"

"I've been told so."

"Do you know what kind of a model it was?"

"You'll have to ask Leebig. As I told you, he's the roboticist who worked with Dr. Delmarre."

"You know nothing about it?"

"Not a thing."

"If you think of anything, let me know."

"I will. And don't think new robot models are all that Dr. Delmarre was interested in. Dr. Delmarre used to say the time would come when unfertilized ova would be stored in banks at liquid-air temperatures and utilized for artificial insemination. In that way, eugenic principles could be truly applied and we could get rid of the last vestige of any need for seeing. I'm not sure that I quite go along with him so far, but he was a man of advanced notions; a very good Solarian."

She added quickly, "Do you want to go outside? The five-through-eight group are encouraged to take part in outdoor play and you could see them in action."

Baley said cautiously, "I'll try that. I may have to come back inside on rather short notice."

"Oh yes, I forgot. Maybe you'd rather not go out at all?"

"No." Baley forced a smile. "I'm trying to grow accustomed to the outdoors."

The wind was hard to bear. It made breathing difficult. It wasn't cold, in a direct physical sense, but the feel of it, the feel of his clothes moving against his body, gave Baley a kind of chill.

His teeth chattered when he tried to talk and he had to force his words out in little bits. It hurt his eyes to look so far at a horizon so hazy green and blue and there was only limited relief when he looked at the pathway immediately before his toes. Above all, he avoided looking up at the empty blue, empty, that is, but for the piled-up white of occasional clouds and the glare of the naked sun.

And yet he could fight off the urge to run, to return to enclosure.

He passed a tree, following Klorissa by some ten paces, and he reached out a cautious hand to touch it. It was rough and hard to the touch. Frondy leaves moved and rustled overhead, but he did not raise his eyes to look at them. A living tree!

Klorissa called out. "How do you feel?"

"All right."

"You can see a group of youngsters from here," she said. "They're involved in some kind of game. The robots organize the games and see to it that the little animals don't kick each other's eyes out. With personal presence you can do just that, you know."

Baley raised his eyes slowly, running his glance along the cement of the pathway out to the grass and down the slope, farther and farther out—very carefully—ready to snap back to his toes if he grew frightened—feeling with his eyes . . .

There were the small figures of boys and girls racing madly about, uncaring that they raced at the very outer rim of a world with nothing but air and space above them. The glitter of an occasional robot moved nimbly among them. The noise of the children was a far-off incoherent squeaking in the air.

"They love it," said Klorissa. "Pushing and pulling and squabbling and falling down and getting up and just generally contacting. Skies above! How do children ever manage to grow up?"

"What are those older children doing?" asked Baley. He pointed at a group of isolated youngsters standing to one side.

"They're viewing. They're not in a state of personal presence. By viewing, they can walk together, talk together, race together, play together. Anything except physical contact."

"Where do children go when they leave here?"

"To estates of their own. The number of deaths is, on the average, equal to the number of graduations."

"To their parents' estates?"

"Skies above, no! It would be an amazing coincidence, wouldn't it, to have a parent die just as a child is of age. No, the children take any one that falls vacant. I don't know that any of them would be particularly happy, any-

145

way, living in a mansion that once belonged to their parents, supposing, of course, they knew who their parents were."

"Don't they?"

She raised her eyebrows. "Why should they?"

"Don't parents visit their children here?"

"What a mind you have. Why should they want to?"

Baley said, "Do you mind if I clear up a point for myself? Is it bad manners to ask a person if they have had children?"

"It's an intimate question, wouldn't you say?"

"In a way."

"I'm hardened. Children are my business. Other people aren't."

Baley said, "Have you any children?"

Klorissa's Adam's apple made a soft but clearly visible motion in her throat as she swallowed. "I deserve that, I suppose. And you deserve an answer. I haven't."

"Are you married?"

"Yes, and I have an estate of my own and I would be there but for the emergency here. I'm just not confident of being able to control all the robots if I'm not here in person."

She turned away unhappily, and then pointed. "Now there's one of them gone tumbling and of course he's crying."

A robot was running with great space-devouring strides.

Klorissa said, "He'll be picked up and cuddled and if there's any real damage, I'll be called in." She added nervously, "I hope I don't have to be."

Baley took a deep breath. He noted three trees forming a small triangle fifty feet to the left. He walked in that direction, the grass soft and loathsome under his shoes, disgusting in its softness (like walking through corrupting flesh, and he nearly retched at the thought).

He was among them, his back against one trunk. It was almost like being surrounded by imperfect walls. The sun was only a wavering series of glitters through the leaves, so disconnected as almost to be robbed of horror.

146

Klorissa faced him from the path, then slowly shortened the distance by half.

"Mind if I stay here awhile?" asked Baley.

"Go ahead," said Klorissa.

Baley said, "Once the youngsters graduate out of the farm, how do you get them to court one another?"

"Court?"

"Get to know one another," said Baley, vaguely wondering how the thought could be expressed safely, "so they can marry."

"That's not their problem," said Klorissa. "They're matched by gene analysis, usually when they are quite young. That's the sensible way, isn't it?"

"Are they always willing?"

"To be married? They never are! It's a very traumatic process. At first they have to grow accustomed to one another, and a little bit of seeing each day, once the initial queasiness is gone, can do wonders."

"What if they just don't like their partner?"

"What? If the gene analysis indicates a partnership what difference does it——"

"I understand," said Baley hastily. He thought of Earth and sighed.

Klorissa said, "Is there anything else you would like to know?"

Baley wondered if there were anything to be gained from a longer stay. He would not be sorry to be done with Klorissa and fetal engineering so that he might pass on to the next stage.

He had opened his mouth to say as much, when Klorissa called out at some object far off, "You, child, you there! What are you doing?" Then, over her shoulder: "Earthman! Baley! Watch out! Watch *out!*"

Baley scarcely heard her. He responded to the note of urgency in her voice. The nervous effort that held his emotions taut snapped wide and he flamed into panic. All the terror of the open air and the endless vault of heaven broke in upon him.

Baley gibbered. He heard himself mouth meaningless

147

sounds and felt himself fall to his knees and slowly roll over to his side as though he were watching the process from a distance.

Also from a distance he heard the sighing hum piercing the air above him and ending with a sharp thwack.

Baley closed his eyes and his fingers clutched a thin tree root that skimmed the surface of the ground and his nails burrowed into dirt.

He opened his eyes (it must only have been moments after). Klorissa was scolding sharply at a youngster who remained at a distance. A robot, silent, stood closer to Klorissa. Baley had only time to notice the youngster held a stringed object in his hand before his eyes sheered away.

Breathing heavily, Baley struggled to his feet. He stared at the shaft of glistening metal that remained in the trunk of the tree against which he had been standing. He pulled at it and it came out readily. It had not penetrated far. He looked at the point but did not touch it. It was blunted, but it would have sufficed to tear his skin had he not dropped when he did.

It took him two tries to get his legs moving. He took a step toward Klorissa and called, "You. Youngster."

Klorissa turned, her face flushed. She said, "It was an accident. Are you hurt?"

"No! What is this thing?"

"It's an arrow. It is fired by a bow, which makes a taut string do the work."

"Like this," called the youngster impudently, and he shot another arrow into the air, then burst out laughing. He had light hair and a lithe body.

Klorissa said, "You will be disciplined. Now leave!"

"Wait, wait," cried Baley. He rubbed his knee where a rock had caught and bruised him as he had fallen. "I have some questions. What is your name?"

"Bik," he said carelessly.

"Did you shoot that arrow at me, Bik?"

"That's right," said the boy.

"Do you realize you would have hit me if I hadn't been warned in time to duck?"

Bik shrugged. "I was aiming to hit."

Klorissa spoke hurriedly. "You must let me explain. Archery is an encouraged sport. It is competitive without requiring contact. We have contests among the boys using viewing only. Now I'm afraid some of the boys will aim at robots. It amuses them and it doesn't hurt the robots. I'm the only adult human on the estate and when the boy saw you, he must have assumed you were a robot."

Baley listened. His mind was clearing, and the natural dourness of his long face intensified. He said, "Bik, did you think I was a robot?"

"No," said the youngster. "You're an Earthman."

"All right. Go now."

Bik turned and raced off whistling. Baley turned to the robot. "You! How did the youngster know I was an Earthman, or weren't you with him when he shot?"

"I was with him, master. I told him you were an Earthman."

"Did you tell him what an Earthman was?"

"Yes, master."

"What is an Earthman?"

"An inferior sort of human that ought not to be allowed on Solaria because he breeds disease, master."

"And who told you that, boy?"

The robot maintained silence.

Baley said, "Do you know who told you?"

"I do not, master. It is in my memory store."

"So you told the boy I was a disease-breeding inferior and he immediately shot at me. Why didn't you stop him?"

"I would have, master. I would not have allowed harm to come to a human, even an Earthman. He moved too quickly and I was not fast enough."

"Perhaps you thought I was just an Earthman, not completely a human, and hesitated a bit."

"No, master."

It was said with quiet calm, but Baley's lips quirked

grimly. The robot might deny it in all faith, but Baley felt that was exactly the factor involved.

Baley said, "What were you doing with the boy?"

"I was carrying his arrows, master."

"May I see them?"

He held out his hand. The robot approached and delivered a dozen of them. Baley put the original arrow, the one that had hit the tree, carefully at his feet, and looked the others over one by one. He handed them back and lifted the original arrow again.

He said, "Why did you give this particular arrow to the boy?"

"No reason, master. He had asked for an arrow some time earlier and this was the one my hand touched first. He looked about for a target, then noticed you and asked who the strange human was. I explained——"

"I know what you explained. This arrow you handed him is the only one with gray vanes at the rear. The others have black vanes."

The robot simply stared.

Baley said, "Did you guide the youngster here?"

"We walked randomly, master."

The Earthman looked through the gap between two trees through which the arrow had hurled itself toward its mark. He said, "Would it happen, by any chance, that this youngster, Bik, was the best archer you have here?"

The robot bent his head. "He is the best, master."

Klorissa gaped. "How did you ever come to guess that?"

"It follows," said Baley dryly. "Now please observe this gray-vaned arrow and the others. The gray-vaned arrow is the only one that seems oily at the point. I'll risk melodrama, ma'am, by saying that your warning saved my life. This arrow that missed me is poisoned."

13 A Roboticist Is Confronted

KLORISSA SAID, "Impossible! Skies above, absolutely impossible!"

"Above or below or any way you wish it. Is there an animal on the farm that's expendable? Get it and scratch it with the arrow and see what happens."

"But why should anyone want to——"

Baley said harshly, "I know why. The question is, who?"

"No one."

Baley felt the dizziness returning and he grew savage. He threw the arrow at her and she eyed the spot where it fell.

"Pick it up," Baley cried, "and if you don't want to test it, destroy it. Leave it there and you'll have an accident if the children get at it."

She picked it up hurriedly, holding it between forefinger and thumb.

Baley ran for the nearest entrance to the building and Klorissa was still holding the arrow, gingerly, when she followed him back indoors.

Baley felt a certain measure of equanimity return with the comfort of enclosure. He said, "Who poisoned the arrow?"

"I can't imagine."

"I suppose it isn't likely the boy did it himself. Would you have any way of telling who his parents were?"

"We could check the records," said Klorissa gloomily.

"Then you do keep records of relationships?"

"We have to for gene analysis."

"Would the youngster know who his parents were?"

"Never," said Klorissa energetically.

"Would he have any way of finding out?"

"He would have to break into the records room. Impossible."

"Suppose an adult visited the estate and wanted to know who his child was——"

Klorissa flushed. "Very unlikely."

"But suppose. Would he be told if he were to ask?"

"I don't know. It isn't exactly illegal for him to know. It certainly isn't customary."

"Would *you* tell him?"

"I'd try not to. I know Dr. Delmarre wouldn't have. He believed knowledge of relationship was for gene analysis only. Before him things may have been looser. . . . Why do you ask all this, anyway?"

"I don't see how the youngster could have a motive on his own account. I thought that through his parents he might have."

"This is all horrible." In her disturbed state of mind Klorissa approached more closely than at any previous time. She even stretched out an arm in his direction. "How can it all be happening? The boss killed; you nearly killed. We have no motives for violence on Solaria. We all have all we can want, so there is no personal ambition. We have no knowledge of relationship, so there is no family ambition. We are all in good genic health."

Her face cleared all at once. "Wait. This arrow can't be poisoned. I shouldn't let you convince me it is."

"Why have you suddenly decided that?"

"The robot with Bik. He would never have allowed poison. It's inconceivable that he could have done anything that might bring harm to a human being. The First Law of Robotics makes sure of that."

Baley said, "Does it? What is the First Law, I wonder?"

Klorissa stared blankly. "What do you mean?"

"Nothing. You have the arrow tested and you will find it poisoned." Baley himself was scarcely interested in the matter. He knew it for poison beyond any internal questionings. He said, "Do you still believe Mrs. Delmarre to have been guilty of her husband's death?"

"She was the only one present."

"I see. And you are the only other human adult present

on this estate at a time when I have just been shot at with a poisoned arrow."

She cried energetically, "I had nothing to do with it."

"Perhaps not. And perhaps Mrs. Delmarre is innocent as well. May I use your viewing apparatus?"

"Yes, of course."

Baley knew exactly whom he intended to view and it was *not* Gladia. It came as a surprise to himself then to hear his voice say, "Get Gladia Delmarre."

The robot obeyed without comment, and Baley watched the manipulations with astonishment, wondering why he had given the order.

Was it that the girl had just been the subject of discussion, or was it that he had been a little disturbed over the manner of the end of their last viewing, or was it simply the sight of the husky, almost overpoweringly practical figure of Klorissa that finally enforced the necessity of a glimpse of Gladia as a kind of counterirritant?

He thought defensively: Jehoshaphat! Sometimes a man has to play things by ear.

She was there before him all at once, sitting in a large, upright chair that made her appear smaller and more defenseless than ever. Her hair was drawn back and bound into a loose coil. She wore pendant earrings bearing gems that looked like diamonds. Her dress was a simple affair that clung tightly at the waist.

She said in a low voice, "I'm glad you viewed, Elijah. I've been trying to reach you."

"Good morning, Gladia." (Afternoon? Evening? He didn't know Gladia's time and he couldn't tell from the manner in which she was dressed what time it might be.) "Why have you been trying to reach me?"

"To tell you I was sorry I had lost my temper last time we viewed. Mr. Olivaw didn't know where you were to be reached."

Baley had a momentary vision of Daneel still bound fast by the overseeing robots and almost smiled. He said,

"That's all right. In a few hours, I'll be seeing you."

"Of course, if—— *Seeing* me?"

"Personal presence," said Baley gravely.

Her eyes grew wide and her fingers dug into the smooth plastic of the chair arms. "Is there any reason for that?"

"It is necessary."

"I don't think——"

"Would you allow it?"

She looked away. "Is it absolutely necessary?"

"It is. First, though, there is someone else I must see. Your husband was interested in robots. You told me that, and I have heard it from other sources, but he wasn't a roboticist, was he?"

"That wasn't his training, Elijah." She still avoided his eyes.

"But he worked with a roboticist, didn't he?"

"Jothan Leebig," she said at once. "He's a good friend of mine."

"He is?" said Baley energetically.

Gladia looked startled. "Shouldn't I have said that?"

"Why not, if it's the truth?"

"I'm always afraid that I'll say things that will make me seem as though—— You don't know what it's like when everyone is sure you've done something."

"Take it easy. How is it that Leebig is a friend of yours?"

"Oh, I don't know. He's in the next estate, for one thing. Viewing energy is just about nil, so we can just view all the time in free motion with hardly any trouble. We go on walks together all the time; or we did, anyway."

"I didn't know you could go on walks together with anyone."

Gladia flushed. "I said *viewing*. Oh well, I keep forgetting you're an Earthman. Viewing in free motion means we focus on ourselves and we can go anywhere we want to without losing contact. I walk on my estate and he walks on his and we're together." She held her chin high. "It can be pleasant."

Then, suddenly, she giggled. "Poor Jothan."

154

"Why do you say that?"

"I was thinking of you thinking we walked together without viewing. He'd die if he thought anyone could think that."

"Why?"

"He's terrible that way. He told me that when he was five years old he stopped seeing people. Insisted on viewing only. Some children are like that. Rikaine"—she paused in confusion, then went on—"Rikaine, my husband, once told me, when I talked about Jothan, that more and more children would be like that too. He said it was a kind of social evolution that favored survival of pro-viewing. Do you think that's so?"

"I'm no authority," said Baley.

"Jothan won't even get married. Rikaine was angry with him, told him he was anti-social and that he had genes that were necessary in the common pool, but Jothan just refused to consider it."

"Has he a right to refuse?"

"No-o," said Gladia hesitantly, "but he's a very brilliant roboticist, you know, and roboticists are valuable on Solaria. I suppose they stretched a point. Except I think Rikaine was going to stop working with Jothan. He told me once Jothan was a bad Solarian."

"Did he tell Jothan that?"

"I don't know. He was working with Jothan to the end."

"But he thought Jothan was a bad Solarian for refusing to marry?"

"Rikaine once said that marriage was the hardest thing in life, but that it had to be endured."

"What did you think?"

"About what, Elijah?"

"About marriage. Did you think it was the hardest thing in life?"

Her expression grew slowly blank as though she were painstakingly washing emotion out of it. She said, "I never thought about it."

Baley said, "You said you go on walks with Jothan Leebig all the time, then corrected yourself and put that

155

in the past. You don't go on walks with him any more, then?"

Gladia shook her head. Expression was back in her face. Sadness. "No. We don't seem to. I viewed him once or twice. He always seemed busy and I didn't like to—— You know."

"Was this since the death of your husband?"

"No, even some time before. Several months before."

"Do you suppose Dr. Delmarre ordered him not to pay further attention to you?"

Gladia looked startled. "Why should he? Jothan isn't a robot and neither am I. How can we take orders and why should Rikaine give them?"

Baley did not bother to try to explain. He could have done so only in Earth terms and that would make things no clearer to her. And if it did manage to clarify, the result could only be disgusting to her.

Baley said, "Only a question. I'll view you again, Gladia, when I'm done with Leebig. What time do you have, by the way?" He was sorry at once for asking the question. Robots would answer in Terrestrial equivalents, but Gladia might answer in Solarian units and Baley was weary of displaying ignorance.

But Gladia answered in purely qualitative terms. "Mid-afternoon," she said.

"Then that's it for Leebig's estate also?"

"Oh yes."

"Good. I'll view you again as soon as I can and we'll make arrangements for seeing."

Again she grew hesitant. "Is it absolutely necessary?"

"It is."

She said in a low voice, "Very well."

There was some delay in contacting Leebig and Baley utilized it in consuming another sandwich, one that was brought to him in its original packaging. But he had grown more cautious. He inspected the seal carefully before breaking it, then looked over the contents painstakingly.

He accepted a plastic container of milk, not quite unfrozen, bit an opening with his own teeth, and drank from it directly. He thought gloomily that there were such things as odorless, tasteless, slow-acting poisons that could be introduced delicately by means of hypodermic needles or high-pressure needle jets, then put the thought aside as being childish.

So far murders and attempted murders had been committed in the most direct possible fashion. There was nothing delicate or subtle about a blow on the head, enough poison in a glass to kill a dozen men, or a poisoned arrow shot openly at the victim.

And then he thought, scarcely less gloomily, that as long as he hopped between time zones in this fashion, he was scarcely likely to have regular meals. Or, if this continued, regular sleep.

The robot approached him. "Dr. Leebig directs you to call sometime tomorrow. He is engaged in important work."

Baley bounced to his feet and roared, "You tell that guy——"

He stopped. There was no use in yelling at a robot. That is, you could yell if you wished, but it would achieve results no sooner than a whisper.

He said in a conversational tone, "You tell Dr. Leebig, or his robot if that is as far as you've reached, that I am investigating the murder of a professional associate of his and a good Solarian. You tell him that I cannot wait on his work. You tell him that if I am not viewing him in five minutes, I will be in a plane and at his estate *seeing* him in less than an hour. You use that word, seeing, so there's no mistake."

He returned to his sandwich.

The five minutes were not quite gone, when Leebig, or at least a Solarian whom Baley presumed to be Leebig, was glaring at him.

Baley glared back. Leebig was a lean man, who held himself rigidly erect. His dark, prominent eyes had a look of intense abstraction about them, compounded now with anger. One of his eyelids dropped slightly.

He said, "Are you the Earthman?"

"Elijah Baley," said Baley, "Plainclothesman C-7, in charge of the investigation into the murder of Dr. Rikaine Delmarre. What is your name?"

"I'm Dr. Jothan Leebig. Why do you presume to annoy me at my work?"

"It's easy," said Baley quietly. "It's my business."

"Then take your business elsewhere."

"I have a few questions to ask first, Doctor. I believe you were a close associate of Dr. Delmarre. Right?"

One of Leebig's hands clenched suddenly into a fist and he strode hastily toward a mantelpiece on which tiny clockwork contraptions went through complicated periodic motions that caught hypnotically at the eye.

The viewer kept focused on Leebig so that his figure did not depart from central projection as he walked. Rather the room behind him seemed to move backward in little rises and dips as he strode.

Leebig said, "If you are the foreigner whom Gruer threatened to bring in——"

"I am."

"Then you are here against my advice. Done viewing."

"Not yet. Don't break contact." Baley raised his voice sharply and a finger as well. He pointed it directly at the roboticist, who shrank visibly away from it, full lips spreading into an expression of disgust.

Baley said, "I wasn't bluffing about seeing you, you know."

"No Earthman vulgarity, please."

"A straightforward statement is what it is intended to be. I will see you, if I can't make you listen any other way. I will grab you by the collar and make you listen."

Leebig stared back. "You are a filthy animal."

"Have it your way, but I will do as I say."

"If you try to invade my estate, I will—I will——"

Baley lifted his eyebrows. "Kill me? Do you often make such threats?"

"I made no threat."

"Then talk now. In the time you have wasted, a good

158

deal might have been accomplished. You were a close associate of Dr. Delmarre. Right?"

The roboticist's head lowered. His shoulders moved slightly to a slow, regular breathing. When he looked up, he was in command of himself. He even managed a brief, sapless smile.

"I was."

"Delmarre was interested in new types of robots, I understand."

"He was."

"What kind?"

"Are you a roboticist?"

"No. Explain it for the layman."

"I doubt that I can."

"Try! For instance, I think he wanted robots capable of disciplining children. What would that involve?"

Leebig raised his eyebrows briefly and said, "To put it very simply, skipping all the subtle details, it means a strengthening of the C-integral governing the Sikorovich tandem route response at the W-65 level."

"Double-talk," said Baley.

"The truth."

"It's double-talk to me. How else can you put it?"

"It means a certain weakening of the First Law."

"Why so? A child is disciplined for its own future good. Isn't that the theory?"

"Ah, the future good!" Leebig's eyes glowed with passion and he seemed to grow less conscious of his listener and correspondingly more talkative. "A simple concept, you think. How many human beings are willing to accept a trifling inconvenience for the sake of a large future good? How long does it take to train a child that what tastes good now means a stomach-ache later, and what tastes bad now will correct the stomach-ache later? Yet you want a robot to be able to understand?

"Pain inflicted by a robot on a child sets up a powerful disruptive potential in the positronic brain. To counteract that by an anti-potential triggered through a realization of future good requires enough paths and bypaths to increase the mass of the positronic brain by 50 per cent, unless other circuits are sacrificed."

Baley said, "Then you haven't succeeded in building such a robot."

"No, nor am I likely to succeed. Nor anyone."

"Was Dr. Delmarre testing an experimental model of such a robot at the time of his death?"

"Not of *such* a robot. We were interested in other more practical things also."

Baley said quietly, "Dr. Leebig, I am going to have to learn a bit more about robotics and I am going to ask you to teach me."

Leebig shook his head violently, and his drooping eyelid dipped further in a ghastly travesty of a wink. "It should be obvious that a course in robotics takes more than a moment. I lack the time."

"Nevertheless, you must teach me. The smell of robots is the one thing that pervades everything on Solaria. If it is time we require, then more than ever I must see you. I am an Earthman and I cannot work or think comfortably while viewing."

It would not have seemed possible to Baley for Leebig to stiffen his stiff carriage further, but he did. He said, "Your phobias as an Earthman don't concern me. Seeing is impossible."

"I think you will change your mind when I tell you what I chiefly want to consult you about."

"It will make no difference. Nothing can."

"No? Then listen to this. It is my belief that throughout the history of the positronic robot, the First Law of Robotics has been deliberately misquoted."

Leebig moved spasmodically. "Misquoted? Fool! Madman! Why?"

"To hide the fact," said Baley with complete composure, "that robots can commit murder."

14 A Motive Is Revealed

LEEBIG'S MOUTH widened slowly. Baley took it for a snarl at first and then, with considerable surprise, decided that it was the most unsuccessful attempt at a smile that he had ever seen.

Leebig said, "Don't say that. Don't ever say that."

"Why not?"

"Because anything, however small, that encourages distrust of robots is harmful. Distrusting robots is a human *disease!*"

It was as though he were lecturing a small child. It was as though he were saying something gently that he wanted to yell. It was as though he were trying to persuade when what he really wanted was to enforce on penalty of death.

Leebig said, "Do you know the history of robotics?"

"A little."

"On Earth, you should. Yes. Do you know robots started with a Frankenstein complex against them? They were suspect. Men distrusted and feared robots. Robotics was almost an undercover science as a result. The Three Laws were first built into robots in an effort to overcome distrust and even so Earth would never allow a robotic society to develop. One of the reasons the first pioneers left Earth to colonize the rest of the Galaxy was so that they might establish societies in which robots would be allowed to free men of poverty and toil. Even *then,* there remained a latent suspicion not far below, ready to pop up at any excuse."

"Have you yourself had to counter distrust of robots?" asked Baley.

"Many times," said Leebig grimly.

"Is that why you and other roboticists are willing to distort the facts just a little in order to avoid suspicion as much as possible?"

"There is no distortion!"

161

"For instance, aren't the Three Laws misquoted?"

"No!"

"I can demonstrate that they are, and unless you convince me otherwise, I will demonstrate it to the whole Galaxy, if I can."

"You're mad. Whatever argument you may think you have is fallacious, I assure you."

"Shall we discuss it?"

"If it does not take too long."

"Face to face? Seeing?"

Leebig's thin face twisted. *"No!"*

"Good-by, Dr. Leebig. Others will listen to me."

"Wait. Great Galaxy, man, wait!"

"Seeing?"

The roboticist's hands wandered upward, hovered about his chin. Slowly a thumb crept into his mouth and remained there. He stared, blankly, at Baley.

Baley thought: Is he regressing to the pre-five-year-old stage so that it will be legitimate for him to see me?

"Seeing?" he said.

But Leebig shook his head slowly. "I can't. I can't," he moaned, the words all but stifled by the blocking thumb. "Do whatever you want."

Baley stared at the other and watched him turn away and face the wall. He watched the Solarian's straight back bend and the Solarian's face hide in shaking hands.

Baley said, "Very well, then, I'll agree to view."

Leebig said, back still turned, "Excuse me a moment. I'll be back."

Baley tended to his own needs during the interval and stared at his fresh-washed face in the bathroom mirror. Was he getting the feel of Solaria and Solarians? He wasn't sure.

He sighed and pushed a contact and a robot appeared. He didn't turn to look at it. He said, "Is there another viewer at the farm, besides the one I'm using?"

"There are three other outlets, master."

"Then tell Klorissa Cantoro—tell your mistress that I

162

will be using this one till further notice and that I am not to be disturbed."

"Yes, master."

Baley returned to his position where the viewer remained focused on the empty patch of room in which Leebig had stood. It was still empty and he settled himself to wait.

It wasn't long. Leebig entered and the room once more jiggled as the man walked. Evidently focus shifted from room center to man center without delay. Baley remembered the complexity of viewing controls and began to feel a kind of appreciation of what was involved.

Leebig was quite master of himself now, apparently. His hair was slicked back and his costume had been changed. His clothes fitted loosely and were of a material that glistened and caught highlights. He sat down in a slim chair that folded out of the wall.

He said soberly, "Now what is this notion of yours concerning First Law?"

"Will we be overheard?"

"No. I've taken care."

Baley nodded. He said, "Let me quote the First Law."

"I scarcely need that."

"I know, but let me quote it, anyway: A robot may not harm a human being or, through inaction, allow a human being to come to harm."

"Well?"

"Now when I first landed on Solaria, I was driven to the estate assigned for my use in a ground-car. The ground-car was a specially enclosed job designed to protect me from exposure to open space. As an Earthman———"

"I know about that," said Leebig impatiently. "What has this to do with the matter?"

"The robots who drove the car did *not* know about it. I asked that the car be opened and was at once obeyed. Second Law. They had to follow orders. I was uncomfortable, of course, and nearly collapsed before the car was enclosed again. Didn't the robots harm me?"

"At your order," snapped Leebig.

"I'll quote the Second Law: A robot must obey the orders given it by human beings except where such orders would conflict with the First Law. So you see, my order should have been ignored."

"This is nonsense. The robot lacked knowledge——"

Baley leaned forward in his chair. "Ah! We have it. Now let's recite the First Law as it should be stated: A robot may do nothing that, *to its knowledge,* will harm a human being; nor, through inaction, *knowingly* allow a human being to come to harm."

"This is all understood."

"I think not by ordinary men. Otherwise, ordinary men would realize robots could commit murder."

Leebig was white. "Mad! Lunacy!"

Baley stared at his finger ends. "A robot may perform an innocent task, I suppose; one that has no damaging effect on a human being?"

"If ordered to do so," said Leebig.

"Yes, of course. If ordered to do so. And a second robot may perform an innocent task, also, I suppose; one that also can have no damaging effect on a human being? If ordered to do so?"

"Yes."

"And what if the two innocent tasks, each completely innocent, completely, amount to murder when added together?"

"What?" Leebig's face puckered into a scowl.

"I want your expert opinion on the matter," said Baley. "I'll set you a hypothetical case. Suppose a man says to a robot, 'Place a small quantity of this liquid into a glass of milk that you will find in such and such a place. The liquid is harmless. I wish only to know its effect on milk. Once I know the effect, the mixture will be poured out. After you have performed this action, forget you have done so.'"

Leebig, still scowling, said nothing.

Baley said, "If I had told the robot to add a mysterious liquid to milk and then offer it to a man, First Law would force it to ask, 'What is the nature of the liquid?

Will it harm a man?' And if it were assured the liquid was harmless, First Law might still make the robot hesitate and refuse to offer the milk. Instead, however, it is told the milk will be poured out. First Law is not involved. Won't the robot do as it is told?"

Leebig glared.

Baley said, "Now a second robot has poured out the milk in the first place and is unaware that the milk has been tampered with. In all innocence, it offers the milk to a man and the man dies."

Leebig cried out, *"No!"*

"Why not? Both actions are innocent in themselves. Only together are they murder. Do you deny that that sort of thing can happen?"

"The murderer would be the man who gave the order," cried Leebig.

"If you want to be philosophical, yes. The robots would have been the immediate murderers, though, the instruments of murder."

"No man would give such orders."

"A man would. A man has. It was exactly in this way that the murder attempt on Dr. Gruer must have been carried through. You've heard about that, I suppose."

"On Solaria," muttered Leebig, "one hears about everything."

"Then you know Gruer was poisoned at his dinner table before the eyes of myself and my partner, Mr. Olivaw of Aurora. Can you suggest any other way in which the poison might have reached him? There was no other human on the estate. As a Solarian, you must appreciate that point."

"I'm not a detective. I have no theories."

"I've presented you with one. I want to know if it is a possible one. I want to know if two robots might not perform two separate actions, each one innocent in itself, the two together resulting in murder. You're the expert, Dr. Leebig. *Is it possible?*"

And Leebig, haunted and harried, said, "Yes," in a voice so low that Baley scarcely heard him.

Baley said, "Very well, then. So much for the First Law."

Leebig stared at Baley and his drooping eyelid winked once or twice in a slow tic. His hands, which had been clasped, drew apart, though the fingers maintained their clawed shape as though each hand still entwined a phantom hand of air. Palms turned downward and rested on knees and only then did the fingers relax.

Baley watched it all in abstraction.

Leebig said, "Theoretically, yes. Theoretically! But don't dismiss the First Law that easily, Earthman. Robots would have to be ordered very cleverly in order to circumvent the First Law."

"Granted," said Baley. "I am only an Earthman. I know next to nothing about robots and my phrasing of the orders was only by way of example. A Solarian would be much more subtle and do much better. I'm sure of that."

Leebig might not have been listening. He said loudly, "If a robot can be manipulated into doing harm to a man, it means only that we must extend the powers of the positronic brain. One *might* say we ought to make the human better. That is impossible, so we will make the robot more foolproof.

"We advance continuously. Our robots are more varied, more specialized, more capable, and more unharming than those of a century ago. A century hence, we will have still greater advances. Why have a robot manipulate controls when a positronic brain can be built into the controls itself? That's specialization, but we can generalize, also. Why not a robot with replaceable and interchangeable limbs. Eh? Why not? If we——"

Baley interrupted. "Are you the only roboticist on Solaria?"

"Don't be a fool."

"I only wondered. **Dr. Delmarre** was the only—uh—fetal engineer, except for an assistant."

"Solaria has over twenty roboticists."

"Are you the best?"

"I am," Leebig said without self-consciousness.

"Delmarre worked with you."

"He did."

Baley said, "I understand that he was planning to break the partnership toward the end."

"No sign of it. What gave you the idea?"

"I understand he disapproved of your bachelorhood."

"He may have. He was a thorough Solarian. However, it did not affect our business relationships."

"To change the subject. In addition to developing new model robots, do you also manufacture and repair existing types?"

Leebig said, "Manufacture and repair are largely robot-conducted. There is a large factory and maintenance shop on my estate."

"Do robots require much in the way of repair, by the way?"

"Very little."

"Does that mean that robot repair is an undeveloped science?"

"Not at all." Leebig said that stiffly.

"What about the robot that was at the scene of Dr. Delmarre's murder?"

Leebig looked away, and his eyebrows drew together as though a painful thought were being barred entrance to his mind. "It was a complete loss."

"Really complete? Could it answer any questions at all?"

"None at all. It was absolutely useless. Its positronic brain was completely short-circuited. Not one pathway was left intact. Consider! It had witnessed a murder it had been unable to halt——"

"Why was it unable to halt the murder, by the way?"

"Who can tell? Dr. Delmarre was experimenting with that robot. I do not know in what mental condition he had left it. He might have ordered it, for instance, to suspend all operations while he checked one particular circuit element. If someone whom neither Dr. Delmarre nor the robot suspected of harm were suddenly to launch a homicidal attack, there might be a perceptible interval before the robot could use First Law potential to overcome Dr. Delmarre's freezing order. The length of the interval would depend on the nature of the attack and the nature of Dr. Delmarre's freezing order. I could invent a dozen other ways of explaining why the robot was unable to prevent the murder. Being unable to do so was a First Law violation, however, and that was sufficient to blast every positronic pathway in the robot's mind."

"But if the robot was physically unable to prevent the murder, was it responsible? Does the First Law ask impossibilities?"

Leebig shrugged. "The First Law, despite your attempts to make little of it, protects humanity with every atom of possible force. It allows no excuses. If the First Law is broken, the robot is ruined."

"That is a universal rule, sir?"

"As universal as robots."

Baley said, "Then I've learned something."

"Then learn something else. Your theory of murder by a series of robotic actions, each innocent in itself, will not help you in the case of Dr. Delmarre's death."

"Why not?"

"The death was not by poisoning, but by bludgeoning. Something had to hold the bludgeon, and that had to be a human arm. No robot could swing a club and smash a skull."

"Suppose," said Baley, "a robot were to push an innocent button which dropped a booby-trap weight on Delmarre's head."

Leebig smiled sourly. "Earthman, I've viewed the scene of the crime. I've heard all the news. The murder was a big thing here on Solaria, you know. So I know there was no sign of any machinery at the scene of the crime, or of any fallen weight."

Baley said, "Or of any blunt instrument, either."

Leebig said scornfully, "You're a detective. Find it."

"Granting that a robot was not responsible for Dr. Delmarre's death, who was, then?"

"Everyone knows who was," shouted Leebig. "His wife! Gladia!"

Baley thought: At least there's a unanimity of opinion.

Aloud he said, "And who was the mastermind behind the robots who poisoned Gruer?"

"I suppose . . ." Leebig trailed off.

"You don't think there are two murderers, do you? If Gladia was responsible for one crime, she must be responsible for the second attempt, also."

"Yes. You must be right." His voice gained assurance. "No doubt of it."

"No doubt?"

"Nobody else could get close enough to Dr. Delmarre to kill him. He allowed personal presence no more than I did, except that he made an exception in favor of his wife, and I make no exceptions. The wiser I." The roboticist laughed harshly.

"I believe you knew her," said Baley abruptly.

"Whom?"

"Her. We are discussing only one 'her.' Gladia!"

"Who told you I knew her any more than I know anyone else?" demanded Leebig. He put his hand to his throat. His fingers moved slightly and opened the neckseam of his garment for an inch downward, leaving more freedom to breathe.

"Gladia herself did. You two went for walks."

"So? We were neighbors. It is a common thing to do. She seemed a pleasant person."

"You approved of her, then?"

Leebig shrugged. "Talking to her was relaxing."

"What did you talk about?"

"Robotics." There was a flavor of surprise about the word as though there were wonder that the question could be asked.

"And she talked robotics too?"

"She knew nothing about robotics. Ignorant! But she listened. She has some sort of field-force rigmarole she plays with; field coloring, she calls it. I have no patience with that, but I listened."

"All this without personal presence?"

Leebig looked revolted and did not answer.

Baley tried again, "Were you attracted to her?"

"What?"

"Did you find her attractive? Physically?"

Even Leebig's bad eyelid lifted and his lips quivered. "Filthy animal," he muttered.

"Let me put it this way, then. When did you cease finding Gladia pleasant? You used that word yourself, if you remember."

"What do you mean?"

"You said you found her pleasant. Now you believe she murdered her husband. That isn't the mark of a pleasant person."

"I was mistaken about her."

"But you decided you were mistaken before she killed her husband, if she did so. You stopped walking with her some time before the murder. Why?"

Leebig said, "Is that important?"

"Everything is important till proven otherwise."

"Look, if you want information from me as a roboticist, ask it. I won't answer personal questions."

Baley said, "You were closely associated with both the murdered man and the chief suspect. Don't you see that personal questions are unavoidable? Why did you stop walking with Gladia?"

Leebig snapped, "There came a time when I ran out of things to say; when I was too busy; when I found no reason to continue the walks."

"When you no longer found her pleasant, in other words."

"All right. Put it so."

"Why was she no longer pleasant?"

Leebig shouted, "I have no reason."

Baley ignored the other's excitement. "You are still someone who has known Gladia well. What could her motive be?"

"Her motive?"

"No one has suggested any motive for the murder.

170

Surely Gladia wouldn't commit murder without a motive."

"Great Galaxy!" Leebig leaned his head back as though to laugh, but didn't. "No one told you? Well, perhaps no one knew. I knew, though. She told me. She told me frequently."

"Told you what, Dr. Leebig?"

"Why, that she quarreled with her husband. Quarreled bitterly and frequently. She hated him, Earthman. Didn't anyone tell you that? Didn't *she* tell you?"

15   A Portrait Is Colored

BALEY TOOK it between the eyes and tried not to show it.

Presumably, living as they did, Solarians considered one another's private lives to be sacrosanct. Questions concerning marriage and children were in bad taste. He supposed then that chronic quarreling could exist between husband and wife and be a matter into which curiosity was equally forbidden.

But even when murder had been committed? Would no one commit the social crime of asking the suspect if she quarreled with her husband? Or of mentioning the matter if they happened to know of it?

Well, Leebig had.

Baley said, "What did the quarrels concern?"

"You had better ask her, I think."

He better had, thought Baley. He rose stiffly, "Thank you, Dr. Leebig, for your co-operation. I may need your help again later. I hope you will keep yourself available."

"Done viewing," said Leebig, and he and the segment of his room vanished abruptly.

For the first time Baley found himself not minding a plane flight through open space. Not minding it at all. It was almost as though he were in his own element.

He wasn't even thinking of Earth or of Jessie. He had been away from Earth only a matter of weeks, yet it might as well have been years. He had been on Solaria only the better part of three days and yet it seemed forever.

How fast could a man adapt to nightmare?

Or was it Gladia? He would be seeing her soon, not viewing her. Was that what gave him confidence and this odd feeling of mixed apprehension and anticipation?

Would she endure it? he wondered. Or would she slip away after a few moments of seeing, begging off as Quemot had done?

She stood at the other end of a long room when he entered. She might almost have been an impressionistic representation of herself, she was reduced so to essentials.

Her lips were faintly red, her eyebrows lightly penciled, her earlobes faintly blue, and, except for that, her face was untouched. She looked pale, a little frightened, and very young.

Her brown-blond hair was drawn back, and her gray-blue eyes were somehow shy. Her dress was a blue so dark as to be almost black, with a thin white edging curling down each side. She wore long sleeves, white gloves, and flat-heeled shoes. Not an inch of skin showed anywhere but in her face. Even her neck was covered by a kind of unobtrusive ruching.

Baley stopped where he was. "Is this close enough, Gladia?"

She was breathing with shallow quickness. She said, "I had forgotten what to expect really. It's just like viewing, isn't it? I mean, if you don't think of it as seeing."

Baley said, "It's all quite normal to me."

"Yes, on Earth." She closed her eyes. "Sometimes I try to imagine it. Just crowds of people everywhere. You walk down a road and there are others walking with you and still others walking in the other direction. Dozens——"

"Hundreds," said Baley. "Did you ever view scenes on Earth in a book-film? Or view a novel with an Earth setting?"

"We don't have many of those, but I've viewed novels set on the other Outer Worlds where seeing goes on all

172

the time. It's different in a novel. It just seems like a multiview."

"Do people ever kiss in novels?"

She flushed painfully. "I don't read that kind."

"Never?"

"Well—there are always a few dirty films around, you know, and sometimes, just out of curiosity—— It's sickening, really."

"Is it?"

She said with sudden animation, "But Earth is so different. So many people. When you walk, Elijah, I suppose you even t-touch people. I mean, by accident."

Baley half smiled. "You even knock them down by accident." He thought of the crowds on the Expressways, tugging and shoving, bounding up and down the strips, and for a moment, inevitably, he felt the pang of homesickness.

Gladia said, "You don't have to stay way out there."

"Would it be all right if I came closer?"

"I think so. I'll tell you when I'd rather you wouldn't any more."

Stepwise Baley drew closer, while Gladia watched him, wide-eyed.

She said suddenly, "Would you like to see some of my field colorings?"

Baley was six feet away. He stopped and looked at her. She seemed small and fragile. He tried to visualize her, something in her hand (what?), swinging furiously at the skull of her husband. He tried to picture her, mad with rage, homicidal with hate and anger.

He had to admit it could be done. Even a hundred and five pounds of woman could crush a skull if she had the proper weapon and were wild enough. And Baley had known murderesses (on Earth, of course) who, in repose, were bunny rabbits.

He said, "What are field colorings, Gladia?"

"An art form," she said.

Baley remembered Leebig's reference to Gladia's art. He nodded. "I'd like to see some."

"Follow me, then."

Baley maintained a careful six-foot distance between them. At that, it was less than a third the distance Klorissa had demanded.

They entered a room that burst with light. It glowed in every corner and every color.

Gladia looked pleased, proprietary. She looked up at Baley, eyes anticipating.

Baley's response must have been what she expected, though he said nothing. He turned slowly, trying to make out what he saw, for it was light only, no material object at all.

The gobbets of light sat on embracing pedestals. They were living geometry, lines and curves of color, entwined into a coalescing whole yet maintaining distinct identities. No two specimens were even remotely alike.

Baley groped for appropriate words and said, "Is it supposed to mean anything?"

Gladia laughed in her pleasant contralto. "It means whatever you like it to mean. They're just light-forms that might make you feel angry or happy or curious or whatever *I* felt when I constructed one. I could make one for you, a kind of portrait. It might not be very good, though, because I would just be improvising quickly."

"Would you? I would be very interested."

"All right," she said, and half-ran to a light-figure in one corner, passing within inches of him as she did so. She did not seem to notice.

She touched something on the pedestal of the light-figure and the glory above died without a flicker.

Baley gasped and said, "Don't do that."

"It's all right. I was tired of it, anyway. I'll just fade the others temporarily so they don't distract me." She opened a panel along one featureless wall and moved a rheostat. The colors faded to something scarcely visible.

Baley said, "Don't you have a robot to do this? Closing contacts?"

"Shush, now," she said impatiently. "I don't keep robots

in here. This is *me*." She looked at him, frowning. "I don't know you well enough. That's the trouble."

She wasn't looking at the pedestal, but her fingers rested lightly on its smooth upper surface. All ten fingers were curved, tense, waiting.

One finger moved, describing a half curve over smoothness. A bar of deep yellow light grew and slanted obliquely across the air above. The finger inched backward a fraction and the light grew slightly less deep in shade.

She looked at it momentarily. "I suppose that's it. A kind of strength without weight."

"Jehoshaphat," said Baley.

"Are you offended?" Her fingers lifted and the yellow slant of light remained solitary and stationary.

"No, not at all. But what is it? How do you do it?"

"That's hard to explain," said Gladia, looking at the pedestal thoughtfully, "considering I don't really understand it myself. It's a kind of optical illusion, I've been told. We set up force-fields at different energy levels. They're extrusions of hyperspace, really, and don't have the properties of ordinary space at all. Depending on the energy level, the human eye sees light of different shades. The shapes and colors are controlled by the warmth of my fingers against appropriate spots on the pedestal. There are all sorts of controls inside each pedestal."

"You mean if I were to put my finger there——" Baley advanced and Gladia made way for him. He put a hesitant forefinger down upon the pedestal and felt a soft throbbing.

"Go ahead. Move your finger, Elijah," said Gladia.

Baley did so and a dirty-gray jag of light lifted upward, skewing the yellow light. Baley withdrew his finger sharply and Gladia laughed and then was instantly contrite.

"I shouldn't laugh," she said. "It's really very hard to do, even for people who've tried a long time." Her own hand moved lightly and too quickly for Baley to follow and the monstrosity he had set up disappeared, leaving the yellow light in isolation again.

"How did you learn to do this?" asked Baley.

"I just kept on trying. It's a new art form, you know, and only one or two really know how——"

"And you're the best," said Baley somberly. "On Solaria everyone is either the only or the best or both."

"You needn't laugh. I've had some of my pedestals on display. I've given shows." Her chin lifted. There was no mistaking her pride.

She continued, "Let me go on with your portrait." Her fingers moved again.

There were few curves in the light-form that grew under her ministrations. It was all sharp angles. And the dominant color was blue.

"That's Earth, somehow," said Gladia, biting her lower lip. "I always think of Earth as blue. All those people and seeing, seeing, seeing. Viewing is more rose. How does it seem to you?"

"Jehoshaphat, I can't picture things as colors."

"Can't you?" she asked abstractedly. "Now you say 'Jehoshaphat' sometimes and that's just a little blob of violet. A little sharp blob because it usually comes out ping, like that." And the little blob was there, glowing just off-center.

"And then," she said, "I can finish it like this." And a flat, lusterless hollow cube of slate gray sprang up to enclose everything. The light within shone through it, but dimmer; imprisoned, somehow.

Baley felt a sadness at it, as though it were something enclosing him, keeping him from something he wanted. He said, "What's that last?"

Gladia said, "Why, the walls about you. That's what's most in you, the way you can't go outside, the way you have to be inside. You *are* inside there. Don't you see?"

Baley saw and somehow he disapproved. He said, "Those walls aren't permanent. I've been out today."

"You have? Did you mind?"

He could not resist a counterdig. "The way you mind seeing me. You don't like it but you can stand it."

She looked at him thoughtfully. "Do you want to come out now? With me? For a walk?"

176

It was Baley's impulse to say: Jehoshaphat, no.

She said, "I've never walked with anyone, seeing. It's still daytime, and it's pleasant weather."

Baley looked at his abstractionist portrait and said, "If I go, will you take away the gray?"

She smiled and said, "I'll see how you behave."

The structure of light remained as they left the room. It stayed behind, holding Baley's imprisoned soul fast in the gray of the Cities.

Baley shivered slightly. Air moved against him and there was a chill to it.

Gladia said, "Are you cold?"

"It wasn't like this before," muttered Baley.

"It's late in the day now, but it isn't really cold. Would you like a coat? One of the robots could bring one in a minute."

"No. It's all right." They stepped forward along a narrow paved path. He said, "Is this where you used to walk with Dr. Leebig?"

"Oh no. We walked way out among the fields, where you only see an occasional robot working and you can hear the animal sounds. You and I will stay near the house though, just in case."

"In case what?"

"Well, in case you want to go in."

"Or in case you get weary of seeing?"

"It doesn't bother me," she said recklessly.

There was the vague rustle of leaves above and an all-pervading yellowness and greenness. There were sharp, thin cries in the air about, plus a strident humming, and shadows, too.

He was especially aware of the shadows. One of them stuck out before him, in shape like a man, that moved as he did in horrible mimicry. Baley had heard of shadows, of course, and he knew what they were, but in the pervasive indirect lighting of the Cities he had never been specifically aware of one.

177

Behind him, he knew, was the Solarian sun. He took care not to look at it, but he knew it was there.

Space was large, space was lonely, yet he found it drawing him. His mind pictured himself striding the surface of a world with thousands of miles and light-years of room all about him.

Why should he find attraction in this thought of loneliness? He didn't want loneliness. He wanted Earth and the warmth and companionship of the man-crammed Cities.

The picture failed him. He tried to conjure up New York in his mind, all the noise and fullness of it, and found he could remain conscious only of the quiet, air-moving chill of the surface of Solaria.

Without quite willing it Baley moved closer to Gladia until he was two feet away, then grew aware of her startled face.

"I beg your pardon," he said at once, and drew off.

She gasped, "It's all right. Won't you walk this way? We have some flower beds you might like."

The direction she indicated lay away from the sun. Baley followed silently.

Gladia said, "Later in the year, it will be wonderful. In the warm weather I can run down to the lake and swim, or just run across the fields, run as fast as I can until I'm just glad to fall down and lie still."

She looked down at herself. "But this is no costume for it. With all this on, I've *got* to walk. Sedately, you know."

"How would you prefer to dress?" asked Baley.

"Halter and shorts at the *most*," she cried, lifting her arms as though feeling the freedom of that in her imagination. "Sometimes less. Sometimes just sandals so you can feel the air with every inch—— Oh, I'm sorry, I've offended you."

Baley said, "No. It's all right. Was that your costume when you went walking with Dr. Leebig?"

"It varied. It depended on the weather. Sometimes I wore very little, but it was viewing, you know. You *do* understand, I hope."

"I understand. What about Dr. Leebig, though? Did he dress lightly too?"

"Jothan dress lightly?" Gladia smiled flashingly. "Oh no. He's very solemn, always." She twisted her face into a thin look of gravity and half winked, catching the very essence of Leebig and forcing a short grunt of appreciation out of Baley.

"This is the way he talks," she said. " 'My dear Gladia, in considering the effect of a first-order potential on positron flow——' "

"Is that what he talked to you about? Robotics?"

"Mostly. Oh, he takes it so seriously, you know. He was always trying to teach me about it. He never gave up."

"Did you learn anything?"

"Not one thing. Nothing. It's just all a complete mix-up to me. He'd get angry with me sometimes, but when he'd scold, I'd dive into the water, if we were anywhere near the lake, and splash him."

"*Splash* him? I thought you were viewing."

She laughed. "You're *such* an Earthman. I'd splash where he was standing in his own room or on his own estate. The water couldn't touch him, but he would duck just the same. Look at that."

Baley looked. They had circled a wooded patch and now came upon a clearing, centered about an ornamental pond. Small bricked walks penetrated the clearing and broke it up. Flowers grew in profusion and order. Baley knew them for flowers from book-films he had viewed.

In a way the flowers were like the light-patterns that Gladia constructed and Baley imagined that she constructed them in the spirit of flowers. He touched one cautiously, then looked about. Reds and yellows predominated.

In turning to look about Baley caught a glimpse of the sun.

He said uneasily, "The sun is low in the sky."

"It's late afternoon," called Gladia back to him. She had run toward the pond and was sitting on a stone bench at its edge. "Come here," she shouted, waving. "You can stand if you don't like to sit on stone."

Baley advanced slowly. "Does it get this low every day?" and at once he was sorry he asked. If the planet rotated, the sun must be low in the sky both mornings and afternoons. Only at midday could it be high.

Telling himself this couldn't change a lifetime of pictured thought. He knew there was such a thing as night and had even experienced it, with a planet's whole thickness interposing safely between a man and the sun. He knew there were clouds and a protective grayness hiding the worst of outdoors. And still, when he thought of planetary surfaces, it was always a picture of a blaze of light with a sun high in the sky.

He looked over his shoulder, just quickly enough to get a flash of sun, and wondered how far the house was if he should decide to return.

Gladia was pointing to the other end of the stone bench.

Baley said, "That's pretty close to you, isn't it?"

She spread out her little hands, palms up. "I'm getting used to it. Really."

He sat down, facing toward her to avoid the sun.

She leaned over backward toward the water and pulled a small cup-shaped flower, yellow without and white-streaked within, not at all flamboyant. She said, "This is a native plant. Most of the flowers here are from Earth originally."

Water dripped from its severed stem as she extended it gingerly toward Baley.

Baley reached for it as gingerly. "You killed it," he said.

"It's only a flower. There are thousands more." Suddenly, before his fingers more than touched the yellow cup, she snatched it away, her eyes kindling. "Or are you trying to imply I could kill a human being because I pulled a flower?"

Baley said in soft conciliation, "I wasn't implying anything. May I see it?"

Baley didn't really want to touch it. It had grown in

180

wet soil and there was still the effluvium of mud about it. How could these people, who were so careful in contact with Earthmen and even with one another, be so careless in their contact with ordinary dirt?

But he held the stalk between thumb and forefinger and looked at it. The cup was formed of several thin pieces of papery tissue, curving up from a common center. Within it was a white convex swelling, damp with liquid and fringed with dark hairs that trembled lightly in the wind.

She said, "Can you smell it?"

At once Baley was aware of the odor that emanated from it. He leaned toward it and said, "It smells like a woman's perfume."

Gladia clapped her hands in delight. "How like an Earthman. What you really mean is that a woman's perfume smells like *that*."

Baley nodded ruefully. He was growing weary of the outdoors. The shadows were growing longer and the land was becoming somber. Yet he was determined not to give in. He wanted those gray walls of light that dimmed his portrait removed. It was quixotic, but there it was.

Gladia took the flower from Baley, who let it go without reluctance. Slowly she pulled its petals apart. She said, "I suppose every woman smells different."

"It depends on the perfume," said Baley indifferently.

"Imagine being close enough to tell. I don't wear perfume because no one is close enough. Except now. But I suppose you smell perfume often, all the time. On Earth, your wife is always with you, isn't she?" She was concentrating very hard on the flower, frowning as she plucked it carefully to pieces.

"She's not always with me," said Baley. "Not every minute."

"But most of the time. And whenever you want to——"

Baley said suddenly, "Why did Dr. Leebig try so hard to teach you robotics, do you suppose?"

The dismembered flower consisted now of a stalk and the inner swelling. Gladia twirled it between her fingers, then tossed it away, so that it floated for a moment on the surface of the pond. "I think he wanted me to be his assistant," she said.

"Did he tell you so, Gladia?"

"Toward the end, Elijah. I think he grew impatient. Anyway, he asked me if I didn't think it would be exciting to work in robotics. Naturally, I told him I could think of nothing duller. He was quite angry."

"And he never walked with you again after that."

She said, "You know, I think that may have been it. I suppose his feelings were hurt. Really, though, what could I do?"

"It was before that, though, that you told him about your quarrels with Dr. Delmarre."

Her hands became fists and held so in a tight spasm. Her body held stiffly to its position, head bent and a little to one side. Her voice was unnaturally high. "What quarrels?"

"Your quarrels with your husband. I understand you hated him."

Her face was distorted and blotched as she glared at him. "Who told you that? Jothan?"

"Dr. Leebig mentioned it. I think it's true."

She was shaken. "You're still trying to prove I killed him. I keep thinking you're my friend and you're only— only a detective."

She raised her fists and Baley waited.

He said, "You know you can't touch me."

Her hands dropped and she began crying without a sound. She turned her head away.

Baley bent his own head and closed his eyes, shutting out the disturbing long shadows. He said, "Dr. Delmarre was not a very affectionate man, was he?"

She said in a strangled way, "He was a very busy man."

Baley said, "You *are* affectionate, on the other hand. You find a man interesting. Do you understand?"

"I c-can't help it. I know it's disgusting, but I can't help it. It's even disgusting t-to talk about it."

"You did talk about it to Dr. Leebig, though?"

"I *had* to do something and Jothan was handy and he didn't seem to mind and it made me feel better."

"Was this the reason you quarreled with your husband? Was it that he was cold and unaffectionate and you resented it?"

"Sometimes I hated him." She shrugged her shoulders helplessly. "He was just a good Solarian and we weren't scheduled for ch—for ch———" She broke down.

Baley waited. His own stomach was cold and open air pressed down heavily upon him. When Gladia's sobs grew quieter, he asked, as gently as he could, "Did you kill him, Gladia?"

"No-no." Then, suddenly, as though all resistance had corroded within her: "I haven't told you everything."

"Well, then, please do so now."

"We were quarreling that time, the time he died. The old quarrel. I screamed at him but he never shouted back. He hardly ever even said anything and that just made it worse. I was so angry, so angry. I don't remember after that."

"Jehoshaphat!" Baley swayed slightly and his eyes sought the neutral stone of the bench. "What do you mean you don't remember?"

"I mean he was dead and I was screaming and the robots came———"

"Did you kill him?"

"I don't remember it, Elijah, and I would remember it if I did, wouldn't I? Only I don't remember anything else, either, and I've been so frightened, so frightened. Help me, please, Elijah."

"Don't worry, Gladia. I'll help you." Baley's reeling mind fastened on the murder weapon. What happened to it? It must have been removed. If so, only the murderer could have done it. Since Gladia was found immediately after the murder on the scene, she could not have done it. The murderer would have to be someone else. No matter how it looked to everyone on Solaria, it had to be someone else.

Baley thought sickly: I've got to get back to the house.

He said, "Gladia——"

Somehow he was staring at the sun. It was nearly at the horizon. He had to turn his head to look at it and his eyes locked with a morbid fascination. He had never seen it so. Fat, red, and dim somehow, so that one could look at it without blinding, and see the bleeding clouds above it in thin lines, with one crossing it in a bar of black.

Baley mumbled, "The sun is so red."

He heard Gladia's choked voice say drearily, "It's always red at sunset, red and dying."

Baley had a vision. The sun was moving down to the horizon because the planet's surface was moving away from it, a thousand miles an hour, spinning under that naked sun, spinning with nothing to guard the microbes called men that scurried over its spinning surface, spinning madly forever, spinning—spinning . . .

It was his head that was spinning and the stone bench that was slanting beneath him and the sky heaving, blue, dark blue, and the sun was gone, with the tops of trees and the ground rushing up and Gladia screaming thinly and another sound . . .

16   A Solution Is Offered

BALEY WAS aware first of enclosure, the absence of the open, and then of a face bending over him.

He stared for a moment without recognition. Then: "Daneel!"

The robot's face showed no sign of relief or of any other recognizable emotion at being addressed. He said, "It is well that you have recovered consciousness, Partner Elijah. I do not believe you have suffered physical injury."

"I'm all right," said Baley testily, struggling to his elbows. "Jehoshaphat, am I in bed? What for?"

"You have been exposed to the open a number of times today. The effects upon you have been cumulative and you need rest."

"I need a few answers first." Baley looked about and tried to deny to himself that his head was spinning just a little. He did not recognize the room. The curtains were drawn. Lights were comfortably artificial. He was feeling much better. "For instance, where am I?"

"In a room of Mrs. Delmarre's mansion."

"Next, let's get something straight. What are *you* doing here? How did you get away from the robots I set over you?"

Daneel said, "It had seemed to me that you would be displeased at this development and yet in the interests of your safety and of my orders, I felt that I had no choice but——"

"What did you *do*? Jehoshaphat!"

"It seems Mrs. Delmarre attempted to view you some hours ago."

"Yes." Baley remembered Gladia saying as much earlier in the day. "I know that."

"Your order to the robots that held me prisoner was, in your words: 'Do not allow him' (meaning myself) 'to establish contact with other humans or other robots, either by seeing or by viewing.' However, Partner Elijah, you said nothing about forbidding other humans or robots to contact me. You see the distinction?"

Baley groaned.

Daneel said, "No need for distress, Partner Elijah. The flaw in your orders was instrumental in saving your life, since it brought me to the scene. You see, when Mrs. Delmarre viewed me, being allowed to do so by my robot guardians, she asked after you and I answered, quite truthfully, that I did not know of your whereabouts, but that I could attempt to find out. She seemed anxious that I do so. I said I thought it possible you might have left the house temporarily and that I would check that matter and would she, in the meanwhile, order the robots in the room with me, to search the mansion for your presence."

"Wasn't she surprised that you didn't deliver the orders to the robots yourself?"

"I gave her the impression, I believe, that as an Auroran

I was not as accustomed to robots as she was; that she might deliver the orders with greater authority and effect a more speedy consummation. Solarians, it is quite clear, are vain of their skill with robots and contemptuous of the ability of natives of other planets to handle them. Is that not your opinion as well, Partner Elijah?"

"And she ordered them away, then?"

"With difficulty. They protested previous orders but, of course, could not state the nature thereof since you had ordered them to tell no one of my own true identity. She overrode them, although the final orders had to be shrilled out in fury."

"And then you left."

"I did, Partner Elijah."

A pity, thought Baley, that Gladia did not consider that episode important enough to relay to him when he viewed her. He said, "It took you long enough to find me, Daneel."

"The robots on Solaria have a network of information through subetheric contact. A skilled Solarian could obtain information readily, but, mediated as it is through millions of individual machines, one such as myself, without experience in the matter, must take time to unearth a single datum. It was better than an hour before the information as to your whereabouts reached me. I lost further time by visiting Dr. Delmarre's place of business after you had departed."

"What were you doing there?"

"Pursuing researches of my own. I regret that this had to be done in your absence, but the exigencies of the investigation left me no choice."

Baley said, "Did you view Klorissa Cantoro, or see her?"

"I viewed her, but from another part of her building, not from our own estate. There were records at the farm I had to see. Ordinarily viewing would have been sufficient, but it might have been inconvenient to remain on our own estate since three robots knew my real nature and might easily have imprisoned me once more."

Baley felt almost well. He swung his legs out of bed and found himself in a kind of nightgown. He stared at it with distaste. "Get me my clothes."

Daneel did so.

As Baley dressed, he said, "Where's Mrs. Delmarre?"

"Under house arrest, Partner Elijah."

"What? By whose order?"

"By my order. She is confined to her bedroom under robotic guard and her right to give orders other than to meet personal needs has been neutralized."

"By yourself?"

"The robots on this estate are not aware of my identity."

Baley finished dressing. "I know the case against Gladia," he said. "She had the opportunity; more of it, in fact, than we thought at first. She did not rush to the scene at the sound of her husband's cry, as she first said. She was there all along."

"Does she claim to have witnessed the murder and seen the murderer?"

"No. She remembers nothing of the crucial moments. That happens sometimes. It turns out, also, that she has a motive."

"What was it, Partner Elijah?"

"One that I had suspected as a possibility from the first. I said to myself, if this were Earth, and Dr. Delmarre were as he was described to be and Gladia Delmarre as she seemed to be, I would say that she was in love with him, or had been, and that he was in love only with himself. The difficulty was to tell whether Solarians felt love or reacted to love in any Earthly sense. My judgment as to their emotions and reactions wasn't to be trusted. It was why I had to see a few. *Not* view them, but see them."

"I do not follow you, Partner Elijah."

"I don't know if I can explain it to you. These people have their gene possibilities carefully plotted before birth and the actual gene distribution tested after birth."

"I know that."

"But genes aren't everything. Environment counts too, and environment can bend into actual psychosis where

187

genes indicate only a potentiality for a particular psychosis. Did you notice Gladia's interest in Earth?"

"I remarked upon it, Partner Elijah, and considered it an assumed interest designed to influence your opinions."

"Suppose it were a real interest, even a fascination. Suppose there were something about Earth's crowds that excited her. Suppose she were attracted against her will by something she had been taught to consider filthy. There was possible abnormality. I had to test it by seeing Solarians and noticing how they reacted to it, and seeing her and noticing how *she* reacted to it. It was why I had to get away from you, Daneel, at any cost. It was why I had to abandon viewing as a method for carrying on the investigation."

"You did not explain this, Partner Elijah."

"Would the explanation have helped against what you conceived your duty under First Law to be?"

Daneel was silent.

Baley said, "The experiment worked. I saw or tried to see several people. An old sociologist tried to see me and had to give up midway. A roboticist refused to see me at all even under terrific force. The bare possibility sent him into an almost infantile frenzy. He sucked his finger and wept. Dr. Delmarre's assistant was used to personal presence in the way of her profession and so she tolerated me, but at twenty feet only. Gladia, on the other hand——"

"Yes, Partner Elijah?"

"Gladia consented to see me without more than a slight hesitation. She tolerated my presence easily and actually showed signs of decreasing strain as time went on. It all fits into a pattern of psychosis. She didn't mind seeing me; she was interested in Earth; she might have felt an abnormal interest in her husband. All of it could be explained by a strong and, for this world, psychotic interest in the personal presence of members of the opposite sex. Dr. Delmarre, himself, was not the type to encourage such a feeling or co-operate with it. It must have been very frustrating for her."

Daneel nodded. "Frustrating enough for murder in a moment of passion."

"In spite of everything, I don't think so, Daneel."

"Are you perhaps being influenced by extraneous motives of your own, Partner Elijah? Mrs. Delmarre is an attractive woman and you are an Earthman in whom a preference for the personal presence of an attractive woman is not psychotic."

"I have better reasons," said Baley uneasily. (Daneel's cool glance was too penetrating and soul-dissecting by half. Jehoshaphat! The thing was only a machine.) He said, "If she were the murderess of her husband, she would also have to be the attempted murderess of Gruer." He had almost the impulse to explain the way murder could be manipulated through robots, but held back. He was not sure how Daneel would react to a theory that made unwitting murderers of robots.

Daneel said, "And the attempted murderess of yourself as well."

Baley frowned. He had had no intention of telling Daneel of the poisoned arrow that had missed; no intention of strengthening the other's already too strong protective complex vis-à-vis himself.

He said angrily, "What did Klorissa tell you?" He ought to have warned her to keep quiet, but then, how was he to know that Daneel would be about, asking questions?

Daneel said calmly, "Mrs. Cantoro had nothing to do with the matter. I witnessed the murder attempt myself."

Baley was thoroughly confused. "You were nowhere about."

Daneel said, "I caught you myself and brought you here an hour ago."

"What are you talking about?"

"Do you not remember, Partner Elijah? It was almost a perfect murder. Did not Mrs. Delmarre suggest that you go into the open? I was not a witness to that, but I feel certain she did."

"She did suggest it. Yes."

"She may even have enticed you to leave the house."

Baley thought of the "portrait" of himself, of the enclosing gray walls. Could it have been clever psychology? Could a Solarian have that much intuitive understanding of the psychology of an Earthman?

"No," he said.

Daneel said, "Was it she who suggested you go down to the ornamental pond and sit on the bench?"

"Well, yes."

"Does it occur to you that she might have been watching you, noticing your gathering dizziness?"

"She asked once or twice if I wanted to go back."

"She might not have meant it seriously. She might have been watching you turn sicker on that bench. She might even have pushed you, or perhaps a push wasn't necessary. At the moment I reached you and caught you in my arms, you were in the process of falling backward off the stone bench and into three feet of water, in which you would surely have drowned."

For the first time Baley recalled those last fugitive sensations. "Jehoshaphat!"

"Moreover," said Daneel with calm relentlessness, "Mrs. Delmarre sat beside you, watching you fall, without a move to stop you. Nor would she have attempted to pull you out of the water. She would have let you drown. She might have called a robot, but the robot would surely have arrived too late. And afterward, she would explain merely that, of course, it was impossible for her to touch you even to save your life."

True enough, thought Baley. No one would question her inability to touch a human being. The surprise, if any, would come at her ability to be as close to one as she was.

Daneel said, "You see, then, Partner Elijah, that her guilt can scarcely be in question. You stated that she would have to be the attempted murderess of Agent Gruer as though this were an argument against her guilt. You see now that she must have been. Her only motive to murder you was the same as her motive for trying to murder Gruer; the necessity of getting rid of an embarrassingly persistent investigator of the first murder."

Baley said, "The whole sequence might have been an innocent one. She might never have realized how the outdoors would affect me."

"She studied Earth. She knew the peculiarities of Earthmen."

"I assured her I had been outdoors today and that I was growing used to it."

"She may have known better."

Baley pounded fist against palm. "You're making her too clever. It doesn't fit and I don't believe it. In any case, no murder accusation can stick unless and until the absence of the murder weapon can be accounted for."

Daneel looked steadily at the Earthman, "I can do that, too, Partner Elijah."

Baley looked at his robot partner with a stunned expression. "How?"

"Your reasoning, you will remember, Partner Elijah, was this. Were Mrs. Delmarre the murderess, then the weapon, whatever it was, must have remained at the scene of the murder. The robots, appearing almost at once, saw no sign of such a weapon, hence it must have been removed from the scene, hence the murderer must have removed it, hence the murderer could not be Mrs. Delmarre. Is all that correct?"

"Correct."

"Yet," continued the robot, "there is one place where the robots did not look for the weapon."

"Where?"

"Under Mrs. Delmarre. She was lying in a faint, brought on by the excitement and passion of the moment, whether murderess or not, and the weapon, whatever it was, lay under her and out of sight."

Baley said, "Then the weapon would have been discovered as soon as she was moved."

"Exactly," said Daneel, "but she was not moved by the robots. She herself told us yesterday at dinner that Dr. Thool ordered the robots to put a pillow under her head

191

and leave her. She was first moved by Dr. Altim Thool, himself, when he arrived to examine her."

"So?"

"It follows, therefore, Partner Elijah, that a new possibility arises. Mrs. Delmarre was the murderess, the weapon was at the scene of the crime, but Dr. Thool carried it off and disposed of it to protect Mrs. Delmarre."

Baley felt contemptuous. He had almost been seduced into expecting something reasonable. He said, "Completely motiveless. Why should Dr. Thool do such a thing?"

"For a very good reason. You remember Mrs. Delmarre's remarks concerning him: 'He always treated me since I was a child and was always so friendly and kind.' I wondered if he might have some motive for being particularly concerned about her. It was for that reason that I visited the baby farm and inspected the records. What I had merely guessed at as a possibility turned out to be the truth."

"What?"

"Dr. Altim Thool was the father of Gladia Delmarre, and what is more, he knew of the relationship."

Baley had no thought of disbelieving the robot. He felt only a deep chagrin that it had been Robot Daneel Olivaw and not himself that had carried through the necessary piece of logical analysis. Even so, it was not complete.

He said, "Have you spoken to Dr. Thool?"

"Yes. I have placed him under house arrest, also."

"What does he say?"

"He admits that he is the father of Mrs. Delmarre. I confronted him with the records of the fact and the records of his inquiries into her health when she was a youngster. As a doctor, he was allowed more leeway in this respect than another Solarian might have been allowed."

"Why should he have inquired into her health?"

"I have considered that, too, Partner Elijah. He was an old man when he was given special permission to have an additional child and, what is more, he succeeded in producing one. He considers this a tribute to his genes and to his physical fitness. He is prouder of the result, perhaps, than is quite customary on this world. Moreover, his position as physician, a profession little regarded on Solaria because it involves personal presences, made it the more important to him to nurture this sense of pride. For that reason, he maintained unobtrusive contact with his offspring."

"Does Gladia know anything of it?"

"As far as Dr. Thool is aware, Partner Elijah, she does not."

Baley said, "Does Thool admit removing the weapon?"

"No. That he does not."

"Then you've got nothing, Daneel."

"Nothing?"

"Unless you can find the weapon and prove he took it, or at the very least induce him to confess, you have no evidence. A chain of deduction is pretty, but it isn't evidence."

"The man would scarcely confess without considerable questioning of a type I myself could not carry through. His daughter is dear to him."

"Not at all," said Baley. "His feeling for his daughter is not at all what you and I are accustomed to. Solaria is different!"

He strode the length of the room and back, letting himself cool. He said, "Daneel, you have worked out a perfect exercise in logic, but none of it is reasonable, just the same." (Logical but not reasonable. Wasn't that the definition of a robot?)

He went on, "Dr. Thool is an old man and past his best years, regardless of whether he was capable of siring a daughter thirty years or so ago. Even Spacers get senile. Picture him then examining his daughter in a faint and his son-in-law dead by violence. Can you imagine the unusual nature of the situation for him? Can you suppose he could have remained master of himself? So much the master of himself, in fact, as to carry out a series of amazing actions?

"Look! First, he would have had to notice a weapon under his daughter, one that must have been so well covered by her body that the robots never noticed it. Secondly, from whatever small scrap of object he noted, he must have deduced the presence of the weapon and seen at once that if he could but sneak off with that weapon, unseen, a murder accusation against his daughter would be hard to substantiate. That's pretty subtle thinking for an old man in a panic. Then, thirdly, he would have had to carry the plan through, also tough for an old man in a panic. And now lastly, he would have to dare to compound the felony further by sticking to his lie. It all may be the result of logical thinking, but none of it is reasonable."

Daneel said, "Do you have an alternate solution to the crime, Partner Elijah?"

Baley had sat down during the course of his last speech and now he tried to rise again, but a combination of weariness and the depth of the chair defeated him. He held out his hand petulantly. "Give me a hand, will you, Daneel?"

Daneel stared at his own hand. "I beg your pardon, Partner Elijah?"

Baley silently swore at the other's literal mind and said, "Help me out of the chair."

Daneel's strong arm lifted him out of the chair effortlessly.

Baley said, "Thanks. No, I haven't an alternate solution. At least, I have, but the whole thing hinges on the location of the weapon."

He walked impatiently to the heavy curtains that lined most of one wall and lifted a corner without quite realizing what he was doing. He stared at the black patch of glass until he became aware of the fact that he was looking out into the early night, and then dropped the curtain just as Daneel, approaching quietly, took it out of his fingers.

In the split fraction of a moment in which Baley watched the robot's hand take the curtain away from him

194

with the loving caution of a mother protecting her child from the fire, a revolution took place within him.

He snatched the curtain back, yanking it out of Daneel's grasp. Throwing his full weight against it, he tore it away from the window, leaving shreds behind.

"Partner Elijah!" said Daneel softly. "Surely you know now what the open will do to you."

"I know," said Baley, "what it will do *for* me."

He stared out the window. There was nothing to see, only blackness, but that blackness was open air. It was unbroken, unobstructed space, even if unlit, and he was facing it.

And for the first time he faced it freely. It was no longer bravado, or perverse curiosity, or the pathway to a solution of a murder. He faced it because he knew he wanted to and because he needed to. That made all the difference.

Walls were crutches! Darkness and crowds were crutches! He must have thought them so, unconsciously, and hated them even when he most thought he loved and needed them. Why else had he so resented Gladia's gray enclosure of his portrait?

He felt himself filling with a sense of victory, and, as though victory were contagious, a new thought came, bursting like an inner shout.

Baley turned dizzily to Daneel. "I know," he whispered. "Jehoshaphat! I know!"

"Know what, Partner Elijah?"

"I know what happened to the weapon; I know who is responsible. All at once, everything falls into place."

17   A Meeting Is Held

DANEEL WOULD allow no immediate action.

"Tomorrow!" he had said with respectful firmness. "That is my suggestion, Partner Elijah. It is late and you are in need of rest."

Baley had to admit the truth of it, and besides there

was the need of preparation; a considerable quantity of it. He had the solution of the murder, he felt sure of that, but it rested on deduction, as much as had Daneel's theory, and it was worth as little as evidence. Solarians would have to help him.

And if he were to face them, one Earthman against half a dozen Spacers, he would have to be in full control. That meant rest and preparation.

Yet he would not sleep. He was certain he would not sleep. Not all the softness of the special bed set up for him by smoothly functioning robots nor all the soft perfume and softer music in the special room of Gladia's mansion would help. He was sure of it.

Daneel sat unobtrusively in one darkened corner.

Baley said, "Are you still afraid of Gladia?"

The robot said, "I do not think it wise to allow you to sleep alone and unprotected."

"Well, have your way. Are you clear as to what I want you to do, Daneel?"

"I am, Partner Elijah."

"You have no reservations under the First Law, I hope."

"I have some with respect to the conference you wish arranged. Will you be armed and careful of your own safety?"

"I assure you, I will."

Daneel delivered himself of a sigh that was somehow so human that for a moment Baley found himself trying to penetrate the darkness that he might study the machine-perfect face of the other.

Daneel said, "I have not always found human behavior logical."

"We need Three Laws of our own," said Baley, "but I'm glad we don't have them."

He stared at the ceiling. A great deal depended on Daneel and yet he could tell him very little of the whole truth. Robots were too involved. The planet, Aurora, had its reasons for sending a robot as representative of their interests, but it was a mistake. Robots had their limitations.

Still, if all went right, this could all be over in twelve hours. He could be heading back to Earth in twenty-four, bearing hope. A strange kind of hope. A kind he could scarcely believe himself, yet it was Earth's way out. It must be Earth's way out.

Earth! New York! Jessie and Ben! The comfort and familiarity and dearness of home!

He dwelled on it, half asleep, and the thought of Earth failed to conjure the comfort he expected. There was an estrangement between himself and the Cities.

And at some unknown point in time it all faded and he slept.

Baley, having slept and then wakened, showered and dressed. Physically he was quite prepared. Yet he was unsure. It was not that his reasoning seemed any less cogent to himself in the pallor of morning. It was rather the necessity of facing Solarians.

Could he be sure of their reactions after all? Or would he still be working blind?

Gladia was the first to appear. It was simple for her, of course. She was on an intramural circuit, since she was in the mansion itself. She was pale and expressionless, in a white gown that draped her into a cold statue.

She stared helplessly at Baley. Baley smiled back gently and she seemed to take comfort from that.

One by one, they appeared now. Attlebish, the Acting Head of Security, appeared next after Gladia, lean and haughty, his large chin set in disapproval. Then Leebig, the roboticist, impatient and angry, his weak eyelid fluttering periodically. Quemot, the sociologist, a little tired, but smiling at Baley out of deep-set eyes in a condescending way, as though to say: We have seen one another, we have been intimate.

Klorissa Cantoro, when she appeared, seemed uneasy in the presence of the others. She glanced at Gladia for a moment with an audible sniff, then stared at the floor. Dr. Thool, the physician, appeared last. He looked haggard, almost sick.

They were all there, all but Gruer, who was slowly recovering and for whom attendance was physically impossible. (Well, thought Baley, we'll do without him.) All were dressed formally; all sat in rooms that were well curtained into enclosure.

Daneel had arranged matters well. Baley hoped fervently that what remained for Daneel to do would work as well.

Baley looked from one Spacer to the other. His heart thudded. Each figure viewed him out of a different room and the clash of lighting, furniture, and wall decoration was dizzying.

Baley said, "I want to discuss the matter of the killing of Dr. Rikaine Delmarre under the heading of motive, opportunity, and means, in that order——"

Attlebish interrupted. "Will this be a long speech?"

Baley said sharply, "It may be. I have been called here to investigate a murder and such a job is my specialty and my profession. I know best how to go about it." (Take nothing from them now, he thought, or this whole thing won't work. Dominate! Dominate!)

He went on, making his words as sharp and incisive as he could. "Motive first. In a way, motive is the most unsatisfactory of the three items. Opportunity and means are objective. They can be investigated factually. Motive is subjective. It may be something that can be observed by others; revenge for a known humiliation, for instance. But it may also be completely unobservable; an irrational, homicidal hate on the part of a well-disciplined person who never lets it show.

"Now almost all of you have told me at one time or another that you believed Gladia Delmarre to have committed the crime. Certainly, no one has suggested an alternate suspect. Has Gladia a motive? Dr. Leebig suggested one. He said that Gladia quarreled frequently with her husband and Gladia later admitted this to me. The rage that can arise out of a quarrel can, conceivably, move a person to murder. Very well.

"The question remains, though, whether she is the

only one with a motive. I wonder. Dr. Leebig, him-self——"

The roboticist almost jumped. His hand extended rigidly in the direction of Baley. "Watch what you say, Earth-man."

"I am only theorizing," said Baley coldly. "You, Dr. Leebig, were working with Dr. Delmarre on new robot models. You are the best man in Solaria as far as robotics is concerned. You say so and I believe it."

Leebig smiled with open condescension.

Baley went on. "But I have heard that Dr. Delmarre was about to break off relations with you for matters con-cerning yourself of which he disapproved."

"False! False!"

"Perhaps. But what if it were true? Wouldn't you have a motive to get rid of him before he humiliated you publicly by breaking with you? I have a feeling you could not easily bear such humiliation."

Baley went on rapidly to give Leebig no chance to retort. "And you, Mrs. Cantoro. Dr. Delmarre's death leaves you in charge of fetal engineering, a responsible position."

"Skies above, we talked about that before," cried Klorissa in anguish.

"I know we did, but it's a point that must be con-sidered, anyway. As for Dr. Quemot, he played chess with Dr. Delmarre regularly. Perhaps he grew annoyed at losing too many games."

The sociologist interposed quietly. "Losing a chess game is insufficient motive surely, Plainclothesman."

"It depends on how seriously you take your chess. Motives can seem all the world to the murderer and com-pletely insignificant to everyone else. Well, it doesn't matter. My point is that motive alone is insufficient. Any-one can have a motive, particularly for the murder of a man such as Dr. Delmarre."

"What do you mean by that remark," demanded Que-mot in indignation.

"Why, only that Dr. Delmarre was a 'good Solarian.'

199

You all described him as such. He rigidly fulfilled all the requirements of Solarian custom. He was an ideal man, almost an abstraction. Who could feel love, or even liking, for such a man? A man without weaknesses serves only to make everyone else conscious of his own imperfections. A primitive poet named Tennyson once wrote: 'He is all fault who has no fault at all.' "

"No one would kill a man for being too good," said Klorissa, frowning.

"You little know," said Baley, and went on without amplification. "Dr. Delmarre was aware of a conspiracy on Solaria, or thought he was; a conspiracy that was preparing an assault on the rest of the Galaxy for purposes of conquest. He was interested in preventing that. For that reason, those concerned in the conspiracy might find it necessary to do away with him. Anyone here could be a member of the conspiracy, including, to be sure, Mrs. Delmarre, but including even the Acting Head of Security, Corwin Attlebish."

"I?" said Attlebish, unmoved.

"You certainly attempted to end the investigation as soon as Gruer's mishap put you in charge."

Baley took a few slow sips at his drink (straight from its original container, untouched by human hands other than his own, or robotic hands, either) and gathered his strength. So far, this was a waiting game, and he was thankful the Solarians were sitting still for it. They hadn't the Earthman's experience of dealing with people at close quarters. They weren't in-fighters.

He said, "Opportunity next. It is the general opinion that only Mrs. Delmarre had opportunity since only she could approach her husband in actual personal presence.

"Are we sure of that? Suppose someone other than Mrs. Delmarre had made up his or her mind to kill Dr. Delmarre? Would not such a desperate resolution make the discomfort of personal presence secondary? If any of you were set on murder, wouldn't you bear personal presence just long enough to do the job? Couldn't you sneak into the Delmarre mansion——"

Attlebish interposed frigidly. "You are ignorant of the matter, Earthman. Whether we would or would not doesn't matter. The fact is that Dr. Delmarre himself would not allow seeing, I assure you. If anyone came into his personal presence, regardless of how valued and long-standing a friendship there was between them, Dr. Delmarre would order him away and, if necessary, call robots to help with the ejection."

"True," said Baley, "*if* Dr. Delmarre were aware that personal presence was involved."

"What do you mean by that?" demanded Dr. Thool in surprise, his voice quavering.

"When you treated Mrs. Delmarre at the scene of the murder," replied Baley, looking full at his questioner, "she assumed you were viewing her, until you actually touched her. So she told me and so I believe. I am, myself, accustomed only to seeing. When I arrived at Solaria and met Security Head Gruer, I assumed I was seeing him. When at the end of our interview, Gruer disappeared, I was taken completely by surprise.

"Now assume the reverse. Suppose that for all a man's adult life, he had been viewing only; never seeing anyone, except on rare occasions his wife. Now suppose someone other than his wife walked up to him in personal presence. Would he not automatically assume that it was a matter of viewing, particularly if a robot had been instructed to advise Delmarre that viewing contact was being set up?"

"Not for a minute," said Quemot. "The sameness of background would give it away."

"Maybe, but how many of you are aware of background now? There would be a minute or so, at least, before Dr. Delmarre would grow aware that something was wrong and in that time, his friend, whoever he was, could walk up to him, raise a club, and bring it down."

"Impossible," said Quemot stubbornly.

"I think not," said Baley. "I think opportunity must be canceled out as absolute proof that Mrs. Delmarre is the murderess. She had opportunity, but so might others."

Baley waited again. He felt perspiration on his forehead,

but wiping it away would have made him look weak. He must maintain absolute charge of the proceedings. The person at whom he was aiming must be placed in self-convinced inferiority. It was hard for an Earthman to do that to a Spacer.

Baley looked from face to face and decided that matters were at least progressing satisfactorily. Even Attlebish looked quite humanly concerned.

"And so we come," he said, "to means, and that is the most puzzling factor of all. The weapon with which the murder was committed was never found."

"We know that," said Attlebish. "If it were not for that point, we would have considered the case against Mrs. Delmarre conclusive. We would never have required an investigation."

"Perhaps," said Baley. "Let's analyze the matter of means, then. There are two possibilities. Either Mrs. Delmarre committed the murder, or someone else did. If Mrs. Delmarre committed the murder, the weapon would have had to remain at the scene of the crime, unless it were removed later. It has been suggested by my partner, Mr. Olivaw of Aurora, who is not present at the moment, that Dr. Thool had the opportunity to remove the weapon. I ask Dr. Thool now, in the presence of all of us, if he did this, if he removed a weapon while examining the unconscious Mrs. Delmarre?"

Dr. Thool was shaking. "No, no. I swear it. I'll abide any questioning. I swear I removed nothing."

Baley said, "Is there anyone who wishes to suggest at this point that Dr. Thool is lying?"

There was a silence, during which Leebig looked at an object outside of Baley's field of vision and muttered something about the time.

Baley said, "The second possibility is that someone else committed the crime and carried the weapon off with him. But if that were so, one must ask why. Carrying the weapon away is an advertisement of the fact that Mrs. Delmarre was not the murderess. If an outsider were the murderer, he would have to be a complete imbecile not

202

to leave the weapon with the corpse to convict Mrs. Delmarre. Either way, then, *the weapon must be there!* Yet it was not seen."

Attlebish said, "Do you take us for fools or for blind men?"

"I take you for Solarians," said Baley calmly, "and therefore incapable of recognizing the particular weapon that was left at the scene of the crime as a weapon."

"I don't understand a word," muttered Klorissa in distress.

Even Gladia, who had scarcely moved a muscle during the course of the meeting, was staring at Baley in surprise.

Baley said, "Dead husband and unconscious wife were not the only individuals on the scene. There was also a disorganized robot."

"Well?" said Leebig angrily.

"Isn't it obvious, then, that, in having eliminated the impossible, what remains, however improbable, is the truth. The robot at the scene of the crime was the murder weapon, a murder weapon none of you could recognize by force of your training."

They all talked at once; all but Gladia, who simply stared.

Baley raised his arms. "Hold it. Quiet! Let me explain!" And once again he told the story of the attempt on Gruer's life and the method by which it could have been accomplished. This time he added the attempt on his own life at the baby farm.

Leebig said impatiently, "I suppose that was managed by having one robot poison an arrow without knowing it was using poison, and having a second robot hand the poisoned arrow to the boy after telling him that you were an Earthman, without its knowing that the arrow was poisoned."

"Something like that. Both robots would be completely instructed."

"Very farfetched," said Leebig.

Quemot was pale and looked as though he might be

sick at any moment. "No Solarian could possibly use robots to harm a human."

"Maybe so," said Baley with a shrug, "but the point is that robots can be so manipulated. Ask Dr. Leebig. He is the roboticist."

Leebig said, "It does not apply to the murder of Dr. Delmarre. I told you that yesterday. How can anyone arrange to have a robot smash a man's skull?"

"Shall I explain how?"

"Do so if you can."

Baley said, "It was a new-model robot that Dr. Delmarre was testing. The significance of that wasn't plain to me until last evening, when I had occasion to say to a robot, in asking for his help in rising out of a chair, 'Give me a hand!' The robot looked at his own hand in confusion as though he thought he was expected to detach it and give it to me. I had to repeat my order less idiomatically. But it reminded me of something Dr. Leebig had told me earlier that day. There was experimentation among robots with replaceable limbs.

"Suppose this robot that Dr. Delmarre had been testing was one such, capable of using any of a number of interchangeable limbs of various shapes for different kinds of specialized tasks. Suppose the murderer knew this and suddenly said to the robot, 'Give me your arm.' The robot would detach its arm and give it to him. The detached arm would make a splendid weapon. With Dr. Delmarre dead, it could be snapped back into place."

Stunned horror gave way to a babble of objection as Baley talked. His last sentence had to be shouted, and, even so, was all but drowned out.

Attlebish, face flushed, raised himself from his chair and stepped forward. "Even if what you say is so, then Mrs. Delmarre is the murderess. She was there, she quarreled with him, she would be watching her husband working with the robot, and would know of the replaceable-limb situation—which I don't believe, by the way. No matter what you do, Earthman, everything points to her."

Gladia began to weep softly.

Baley did not look at her. He said, "On the contrary, it is easy to show that, whoever committed the murder, Mrs. Delmarre did not."

Jothan Leebig suddenly folded his arms and allowed an expression of contempt to settle on his face.

Baley caught that and said, "You'll help me do so, Dr. Leebig. As a roboticist, you know that maneuvering robots into actions such as indirect murder takes enormous skill. I had occasion yesterday to try to put an individual under house arrest. I gave three robots detailed instructions intended to keep this individual safe. It was a simple thing, but I am a clumsy man with robots. There were loopholes in my instructions and my prisoner escaped."

"Who was the prisoner?" demanded Attlebish.

"Beside the point," said Baley impatiently. "What *is* the point is the fact that amateurs can't handle robots well. And some Solarians may be pretty amateurish as Solarians go. For instance, what does Gladia Delmarre know about robotics? . . . Well, Dr. Leebig?"

"What?" The roboticist stared.

"You tried to teach Mrs. Delmarre robotics. What kind of a pupil was she? Did she learn anything?"

Leebig looked about uneasily. "She didn't . . ." and stalled.

"She was completely hopeless, wasn't she? Or would you prefer not to answer?"

Leebig said stiffly, "She might have pretended ignorance."

"Are you prepared to say, as a roboticist, that you think Mrs. Delmarre is sufficiently skilled to drive robots to indirect murder?"

"How can I answer that?"

"Let me put it another way. Whoever tried to have me killed at the baby farm must have had to locate me by using interrobot communications. After all, I told no human where I was going and only the robots who conveyed me from point to point knew of my whereabouts.

My partner, Daneel Olivaw, managed to trace me later in the day, but only with considerable difficulty. The murderer, on the other hand, must have done it easily, since, in addition to locating me, he had to arrange for arrow poisoning and arrow shooting, all before I left the farm and moved on. Would Mrs. Delmarre have the skill to do that?"

Corwin Attlebish leaned forward. "Who do you suggest would have the necessary skill, Earthman?"

Baley said, "Dr. Jothan Leebig is self-admittedly the best robot man on the planet."

"Is that an accusation?" cried Leebig.

"Yes!" shouted Baley.

The fury in Leebig's eyes faded slowly. It was replaced not by calm, exactly, but by a kind of clamped-down tension. He said, "I studied the Delmarre robot after the murder. It had no detachable limbs. At least, they were detachable only in the usual sense of requiring special tools and expert handling. So the robot wasn't the weapon used in killing Delmarre and you have no argument."

Baley said, "Who else can vouch for the truth of your statement?"

"My word is not to be questioned."

"It is here. I'm accusing you, and your unsupported word concerning the robot is valueless. If someone else will bear you out, that would be different. Incidentally, you disposed of that robot quickly. Why?"

"There was no reason to keep it. It was completely disorganized. It was useless."

"Why?"

Leebig shook his finger at Baley and said violently, "You asked me that once before, Earthman, and I told you why. It had witnessed a murder which it had been powerless to stop."

"And you told me that that always brought about complete collapse; that that was a universal rule. Yet when Gruer was poisoned, the robot that had presented him with the poisoned drink was harmed only to the extent of a limp and a lisp. It had actually itself been the agent of what looked like murder at that moment, and not merely a witness, and yet it retained enough sanity to be questioned.

"This robot, the robot in the Delmarre case, must therefore have been still more intimately concerned with murder than the Gruer robot. This Delmarre robot must have had its own arm used as the murder weapon."

"All nonsense," gasped out Leebig. "You know nothing about robotics."

Baley said, "That's as may be. But I will suggest that Security Head Attlebish impound the records of your robot factory and maintenance shop. Perhaps we can find out whether you have built robots with detachable limbs and, if so, whether any were sent to Dr. Delmarre, and, if so, when."

"No one will tamper with my records," cried Leebig.

"Why? If you have nothing to hide, why?"

"But why on Solaria should I want to kill Delmarre? Tell me that. What's my motive?"

"I can think of two," said Baley. "You were friendly with Mrs. Delmarre. Overly friendly. Solarians are human, after a fashion. You never consorted with women, but that didn't keep you immune from, shall we say, animal urges. You saw Mrs. Delmarre—I beg your pardon, you viewed her—when she was dressed rather informally and——"

"No," cried Leebig in agony.

And Gladia whispered energetically, "No."

"Perhaps you didn't recognize the nature of your feelings yourself," said Baley, "or if you had a dim notion of it, you despised yourself for your weakness, and hated Mrs. Delmarre for inspiring it. And yet you might have hated Delmarre, too, for having her. You did ask Mrs. Delmarre to be your assistant. You compromised with your libido that far. She refused and your hatred was the keener for that. By killing Dr. Delmarre in such a way as to throw suspicion on Mrs. Delmarre, you could be avenged on both at once."

"Who would believe that cheap, melodramatic filth?"

demanded Leebig in a hoarse whisper. "Another Earthman, another animal, maybe. No Solarian."

"I don't depend on that motive," said Baley. "I think it was there, unconsciously, but you had a plainer motive, too. Dr. Rikaine Delmarre was in the way of your plans, and had to be removed."

"What plans?" demanded Leebig.

"Your plans aiming at the conquest of the Galaxy, Dr. Leebig," said Baley.

18   A Question Is Answered

"THE EARTHMAN is mad," cried Leebig, turning to the others. "Isn't that obvious?"

Some stared at Leebig wordlessly, some at Baley.

Baley gave them no chance to come to decisions. He said, "You know better, Dr. Leebig. Dr. Delmarre was going to break off with you. Mrs. Delmarre thought it was because you wouldn't marry. I don't think so. Dr. Delmarre himself was planning a future in which ectogenesis would be possible and marriage unnecessary. But Dr. Delmarre was working with you; he would know, and guess, more about your work than anyone else. He would know if you were attempting dangerous experiments and he would try to stop you. He hinted about such matters to Agent Gruer, but gave no details, because he was not yet certain of the details. Obviously, you discovered his suspicions and killed him."

"Mad!" said Leebig again. "I will have nothing more to do with this."

But Attlebish interrupted. "Hear him out, Leebig!"

Baley bit his lip to keep from a premature display of satisfaction at the obvious lack of sympathy in the Security Head's voice. He said, "In the same discussion with me in which you mentioned robots with detachable limbs, Dr. Leebig, you mentioned spaceships with built-in positronic brains. You were definitely talking too much then. Was it that you thought I was only an Earthman and incapable of understanding the implications of robotics? Or was it that you had just been threatened with personal presence, had the threat lifted, and were a little delirious with relief? In any case, Dr. Quemot had already told me that the secret weapon of Solaria against the Outer Worlds was the positronic robot."

Quemot, thus unexpectedly referred to, started violently, and cried, "I meant——"

"You meant it sociologically, I know. But it gives rise to thoughts. Consider a spaceship with a built-in positronic brain as compared to a manned spaceship. A manned spaceship could not use robots in active warfare. A robot could not destroy humans on enemy spaceships or on enemy worlds. It could not grasp the distinction between friendly humans and enemy humans.

"Of course, a robot could be told that the opposing spaceship had no humans aboard. It could be told that it was an uninhabited planet that was being bombarded. That would be difficult to manage. A robot could see that its own ship carried humans; it would know its own world held humans. It would assume that the same was true of enemy ships and worlds. It would take a real expert in robotics, such as you, Dr. Leebig, to handle them properly in that case, and there are very few such experts.

"But a spaceship that was equipped with its own positronic brain would cheerfully attack any ship it was directed to attack, it seems to me. It would naturally assume all other ships were unmanned. A positronic-brained ship could easily be made incapable of receiving messages from enemy ships that might undeceive it. With its weapons and defenses under the immediate control of a positronic brain, it would be more maneuverable than any manned ship. With no room necessary for crewmen, for supplies, for water or air purifiers, it could carry more armor, more weapons and be more invulnerable than any ordinary ship. One ship with a positronic brain could defeat fleets of ordinary ships. Am I wrong?"

The last question was shot at Dr. Leebig, who had risen

from his seat and was standing, rigid, almost cataleptic with—what? Anger? Horror?

There was no answer. No answer could have been heard. Something tore loose and the others were yelling madly. Klorissa had the face of a Fury and even Gladia was on her feet, her small fist beating the air threateningly.

And all had turned on Leebig.

Baley relaxed and closed his eyes. He tried for just a few moments to unknot his muscles, unfreeze his tendons.

It had worked. He had pressed the right button at last. Quemot had made an analogy between the Solarian robots and the Spartan Helots. He said the robots could not revolt so that the Solarians could relax.

But what if some human threatened to teach the robots how to harm humans; to make them, in other words, capable of revolting?

Would that not be the ultimate crime? On a world such as Solaria would not every last inhabitant turn fiercely against anyone even suspected of making a robot capable of harming a human; on Solaria, where robots outnumbered humans by twenty thousand to one?

Attlebish cried, "You are under arrest. You are absolutely forbidden to touch your books or records until the government has a chance to inspect them——" He went on, almost incoherent, scarcely heard in the pandemonium.

A robot approached Baley. "A message, master, from the master Olivaw."

Baley took the message gravely, turned, and cried, "One moment."

His voice had an almost magical effect. All turned to look at him solemnly and in no face (outside Leebig's frozen glare) was there any sign of anything but the most painful attention to the Earthman.

Baley said, "It is foolish to expect Dr. Leebig to leave his records untouched while waiting for some official to reach them. So even before this interview began, my partner, Daneel Olivaw, left for Dr. Leebig's estate. I have just heard from him. He is on the grounds now and will be with Dr. Leebig in a moment in order that he may be put under restraint."

"Restraint!" howled Leebig in an almost animal terror. His eyes widened into staring holes in his head. "Someone coming here? Personal presence? No! No!" The second "No" was a shriek.

"You will not be harmed," said Baley coldly, "if you co-operate."

"But I won't see him. I can't see him." The roboticist fell to his knees without seeming aware of the motion. He put his hands together in a desperate clasped gesture of appeal. "What do you want? Do you want a confession? Delmarre's robot had detachable limbs. Yes. Yes. Yes. I arranged Gruer's poisoning. I arranged the arrow meant for you. I even planned the spaceships as you said. I haven't succeeded, but, yes, I planned it. Only keep the man away. Don't let him come. Keep him away!"

He was babbling.

Baley nodded. Another right button. The threat of personal presence would do more to induce confession than any physical torture.

But then, at some noise or movement outside the field of sound or vision of any of the others, Leebig's head twisted and his mouth opened. He lifted a pair of hands, holding something off.

"Away," he begged. "Go away. Don't come. Please don't come. Please——"

He scrambled away on hands and knees, then his hand went suddenly to a pocket in his jacket. It came out with something and moved rapidly to his mouth. Swaying twice, he fell prone.

Baley wanted to cry: You fool, it isn't a human that's approaching; only one of the robots you love.

Daneel Olivaw darted into the field of vision and for a moment stared down at the crumpled figure.

Baley held his breath. If Daneel should realize it was his own pseudo humanity that had killed Leebig, the effect on his First Law-enslaved brain might be drastic.

But Daneel only knelt and his delicate fingers touched

Leebig here and there. Then he lifted Leebig's head as though it were infinitely precious to him, cradling it, caressing it.

His beautifully chiseled face stared out at the others and he whispered, "A human is dead!"

Baley was expecting her; she had asked for a last interview; but his eyes widened when she appeared.

He said, "I'm seeing you."

"Yes," said Gladia, "how can you tell?"

"You're wearing gloves."

"Oh." She looked at her hands in confusion. Then, softly, "Do you mind?"

"No, of course not. But why have you decided to see, rather than view?"

"Well"—she smiled weakly—"I've got to get used to it, don't I, Elijah? I mean, if I'm going to Aurora."

"Then it's all arranged?"

"Mr. Olivaw seems to have influence. It's all arranged. I'll never come back."

"Good. You'll be happier, Gladia. I know you will."

"I'm a little afraid."

"I know. It will mean seeing all the time and you won't have all the comforts you had on Solaria. But you'll get used to it and, what's more, you'll forget all the terror you've been through."

"I don't want to forget everything," said Gladia softly.

"You will." Baley looked at the slim girl who stood before him and said, not without a momentary pang, "And you will be married someday, too. Really married, I mean."

"Somehow," she said mournfully, "that doesn't seem so attractive to me—right now."

"You'll change your mind."

And they stood there, looking at each other for a wordless moment.

Gladia said, "I've never thanked you."

Baley said, "It was only my job."

"You'll be going back to Earth now, won't you?"

"Yes."

"I'll never see you again."

"Probably not. But don't feel badly about that. In forty years at most, I'll be dead and you won't look a bit different from the way you do now."

Her face twisted. "Don't say that."

"It's true."

She said rapidly, as though forced to change the subject, "It's all true about Jothan Leebig, you know."

"I know. Other roboticists went over his records and found experiments toward unmanned intelligent spaceships. They also found other robots with replaceable limbs."

Gladia shuddered, "Why did he do such a horrible thing, do you suppose?"

"He was afraid of people. He killed himself to avoid personal presence and he was ready to kill other worlds to make sure that Solaria and its personal-presence taboo would never be touched."

"How could he feel so," she murmured, "when personal presence can be so very——"

Again a silent moment while they faced each other at ten paces.

Then Gladia cried suddenly, "Oh, Elijah, you'll think it abandoned of me."

"Think what abandoned?"

"May I touch you? I'll never see you again, Elijah."

"If you want to."

Step by step, she came closer, her eyes glowing, yet looking apprehensive, too. She stopped three feet away, then slowly, as though in a trance, she began to remove the glove on her right hand.

Baley started a restraining gesture. "Don't be foolish, Gladia."

"I'm not afraid," said Gladia.

Her hand was bare. It trembled as she extended it.

And so did Baley's as he took her hand in his. They remained so for one moment, her hand a shy thing, frightened as it rested in his. He opened his hand and hers

213

escaped, darted suddenly and without warning toward his face until her fingertips rested feather-light upon his cheek for the barest moment.

She said, "Thank you, Elijah. Good-by."

He said, "Good-by, Gladia," and watched her leave.

Even the thought that a ship was waiting to take him back to Earth did not wipe out the sense of loss he felt at that moment.

Undersecretary Albert Minnim's look was intended to be one of prim welcome. "I am glad to see you back on Earth. Your report, of course, arrived before you did and is being studied. You did a good job. The matter will look well in your record."

"Thank you," said Baley. There was no room for further elation in him. Being back on Earth; being safe in the Caves; being in hearing of Jessie's voice (he had spoken to her already) had left him strangely empty.

"However," said Minnim, "your report concerned only the murder investigation. There was another matter we were interested in. May I have a report on that, verbally?"

Baley hesitated and his hand moved automatically toward the inner pocket where the warm comfort of his pipe could once more be found.

Minnim said at once, "You may smoke, Baley."

Baley made of the lighting process a rather drawn-out ritual. He said, "I am not a sociologist."

"Aren't you?" Minnim smiled briefly. "It seems to me we discussed that once. A successful detective must be a good rule-of-thumb sociologist even if he never heard of Hackett's Equation. I think, from your discomfort at the moment, that you have notions concerning the Outer Worlds but aren't sure how it will sound to me?"

"If you put it that way, sir . . . When you ordered me to Solaria, you asked a question; you asked what the weaknesses of the Outer Worlds were. Their strengths were their robots, their low population, their long lives, but what were their weaknesses?"

"Well?"

214

"I believe I know the weaknesses of the Solarians, sir."

"You can answer my question? Good. Go ahead."

"Their weaknesses, sir, are their robots, their low population, their long lives."

Minnim stared at Baley without any change of expression. His hands worked in jerky finger-drawn designs along the papers on his desk.

He said, "Why do you say that?"

Baley had spent hours organizing his thoughts on the way back from Solaria; had confronted officialdom, in imagination, with balanced, well-reasoned arguments. Now he felt at a loss.

He said, "I'm not sure I can put them clearly."

"No matter. Let me hear. This is first approximation only."

Baley said, "The Solarians have given up something mankind has had for a million years; something worth more than atomic power, cities, agriculture, tools, fire, everything; because it's something that made everything else possible."

"I don't want to guess, Baley. What is it?"

"The tribe, sir. Co-operation between individuals. Solaria has given it up entirely. It is a world of isolated individuals and the planet's only sociologist is delighted that this is so. That sociologist, by the way, never heard of sociomathematics, because he is inventing his own science. There is no one to teach him, no one to help him, no one to think of something he himself might miss. The only science that really flourishes on Solaria is robotics and there are only a handful of men involved in that, and when it came to an analysis of the interaction of robots and men, they had to call in an Earthman to help.

"Solarian art, sir, is abstract. We have abstract art on Earth as *one* form of art; but on Solaria it is the *only* form. The human touch is gone. The looked-for future is one of ectogenesis and complete isolation from birth."

Minnim said, "It all sounds horrible. But is it harmful?"

"I think so. Without the interplay of human against human, the chief interest in life is gone; most of the intellectual values are gone; most of the reason for living is gone. Viewing is no substitute for seeing. The Solarians, themselves, are conscious that viewing is a long-distance sense.

"And if isolation isn't enough to induce stagnation, there is the matter of their long lives. On Earth, we have a continuous influx of young people who are willing to change because they haven't had time to grow hard-set in their ways. I suppose there's some optimum. A life long enough for real accomplishment and short enough to make way for youth at a rate that's not too slow. On Solaria, the rate *is* too slow."

Minnim still drew patterns with his finger. "Interesting! Interesting!" He looked up, and it was as though a mask had fallen away. There was glee in his eyes. "Plainclothesman, you're a man of penetration."

"Thank you," said Baley stiffly.

"Do you know why I encouraged you to describe your views to me?" He was almost like a little boy, hugging his pleasure. He went on without waiting for an answer. "Your report has already undergone preliminary analysis by our sociologists and I was wondering if you had any idea yourself as to the excellent news for Earth you had brought with you. I see you have."

"But wait," said Baley. "There's more to this."

"There is, indeed," agreed Minnim jubilantly. "Solaria cannot possibly correct its stagnation. It has passed a critical point and their dependence on robots has gone too far. Individual robots can't discipline an individual child, even though discipline may do the child eventual good. The robot can't see past the immediate pain. And robots collectively cannot discipline a planet by allowing its institutions to collapse when the institutions have grown harmful. They can't see past the immediate chaos. So the only end for the Outer Worlds is perpetual stagnation and Earth will be freed of their domination. This new data changes everything. Physical revolt will not even be necessary. Freedom will come of itself."

"Wait," said Baley again, more loudly. "It's only Solaria we're discussing, not any other Outer World."

"It's the same thing. Your Solarian sociologist—Kimot——"

"Quemot, sir."

"Quemot, then. He said, did he not, that the other Outer Worlds were moving in the direction of Solaria?"

"He did, but he knew nothing about the other Outer Worlds first-hand, and he was no sociologist. Not really. I thought I made that clear."

"Our own men will check."

"They'll lack data too. We know nothing about the really big Outer Worlds. Aurora, for instance; Daneel's world. To me, it doesn't seem reasonable to expect them to be anything like Solaria. In fact, there's only one world in the Galaxy which resembles Solaria——"

Minnim was dismissing the subject with a small, happy wave of his neat hand. "Our men will check. I'm sure they will agree with Quemot."

Baley's stare grew somber. If Earth's sociologists were anxious enough for happy news, they would find themselves agreeing with Quemot, at that. Anything could be found in figures if the search were long enough and hard enough and if the proper pieces of information were ignored or overlooked.

He hesitated. Was it best now to speak while he had the ear of a man high in the government or——

He hesitated a trifle too long. Minnim was speaking again, shuffling a few papers and growing more matter-of-fact. "A few minor matters, Plainclothesman, concerning the Delmarre case itself and then you will be free to go. Did you intend to have Leebig commit suicide?"

"I intended to force a confession, sir. I had not anticipated suicide at the approach, ironically, of someone who was only a robot and who would not really be violating the taboo against personal presence. But, frankly, I don't regret his death. He was a dangerous man. It will be a long time before there will be another man who will combine his sickness and his brilliance."

"I agree with that," said Minnim dryly, "and consider his death fortunate, but didn't you consider your danger if the Solarians had stopped to realize that Leebig couldn't possibly have murdered Delmarre?"

Baley took his pipe out of his mouth and said nothing.

"Come, Plainclothesman," said Minnim. "You know he didn't. The murder required personal presence and Leebig would die rather than allow that. He *did* die rather than allow it."

Baley said, "You're right, sir. I counted on the Solarians being too horrified at his misuse of robots to stop to think of that."

"Then who did kill Delmarre?"

Baley said slowly, "If you mean who struck the actual blow, it was the person everyone knew had done so. Gladia Delmarre, the man's wife."

"And you let her go?"

Baley said, "Morally, the responsibility wasn't hers. Leebig knew Gladia quarreled bitterly with her husband, and often. He must have known how furious she could grow in moments of anger. Leebig wanted the death of the husband under circumstances that would incriminate the wife. So he supplied Delmarre with a robot and, I imagine, instructed it with all the skill he possessed to hand Gladia one of its detachable limbs at the moment of her full fury. With a weapon on her hand at the crucial moment, she acted in a temporary black-out before either Delmarre or the robot could stop her. Gladia was as much Leebig's unwitting instrument as the robot itself."

Minnim said, "The robot's arm must have been smeared with blood and matted hair."

"It probably was," said Baley, "but it was Leebig who took the murder robot in charge. He could easily have instructed any other robots who might have noticed the fact to forget it. Dr. Thool might have noticed it, but he inspected only the dead man and the unconscious woman. Leebig's mistake was to think that guilt would rest so obviously on Gladia that the matter of the absence of an obvious weapon at the scene wouldn't save her. Nor could he anticipate that an Earthman would be called in to help with the investigation."

"So with Leebig dead, you arranged to have Gladia leave Solaria. Was that to save her in case any Solarians began thinking about the case?"

Baley shrugged. "She had suffered enough. She had been victimized by everyone; by her husband, by Leebig, by the world of Solaria."

Minnim said, "Weren't you bending the law to suit a personal whim?"

Baley's craggy face grew hard. "It was not a whim. I was not bound by Solarian law. Earth's interests were paramount, and for the sake of those interests, I had to see that Leebig, the dangerous one, was dealt with. As for Mrs. Delmarre." He faced Minnim now, and felt himself taking a crucial step. He *had* to say this. "As for Mrs. Delmarre, I made her the basis of an experiment."

"What experiment?"

"I wanted to know if she would consent to face a world where personal presence was permitted and expected. I was curious to know if she had the courage to face disruption of habits so deeply settled in her. I was afraid she might refuse to go; that she might insist on remaining on Solaria, which was purgatory to her, rather than bring herself to abandon her distorted Solarian way of life. But she chose change and I was glad she did, because to me it seemed symbolic. It seemed to open the gates of salvation for *us*."

"For *us*?" said Minnim with energy. "What the devil do you mean?"

"Not for you and me, particularly, sir," said Baley gravely, "but for all mankind. You're wrong about the other Outer Worlds. They have few robots; they permit personal presence; and they have been investigating Solaria. R. Daneel Olivaw was there with me, you know, and he'll bring back a report. There is a danger they may become Solarias someday, but they will probably recognize that danger and work to keep themselves in a reasonable balance and in that way remain the leaders of mankind."

"That is your opinion," said Minnim testily.

"And there's more to it. There *is* one world like Solaria and that's Earth."

"Plainclothesman Baley!"

"It's so, sir. We're Solaria inside out. They retreated into isolation from one another. We retreated into isolation from the Galaxy. They are at the dead end of their inviolable estates. We are at the dead end of underground Cities. They're leaders without followers, only robots who can't talk back. We're followers without leaders, only enclosing Cities to keep us safe." Baley's fists clenched.

Minnim disapproved. "Plainclothesman, you have been through an ordeal. You need a rest and you will have one. A month's vacation, full pay, and a promotion at the end of it."

"Thank you, but that's not all I want. I want you to listen. There's only one direction out of our dead end and that's outward, toward Space. There are a million worlds out there and the Spacers own only fifty. They are few and long-lived. We are many and short-lived. We are better suited than they for exploration and colonization. We have population pressure to push us and a rapid turnover of generation to keep us supplied with the young and reckless. It was our ancestors who colonized the Outer Worlds in the first place."

"Yes, I see—but I'm afraid our time is up."

Baley could feel the other's anxiety to be rid of him and he remained stolidly in place. He said, "When the original colonization established worlds superior to our own in technology, we escaped by building wombs beneath the ground for ourselves. The Spacers made us feel inferior and we hid from them. That's no answer. To avoid the destructive rhythm of rebellion and suppression, we must *compete* with them, follow them, if we must, lead them, if we can. To do that, we must face the open; we must teach ourselves to face the open. If it is too late to teach ourselves, then we must teach our children. It's vital!"

"You need a rest, Plainclothesman."

Baley said violently, "Listen to me, sir. If the Spacers

220

are strong and we remain as we are, then Earth will be destroyed within a century. That has been computed, as you yourself told me. If the Spacers are really weak and are growing weaker, then we may escape, but who says the Spacers are weak? The Solarians, yes, but that's all we know."

"But——"

"I'm not through. One thing we *can* change, whether the Spacers are weak or strong. We can change the way we are. Let us face the open and we'll never need rebellion. We can spread out into our own crowd of worlds and become Spacers ourselves. If we stay here on Earth, cooped up, then useless and fatal rebellion can't be stopped. It will be all the worse if the people build any false hopes because of supposed Spacer weakness. Go ahead, ask the sociologists. Put my argument to them. And if they're still in doubt, find a way to send me to Aurora. Let me bring back a report on the *real* Spacers, and you'll see what Earth must do."

Minnim nodded. "Yes, yes. Good day, now, Plainclothesman Baley."

Baley left with a feeling of exaltation. He had not expected an open victory over Minnim. Victories over ingrained patterns of thought are not won in a day or a year. But he had seen the look of pensive uncertainty that had crossed Minnim's face and had blotted out, at least for a while, the earlier uncritical joy.

He felt he could see into the future. Minnim would ask the sociologists and one or two of them would be uncertain. They would wonder. They would consult Baley.

Give it one year, thought Baley, one year, and I'll be on my way to Aurora. One generation, and we'll be out in space once more.

Baley stepped onto the northbound Expressway. Soon he would see Jessie. Would *she* understand? And his son, Bentley, now seventeen. When Ben had a seventeen-year-old of his own, would he be standing on some empty world, building a spacious life?

221

It was a frightening thought. Baley still feared the open. But he no longer feared the fear! It was not something to run from, that fear, but something to fight.

Baley felt as though a touch of madness had come over him. From the very first the open had had its weird attraction over him; from the time in the ground-car when he had tricked Daneel in order to have the top lowered so that he might stand up in the open air.

He had failed to understand then. Daneel thought he was being perverse. Baley himself thought he was facing the open out of professional necessity, to solve a crime. Only on that last evening on Solaria, with the curtain tearing away from the window, did he realize his need to face the open for the open's own sake; for its attraction and its promise of freedom.

There must be millions on Earth who would feel that same urge, if the open were only brought to their attention, if they could be made to take the first step.

He looked about.

The Expressway was speeding on. All about him was artificial light and huge banks of apartments gliding backward and flashing signs and store windows and factories and lights and noise and crowds and more noise and people and people and people . . .

It was all he had loved, all he had hated and feared to leave, all he had thought he longed for on Solaria.

And it was all strange to him.

He couldn't make himself fit back in.

He had gone out to solve a murder and something had happened to him.

He had told Minnim the Cities were wombs, and so they were. And what was the first thing a man must do before he can be a man? He must be born. He must leave the womb. And once left, it could not be re-entered.

Baley had left the City and could not re-enter. The City was no longer his; the Caves of Steel were alien. This *had* to be. And it would be so for others and Earth would be born again and reach outward.

His heart beat madly and the noise of life about him sank to an unheard murmur.

He remembered his dream on Solaria and he understood it at last. He lifted his head and he could see through all the steel and concrete and humanity above him. He could see the beacon set in space to lure men outward. He could see it shining down. The naked sun!

Isaac Asimov

☐	BEFORE THE GOLDEN AGE, Book I	C2913	1.95
☐	BEFORE THE GOLDEN AGE, Book II	Q2452	1.50
☐	BEFORE THE GOLDEN AGE, Book III	Q2525	1.50
☐	THE BEST OF ISAAC ASIMOV	23018-X	1.75
☐	BUY JUPITER AND OTHER STORIES	23062-7	1.50
☐	THE CAVES OF STEEL	Q2858	1.50
☐	THE CURRENTS OF SPACE	P2495	1.25
☐	EARTH IS ROOM ENOUGH	Q2801	1.50
☐	THE END OF ETERNITY	Q2832	1.50
☐	THE GODS THEMSELVES	X2883	1.75
☐	I, ROBOT	Q2829	1.50
☐	THE MARTIAN WAY	23158-5	1.50
☐	THE NAKED SUN	Q2648	1.50
☐	NIGHTFALL AND OTHER STORIES	23188-7	1.75
☐	NINE TOMORROWS	Q2688	1.50
☐	PEBBLE IN THE SKY	Q2828	1.50
☐	THE STARS, LIKE DUST	Q2780	1.50
☐	WHERE DO WE GO FROM HERE?—Ed.	X2849	1.75